CLUBLAND

Kevin Sampson lives and works on Merseyside, where the nightlife is as good as it's ever been just now. He is the author of four other novels, *Awaydays*, *Powder*, *Leisure* and *Outlaws*, and a book of non-fiction, *Extra Time*.

D1386162

ALSO BY KEVIN SAMPSON

Fiction

Awaydays
Powder
Leisure
Outlaws

NonFiction

Extra Time

Kevin Sampson

CLUBLAND

VINTAGE

Published by Vintage 2003

2 4 6 8 10 9 7 5 3 1

Copyright © Kevin Sampson 2002

Kevin Sampson has asserted his right under the Copyright, Designs and Patents Act, 1988 to be identified as the author of this work

First published in Great Britain in 2002 by
Jonathan Cape

Vintage
Random House, 20 Vauxhall Bridge Road,
London SW1V 2SA

Random House Australia (Pty) Limited
20 Alfred Street, Milsons Point, Sydney
New South Wales 2061, Australia

Random House New Zealand Limited
18 Poland Road, Glenfield,
Auckland 10, New Zealand

Random House (Pty) Limited
Endulini, 5A Jubilee Road, Parktown 2193,
South Africa

The Random House Group Limited Reg. No. 954009
www.randomhouse.co.uk

A CIP catalogue record for this book
is available from the British Library

ISBN 0 09 928976 8

Papers used by Random House are natural, recyclable products made from wood grown in sustainable forests. The manufacturing processes conform to the environmental regulations of the country of origin

Printed and bound in Great Britain by
Bookmarque Ltd, Croyden, Surrey

For Helen

Endgame 1

Ged

They've left us no alternative. With all of what's went on back there, they really have not give myself a choice in the matter. It is what it is. I went down that road before with the other fella – forgive and forget. Not this time, by the way. Will not make the same mistake twice. They've give us no choice.

The Rules 1

Margueritte

Not only am I almost laughing, I'm laughing in admiration. As stitch-ups go, I've got to hand it to them – they've done me good and proper. How did I not see this coming? I'm a fucking lawyer, for fuck's sake! I should've seen it coming. But I'm not laughing, of course. I'm dying. Inside, right now, from now on in, I'll be dying a slow and excruciating death. That's their mistake. They should've killed me off. While I'm here to watch this happen around me, I'm also here to hurt them. And I will. I will do that. I will fucking hurt the bastards that moved me over. Rule One. Always kill off the enemy.

Goodfellas 1

Mini Me

I've been stood here a quarter of a hour and the procession's still going past. Fucking better it is, man. Ratter had loads out for his, but this turn out for Mikey G is different class. Fucking quality, it is. Some of the fucking motors, man. There's Mercs, Lexus, Beamers, Mitzis, all kinds of fuck-off four wheel drives and that – pure quality, la.

You don't know what to believe round here, but from what I got told Mikey got shot up in the same thingio as what done Rico in. Two big mobs of lads are having a dispute over some gear down by Otterspool and next thing guns are getting let off and lads are going down. Rico's shot Mikey Green, about five of his lads goes after Rico popping him one after another after another. He gets popped like twenty-thirty times and all hands is getting zapped. Fucking better.

But our Darren reckons it was Ratter what's behind it. Ratter's been into all kinds. He's half Ged Brennan's brother and he's a big hitter in the Brennan firm and that, but he's been skanking him bad style, doing his own little thingio and what have you. Like, Ratter and his girl Margueritte – wanna see her man, fuckinell la that is one boss fucking Judy that is. Her and Ratter's got no end of this and that going on, auld buildings what they're doing up and that, but it's all a big mad front for the gear Ratter's bringing in. Serious – our Darren swears on their Michael's life that this is all straight up. Ratter's in deep with the Irish and the Turks and he's bringing all kinds of brown into the city and what he's gone and done is, he's turned round and fitted their Ged up. He's handed Ged Brennan to Mikey Green on a plate – that's how come them fellas is all shooting one another to bits down at Otterspool. Best of it is la, Ged gets wind of what's going down and he don't show at Otterspool. He was meant to be getting done in man, but he never. Here's here.

This is all like last week. Tell you la, our Darren told us that the champagne was flowing all over the South End when Mikey G got popped, but he's got some fucking turn out for a fella what no cunt liked. Different fucking class, this. They're *still* going past. *That Bloomin Flower Shop* on Parky must've cleaned up. Fucking what? Flowers on some of these cars, man. This big fucking limo's just gone past with a Ethiopia flag on the roof in flowers and that. Fucking boss, man!

He's in big with the Brennans, our Darren. Well, he half knows them to let onto in town. He can send a drink over and what have you. That's what I want – to be like that. By the time I'm fucking twenty la, fellas'll be sending over bottles of champagne and all kinds. Is fucking right.

Ged

What's gone on is, Ernie's come right up to myself the minute the service is done with. He's sound, Ernie. Got a lot of time for the lad, no matter that he's Mikey's aul' fella and what have you. How he come to bring up a wrong 'un like Mikey is beyond the likes of myself, but that's all by the by. He's gone now. Can't say as I'm even that thingio, to be fair – could not honestly say that I give a fuck. Knew the lad when we was kiddies and that, but that's as far as it goes. I've come to the funeral to pay my respects. Do the right thing by his

3

mam and his family and that. Is right. Would've been wrong not to in all fairness, but I am getting chocker with it all. It's not even a fortnight since it's all gone off, is it? The other fella – still at, he were. Fucking Ratter. Still at it just them few fucking days ago and that, trying to do me in. Makes you think, at the end of the day.

Four funerals in three days, there's been. I can't be doing with it myself. Women in bits, horse-drawn carriages, big mad flower displays, fucking police escorts and what have you, sermons in the fucking *Echo*'s obit pages, all of that carry-on. Ghouls and all, too. All kinds of ghouls and scary cunts stood outside the churches getting a eyeful of the processions and that. In all fairness, though, it were a fucking boss turnout for the lad – could not put a number on how many top fellas' cars followed the main fucking thingio, but there must've been over thirty official cars in Mikey G's main funeral cortège, at least. So people *are* going to stop and stare and that. But there's got to be limits, hasn't there? Got to be a little bit of thingio when all's said and done – bit of respect for the nearest and dearest and that. Women and family in bits, by the way, in fucking bits they are and there's all these fucking emptyheads stood outside, staring. I can't be doing with funerals myself and that's the God's honest truth.

And the *poems*, la – tell you what! Telling you, la, some of them verses in the fucking *Echo* are criminal, no two ways about it. You wouldn't think that these are the cream of Liverpool's boys putting them messages in, by the way. Fucking sinful, some of them. What?

> *May the merciful tears of Our Lord above*
> *Water the roots of your boundless love.*

4

What's all that about, by the way? We're talking about Mikey Green here, not Hughie fucking Greene. Man was a dog at the end of the day, no two ways about it. Lad was a fucking dog. No way in the world is Our Lord even going to give MG the time of day, let alone cry on the cunt. Pure is not going to happen that, by the way. End of the day, the good Lord knows the score. Mikey Green was a fucking dog. End of. Not that his mam's going to see it that way, in fairness.

> *You liked to come on hard*
> *But my little boy I swear*
> *You weren't no flashing blade*
> *You're my little teddy bear.*

To be totally fair to Mikey, he'd a been chocker with her if he'd a seen that. Would not have liked that one little bit, by the way. She's sound and all too, his ma. June. In bits, she is. Destroyed. To us and that, Mikey was just a gobshite. Pure wrong 'un, Mikey Green. But to June, well – it's her little fella, isn't it? Makes you think.

I'm stood there outside wondering whether it's all right just to do one, but Ernie's come over. He's come right over and he's looked us in the eye and he's gone: 'I want this to be an end of all the killing now, Ged. Don't let it be the start. Let this be the end.'

And he gives myself a big moody stare – just showing that he's a man of sincerity and honour and all of that, but in fairness I was that close to cracking up. I gets like that at moments of, knowmean, where you're expected to be that bit solemn and what have you. I just fucking thingio, I don't know what it is. I'm in bulk. I just feel this big mad fit of the chuckles coming on and it's all's I can do to keep on top of it. Funerals and that, they do your head in. It was George first. Then soft lad yesterday – still can not bring myself to call him by name after all what he done. Fucking one of our own and all, too. Still can not believe what he done and that – or what he was *trying* to do. Then Rico this morning and now Mikey. Too much, la. Ernie's right. This has got to be the end of all that.

He puts his arm around myself and steers us off into a little quiet part where the grass is longer and still wet. I can feel the wet on the bottom of my kecks and Ernie's saying to us: he's saying this. He never was that into what Mikey was up to. Didn't want none of that caper. Was always happy enough to do his own little thing around Granby. He was half made up that Mikey had made a name for hisself, but Ernie don't want nothing to do with Town. The bars, the lap-dance joints, the tanning studios, all of that – does not want none of it. So he's saying to myself, knowmean, this is where the foolishness stops. Do us a favour. Take all Mikey's clubs and that off've my hands.

'You're a businessman, Gerrard. You could make some good dough out of these places. Have them. Give me what you think.'

And I would've. I would've well took them over. Would've give it proper thought and that at least, anyways. That was half where my head was at, weren't it – fucking do something in town, Ged lad. Do yourself a favour. But then the funny girl got in touch. Auld butch arse from the council cut in from the left, didn't she? That changed every fucking thing.

6

Margueritte

I don't even know what I think about all this. I'm numb. What I do know is they'll be right. There'll be no loophole, no lifeline, nothing for me to cling to. It's over. I'm out. His ashes hadn't even gone cold before the letter was on the mat. Phoney condolences and apologies for having to bring up such a sensitive matter at such a time, but can we schedule a meeting at your convenience blah blah blah – i.e. *now*.

The bottom line? The South Village is going to be taken away from me. Not that it would've made a great deal of difference if John-Paul and I *had* been married, but that's what they're offering up as their excuse. Really. We were partners in law but not, it would now seem, in the eyes of Liverpool City Council's lawyers. Byzantium was the preferred developer but, with John-Paul gone, all that is going to change. All the grant aid, the matched money, the regeneration funding, the European top-up – that was valid for as long as John-Paul Brennan was living and breathing. The bastards. That is so, so wrong. It was his name on the contracts, his guarantee, his fucking signature – but the animus that brought that whole thing into being was mine. It was me. Other people saw a great, dead monolith. They saw a useless storage depot. A tramshed. I saw the South Village. Ratter would've had you believe it was all him, but it took me *years* to open his eyes to that one enormous but simple reality – it was city-centre land. The location, the extent, the potential – it was all prime. No matter that it was a fucked-up piece of land with a vast white elephant smack in the centre – it was a huge tract of city land. It was just . . . *perfect*. I saw that. I knew it.

And now I know two more things. One is that some other fucker is going to take over a project that's fully-funded and almost three-quarters finished. The other is that there is not a fucking thing I can do about it. I can go through the motions, go to appeal, take it all the way to Europe if I want to be a real pain in the arse, but really, what would be the point? It's already a done thing. I'm a lawyer and I've let those bastards take my baby away from me.

Moby

Bit weird what our Gerrard's been saying to us and that. Saying that whole part of town that Mikey's had is wide open. It's only bits and bobs and that. It's not like it's *town* town, just a few places he had. Chinatown more or less, but it's only a three-minute walk from the Cream, know where I'm going. Three minutes the other way from the Moathouse and the dock and that. Not what you'd call Town, but fuckinell – not exactly Widnes, neither.

One of his lap-dance gaffs is just there. That'd be a all right place to have. Ultimo it is, the one just off've Duke Street. Not in the same league as Nirvana, to be fair, but that don't bother my good self. End of the day, it don't bother Mr Moby whereabouts in town the gaff is. I just want in. That's the bottom line for YT. End of the day, I would not half mind having my own place. Ged's right, by the way – I'd make a fucking good go of it. Better than some of the other cowboys that's got bars and what have you. I could fill it and all, too. People I know – I could well make a go of it. There's a lot of shite that comes with having a gaff in town, but for myself, I don't see a lot of that coming on top. If it happens, it happens. Bring it on.

Re-start Schemes 1

Ged

I'm not one for looking a gift horse in the mouth at the best of times, but this has come right out the blue and just when I needed it, in fairness. After the other fella, after all of what's went on in the run-up to Chrimbo, my plan was to get New Year out the way then have a proper think about where I'm going with all of this.

For one thing, there is no way in the world that we're doing no more jobs. That's finito, that is. As of that last one – Christmas Eve, if you will – that whole caper is done with. Serious. That's my good self done with the blags and that for good.

And that weren't just me being thingio with all the deaths and that – I weren't being morose and what have you. It's like with the players. They always say they'll be the first to know when it's time to pack it in. That was myself over Christmas. Fucking chocker, I were. Wanted out. Badly wanted out of that whole caper. That last one, right: fucking lunacy, that were. Easy-peasy, but fucking . . . I don't know. Do I want to be pulling a fucking stocking over my grid on Christmas Eve – on Christmas fucking Eve, by the way, and I'm jumping out and shouting 'Stand and deliver!' Is that what I'm after doing for the rest of my life – is it fuck, by the way. I knew the moment I'd give the swag to Eli that that was it. Game over.

And it's not like as though the cabs don't give us a

good enough living, mind you. That's all well and good. But there's things going on in this city that pure do my head in. There's no-marks and dickheads driving big boss cars, making proper dough and giving it the big I Am. It's that fucking easy for them. Now I would never, never want to be seen in that way. I'm not a gangster, never have been, never will be. So good luck to them, by the way. But some of the teds that's getting away with it in town, tell you, la – should not be allowed. Lads like that – I can't believe they're getting away with what they're getting away with. And the fact of the matter is that they're not just getting by. These cunts are *wadded*. Tell you, the cunts are making fucking Brewster's. Not happy about it, by the way, seeing lads like that fucking weighed down with dosh. I want some of that kind of dough for myself, is all.

End of the day, I didn't know much more than that. Did not know what to think. I wanted in on the big dough. Did not see why some no-mark could get away with it while I myself was still half grafting, knowmean. No way in the world am I going to start doing the other thing, by the way, but, by the same thingio, I am a fucking big name in this city and what's good for a no-mark had better be good for YT. That's about as far as I got. I was thinking maybe to go and have a little word with some of the lads, leave it till after the New Year then go and see what possibilities might exist. But I never had to, did I? Never got that far in fairness.

Just after Ernie come to us with his proposition, I gets a call. The funny girl from the council, isn't it – fucking Milly Tant. Shelagh Cormack. Her. Always in the *Echo* and that, legalise drugs, regulate brasses, all of that. Do not understand the half of what she's going on about, in fairness, but the thing she's got myself down for – it's fucking gorgeous. Our John-Paul had been half wrapped up in it, but it's not one of them. It's kosher. It's all one hundred per cent above board. It's something I could be proud to put my name to. Our Stephen'll be made up when I tells him. And little Shy. They'll love it, they will. Property and that, tarting up the city centre and what have you, it's all that. Can half remember having a laugh at Tarzan when he come round the barrio, telling us he was going to do this and that. He was going to turn Tocky into the Garden of Eden, he were. There weren't nothing aul' Heseltine weren't going to do for us. End of the day, he sealed off all the roads so's it took us that little bit longer to get off from Plod, and he planted trees. Nice one and that. Get paid. But I'm half thingio about him, now. Aul' Tarzan and that – it was him started all the tarting up the city at the end of the day.

That's my good self from now on, that is. Gerrard Brennan – local entrepreneur and that. Is right. Just what the doctor ordered, that is. I just need to dot the t's and then it's all sorted.

Re-start Schemes 2

Cormack

Can't say as we're completely sure about Gerrard Brennan, but he's far and away our safest bet. We'd been wanting his brother off the project for a long time, matter of fact. He was bringing in some very good grant aid for his projects, but his scope was *so* limited. He could have done so much more. This was another thing that went against his partner, the able Margueritte. She wasn't able to prevent her common-law chap from using Byzantium as a front for his other interests. She liked to come on as though she was the brains behind the business – she was certainly the beauty – but it's clear that Ratter had the run of the show.

As soon as we moved over to Regen and started looking into some of those sub-leases we knew we'd have a fight to win John-Paul Brennan over. Let's be blunt about old Ratter: why would a drug dealer want to cooperate in a scheme that ultimately will negate or undermine the role of illegal, unchecked and overpriced narcotic supply? He wouldn't. He'd do everything in his power to stop it. And the longer this project stalls, the more pressure from Brussels. It's a very delicate balancing act, Europolitics. The EEC money is there, it's *there* – but we have to keep on spending it, and spending it the way Brussels wants – in order to draw down the next tranche. Truthfully? Margueritte's partner, the great John-Paul Brennan, was cutting up his nose to spite his face. So I couldn't say we cried ourselves to sleep when we heard of his demise.

Bennett's been demised, too. He's only got himself to blame. He was given plenty enough time to act, but he sat on the fence and dithered, trying to see which way the leaves might blow. You can't play the fiddle in local government any more. Those days are gone. Councillor Bennett had to declare. He had to act. He didn't. He's gone. We've given him the dignified option of retirement on health grounds without having to bring in the party whip et cetera. And with Bennett out of the way, the opportunity to do something magnificent with The Loin can not – must not – be missed.

In some ways, their departure has only thrown up different problems, though. We knew we had to move fast. In Regen, you know you're always one wrong turn away from a stab in the back, but meantime you do the job as best you can. And for us, this goes beyond mere job satisfaction. This is a mission. This, The Loin, is something we believe in. It's history in the making. So the selection of a preferred partner for this particular scheme was always limited by law and fraught with complication. Our best protection comes in the way the Brussels funding is paid through. For, while it's fair to say that John-Paul Brennan's kith and kin have some claim on the *land*, his successors still need to hit some pretty rigorous deadlines – and qualitative *guide*lines – if they want the Euro-grants to come on line, on time. This is why we've selected Ged Brennan to head up the operation. It's a risk. There's no doubt about it – he's the best of a very bad bunch of options. But we think it could work. We believe Ged Brennan is workable.

The Rules 2

Margueritte

What stings, what's really starting to hurt about this, is not just the feeling of being completely out-thought, outflanked and just plain fucked over. It's the knowledge that it's a woman who's behind the big putsch. She's not many people's vision of femininity, Shelagh Cormack. Elvis in the burger years, robust sideburns and all, is being kind to her. But behind the cigar and the suit, underneath that whole clichéd butch lesbo Player thing, there operates a shrewd and brilliant female mind. She's a proper feminist. Not one of your fucking know-nothing, done-nothing Andrea Dworkin types. Shelagh Cormack strikes me as a woman who's lived it. She can pull it off now because she's been through it all, all the shite that drives you on. She's taken the boys on and she's beat them at their own game. That's important to me. I fucking *want* women like that in office. I want to *work* with the Shelagh Cormacks of this world. She's singing from my own fucking hymn sheet. The Rules. The ones I thought I'd made up and customised for my own gorgeous gratification over the years. Me and Shelagh, Shelagh and me – we should be allies. Forget all the sister crap – women like Shelagh Cormack and I are rare and dazzling creatures. People with our abilities and outlook and intellect, we don't happen along all that often. We should be scheming together, and we're not. We're not.

Fuck it, I don't *know* how I feel. More than anything, I just feel like a silly little girl. It's bad enough that my whole agenda, my politics, my method of making the world work for *me* has crumbled to dust. But to be worked over by the one woman who could have made the difference – it's too much to bear. We could've been such allies.

I've followed her progress with interest, Shelagh Cormack. Came here as a student from Scotland. Studied Politics, I think – had a twin sister who went off the rails, went on the game so the legend goes. Shelagh first comes to prominence when she's at the Chamber of Commerce. Plod are trying to close down Cream –

14

trying to oppose its licence on grounds of excessive drug use on the premises. Now, Cream has gone through the roof at this point – there's The Ministry and there's Cream and they're the two biggest *uberclubs* in fucking Europe. Students are signing up for Liverpool University in their *droves* you know, and thousands of them are citing Cream as the reason they want to come to Liverpool. There's the Beatles, there's Liverpool Football Club and now there's Cream – the third grace. Hotel trade is booming, taxis are making a mint, the bars and restaurants and takeaways are all coining it, all because of a banging disco in the heart of clubland. And the law wants to close it down. Guess who talked them out of it? Guess which odd-looking, gruff, plain-talking Scots lady made the police see the bigger picture? Rumour has it she was a mid-ranking officer at the Chamber of Commerce – but she made her name as one to watch with the paper she wrote on Cream's significance to the economy of Liverpool. Since then, I've been watching her.

That's why this is killing me. I know that she's behind it – I *know* she is. We could've been so strong together. But she's done me in. She's fucked me. And it's my own stupid fault for not seeing it coming. With John-Paul, he was so sure that our eggs were in the right basket. He greased old Bennet up so much, I'm now tarred with the same brush. I could have cultivated Shelagh Cormack, but I didn't. How was I to know she'd move into this field, into Regeneration? *I couldn't* have known. But that doesn't make this any easier to bear. I don't know what to do. I feel like running away. And perhaps it is time for a change of scenery, anyway.

Right 1

Cormack

All it is, is common sense – but when did simple sense, when did the right thing ever have a place in politics? We've bided our time, got into the right position to guide things gently through at exactly the right time in history, and this now stands a chance of leaving its hallmark. And this is not a parochial move. If this works, it'll reverberate around the world. That's not nothing. That's a thing that made your lives useful.

And it *is* so straightforward, The Loin. We've done it the right way. We've got the academics, the right political voices, the visionaries and the policymakers with our thinking onside. Crucially, we've got some major figureheads from the clergy with us, too. Unimaginable, not so long ago, but even the churches are feeling it now. Priests get turned over by heroin addicts, rectories get screwed for change, baby whores take shelter in the pews of city-centre chapels. The church was never immune from the tendrils of streetlife, but it's seldom felt it like it does today. The clergy of this city are with us. At least, they're not against us. They're not going to oppose The Loin.

The Loin. A small chunk of the city centre. Not even a chunk. Just a few streets and alleyways on the fringes of Clubland. We'll take the streets that no one wants, the clubs where no one goes. And with those streets we'll face up to some of history's shocking universal truths. People like to get high. Men get benefit from the services of prostitutes. Women use prostitutes, too, and even more would love to if the sleaze and the stigma were removed. It's a good thing that we're proposing here – a *good* thing. Sex workers of all kinds have a valid and useful role in society's equilibrium and as such deserve the recognition and working conditions of other workers in the city centre. We don't just acknowledge these truths, we embrace them. These bare facts inform our reality.

And the indication is that government – as in Westminster – is ready to roll with us on this. The precedents have been good. We've just had another progressive and *very* successful NHS conference, and the big breakthrough came with the level of support for a widened availability of prescription drugs. It's not just the Lib-Dems saying decriminalise – we've had support from *everyone*. Even some of the chiefs of police are now telling the nation that we have to legalise smack if we're going to pull society, in the wider sense, out of its grip. Everybody is watching our move with interest.

Our interest is in creating a properly regulated tolerance zone. Heroin would most certainly be tolerated and taxed, and tested for purity and quality. This is an astoundingly brave initiative. Government *ought* to support us. We have much common ground in terms of our policies and thinking. In every practical sense, government has said it's OK to smoke pot for Christ's sake, so it's fair to say that they're more than aware and more than interested in what we're doing here in Liverpool. Prince *Charles* is interested. If we get this right . . .

If only it were that simple. All of this needs to be handled with *incredible* sensitivity – getting a government green light to push on with the trial is only a small part of the process. Our forward-thinking government may well back us, but no way can they be *seen* to back us. We'll need to reach out to Europe for the bulk of the funding. Fundamentally, Brussels will fund us – so we need to be careful and sensitive and experimental, while still keeping an eye on the clock. This needs to happen *now*. But we're in control. We know what we're doing, here.

What we're doing is this: in a strictly defined area, we will offer a regulated service – the controlled and guaranteed source of narcotics, prostitution and other adult leisure options. This project is so sensitive to emotional overreaction that it almost has not been worth the blood, sweat and tears thus far. Its mere mention makes gentle men and women apoplectic with rage. The reality is that at other points in history we would have been shot down and run out of town long before we reached this point. Serious thinkers like ourselves would have been demonised as the second coming of their feared and hated Militants of yore. But the time has come for this scheme. Those who would automatically say no are seeing the other side: that, if prostitution is a fact of life, should it not then be made safe for all involved? For *all* involved.

And they're *starting* to see the sense of a new approach to narcotics, too. If drug users can buy a certified product at fair cost, they don't need to rob you to pay for it. They don't need to source from a dealer. The dealer might look for other illegal ways of making his living, but drug dealing as an underworld trade would be hit inevitably, and fatally.

And who gains? Well, we do for one – and we're pleased to say so. This, more than anything, is where our council leadership will ultimately come to back us. So far, they've adopted a sort of mute collaboration stance. If we fail, they knew nothing of our libertine plot. But if we win, we win big. The council stands to earn more revenue than we do even from parking tickets. And The Loin, the area where prostitutes can work safely and without intimidation, where customers know they're using a health-checked service in an upbeat and well-lit environment, where pot smokers can puff in bars and cokeheads can score in peace, becomes a prime leisure destination. It's another unique barrio in a singular city. Come To Liverpool and Party. And they will. They'll come in droves. But first we have to bring the South Village back on line. No kidding. In every practical sense, the future of this staggering and wonderful project depends upon the cooperation of Mr Gerrard Brennan. If only he knew.

Don't Look Down (On Me)

Ged

Driving back from the meeting, a little baby fox cuts right across the M53. Lucky to stay alive, it were. That's the weather, by the way. Soon as we gets a cold snap, the foxes are out on the forage. When the ground freezes up they can't get their snouts into the soil to get at the grubs and that, so they has to head off to the tip. That's where the fucking wheelie bins have done them in. In the olden days, your foxes could just get into a bin liner like that, sniff out the takeaways and the thrown-out dinners and that and they'd be right into them. Get paid. But with the wheelie bins now, only the really clever foxes are getting a break – the clever ones and the hard ones. They'll suss out that they need to go that little bit further. Might have to go to Bidston tip if you don't want to go hungry, by the way. This one here, he'll be sound.

She's told us a lot more about the project, the South Village and what have you. To be fair, I've always felt that little bit wary of the construction game. I mean, we had our own kennel built and that, but that was all done by lads I'd known for years, in fairness. Even saying that, there was that much to it. Foundations; footings; frames; joists; this, that and the fucking other – too much to take in, for my money. With myself, I've always wanted to be in charge, know where I'm going. Not loony tunes stuff, I'm not thingio. Not a control maniac and what have you. But I do want to know where everything goes. I need to know how it all works so's I can know how they're going to get me. That's the secret in business. Know thine enemy, and double know thine employee – for he will shaft you.

But the way this Cormack is laying it out, there isn't really too many reasons not to go for it. She's as good as paying us to take over a project that's guaranteed to make money. It can't *not* make money. One thing I'll say for the other fella, fucking snake though he were, he did know how to make dough. End of the day, fucking Ratter was one clever cunt. He was a sure thing, and this South Village is a sure thing.

Cormack's given us a bit of the SP about some of the thinking behind the development and that. The joint venture thing – I know where she's coming from and, to be perfectly fair, I don't mind if she does wag my tail a bit on that. The council's been as good as its word and weighed in with this grant and that loan, they've got a right to have a say in how the place is run. Just so long as there's nothing shady. Soft lad was in deep with the Irish connection for starters, and at the end of the day that's what's done him in. Do not want none of that. That's one of their thingios, the Irish – the building game and that. If there's any of that, anything jarg about this development and what have you, I'm doing one. Finito.

Weird coming from myself all that, but that's a big part of what's in it for me. One of the big things for myself over all of what's happened before Chrimbo is the way the likes of Ray Cole dropped us like a piece of shite. Me and Coley – we done all right together. To be fair, I was never going to be captain of the golf team. I was never going to get through the fucking golf club's front door and deep down I knew all that. I weren't that arsed. But I always thought that Coley liked working with myself, come what may. We done good work for the charities and that and we always had plenty to talk about away from all the fund-raising. We was mates. I was a robber and he was Plod, but we got along great. I always thought he half had a inkling of what I done, but he weren't arsed so long as I never thingio, never compromised him and that. He liked my company and that was that.

Not quite, by the way. Soon as he was put in the picture about YT he was gone with the wind. I've thought about that a lot. I accept why he had to do one on us like that. I do – I'm not a knobhead. I'm a villain and I can't expect fellas like Coley to treat me like I'm not. But I don't like it. I don't want that no more. I don't want fellas looking down on me.

The Stables

Cormack

It's been such a maze of legalities and technicalities that we almost wanted to push on with The Loin without integrating the South Village into the zone. If we'd waited too long for a tame developer who could satisfy all the legal criteria, then we might've missed the window altogether. One thing we don't have here is time. If history has shown us anything it's that your moment comes. The moment for The Loin is upon us. We thought of Ged almost out of hopelessness.

We don't for one second think that Ged Brennan is docile. Far from it – one quality that shines through about the man is a near-infuriating sense of propriety. The questions, the questions, the plodding, idiot-savant questions – a schoolboy's mind would work faster. But either he's cleverer than we're giving him credit for – or he's heaven-sent. What we mean by that is that he seems dead keen to take over the South Village as the council's preferred developer. But he also seems happy enough to complete the development along the aesthetic lines we are recommending – and Brussels is watching with interest.

The Euro element could scarcely be more important. The Loin has become one of their pet projects, but their stipulations for funding – architectural, socio-economic and in terms of hard-nosed sustainability – are stringent, and time sensitive. We need to carry on hitting those deadlines, yes – but now we can fold the Village and, crucially, the Stables into all of this, too. The Stables, really, are key to bringing this whole area to life.

That's why we need Ged. Take this outside the

Brennan umbrella, risk a long-running claim against the scheme, the council, the lot and we're suddenly and irreversibly out of time. It *is* tricky. He *is* a complex man. But he is also our only realistic choice. So we don't want to scare him off by rushing into every single detail. We can do that one step at a time. What has to happen here is a very delicate balancing act. We need the physical development to continue, quickly, and with taste. This has to be a world-class product. But we need to do this within the parameters of the law, sadly. Put simply, we still need a Brennan on board.

Oh, but how we would have loved to be able to risk it with Margueritte. Given the time to groom her properly, she might have been just the ticket – given *time*. We would've loved to have her front the whole thing up, of course we would – but the reality was just too dangerous. It's a highly sensitive and hugely controversial development scheme as it is, and Margueritte was just too easy a target. Single black female – too, too easy to shoot down. She's great-looking, articulate, spiky, clever – perfect *Question Time* persona and image. Make her MP for the Granby ward and she'd be PM within ten years. But throw her into the fray of a front-page 'Council-Run Brothel' scandal and she'd get chewed up in seconds. We know how hard these next months are going to be. Margueritte was just too much of a risk. Her moment will come, though. That is an absolute certainty.

What counts, what really counts now is how Ged goes about refurbishing the Stables. The old stables, at the tip of the South Village – just where it merges with The Loin – is a still-cobbled, long-neglected and almost intact piece of early Victorian street scene. It was discovered purely by chance a couple of years ago, when an old paper-storage warehouse started to buckle and had to be brought down, brick by brick. The council's engineers found a small but perfectly preserved street crammed between two warehouses, with stables at one end. A perfect, jerry-built street, hardly touched by time *and* with near-intact stables – unimaginable in a modern city centre, and still hard to visualise without actually seeing them. We still can't believe our luck in stumbling across such a heritage treasure.

Honestly? We're glad Ratter's no longer an element in this. Under him, the street would have become yet more 'cottages' for production companies and the stables would've become a cyberstudio, or penthouse apartments or another damned gym. Now though, *now*, it seems as though his despised stepbrother might use the opportunity properly. The Stables, our generic name for the entire street, restored and lit sensitively, could so well serve as adult leisure units. Perhaps a smokers' café, perhaps a warren of whores' nests. What is beyond dispute is that it's a key portal in our vision. It's going to be one of the major gateways into The Loin. And it's back in the blueprint. The South Village will come on line – Ged Brennan will see to that.

Weirdness 1

Ged

Due diligence. Getting to the bottom line. Is this thing kosher? Will it make dough? What's the risk? These are some of the things you want to know. It takes time, to be fair. All of this fucking carry-on takes time, but you've got to ask the questions. There's another for myself and all, too. Is there any fucking weirdness attached to all of this? In my heart of hearts, I know this whole thingio can not be this simple. There's bound to be weirdness somewhere. I know there is. I do. I fucking know it.

Sex Work

Jade

The new guy's meant to be coming in today. I'll give anybody a chance, yeah – but this fella's got, like, a *really* bad rep. Like, some of the girls here used to work Nirvana. And they know this Moby guy from there? He's a monster. Not just a lech, yeah, but a beast. I don't know. The girls in this game are the worst in the world for stories. Like, if it's not some Asian guy who's travelling the country making a composite corpse from the best parts of various lap dancers, it's a fella with a half-inch dick who sits there wanking himself off in front of them. They just love the camaraderie of the gossip, is my theory. I'd be the first to admit that I have too many theories, yeah, but there we go. Lap dancers love to gossip.

I quite miss the buzz of that shitty little changing room, sometimes. The odour of orange peel (some dolts think it's a special perfume known only to the lap-dance trade! Hah! *Eau d'orange peel*, guaranteed to smother all and any BO associated with the kit-off game); the confessions and pipe dreams and all the gossip; brutal bouncer boyfriends, boob jobs gone horribly wrong, secret foo-lesbian affairs. I liked being part of all that.

Like, it definitely helped with the degree. You can read all the textbooks you want – and some of them are superb on the academic side? But you can't substitute books for the intimate inside track of the practitioner in the sex trade. And that's not a theory.

It's like, I hardly ever get my kit off any more, but that's just the way things have panned out. Let's be, like, *crystal* clear – I'm not someone who ever saw anything remotely embarrassing, or wrong or demeaning about lap dancing, yeah. Quite the opposite, actually – I found it, if anything, strangely empowering. And if anyone wants to be snotty about it, I can assure them there's nothing remotely embarrassing about bringing in like £800 a *week* for a part-time job. I'll be absolutely clear once again. I did not hate taking my clothes off for men. I didn't even get into any of this via the usual cliché of needing to supplement my student loan. It was one hundred per cent a choice thing? No one, but no one was forcing my hand. Certainly, nobody was making me work five nights a week, yeah. Like, if this place was open, I'd be down here. I'm not saying I fucking *loved* it, yeah, but no way was it a grind, either. I definitely got something out of it. Over the first few weeks, I'd tell myself it was a logical continuation of the research I'd started – first-rate coursework – but it was something else, too. Call it what you want, but I was tapping into a different way of life. I liked it. I was meeting girls who think the way I think.

Some of those girls gave me the courage and the strength to undertake that unique piece of coursework that ended up as my now infamous paper, 'Streetlife'. Pride sounds like the wrong emotion to attach to my working as a street prostitute, yeah, but I'm far from ashamed of what I did. It was a thorough piece of field research and the thesis that resulted from it is nothing short of dazzling in its insight. It is – it's a fucking masterpiece. Rick Knighton, my professor at the time, described it as the most enlightened, intellectually rigorous and brilliant student paper he had ever seen. But even in the world of academia, people can't quite separate the remarkable wisdom of the paper from the fact that I am blonde, very cute, and have quite large breasts. What is it about breasts? Girls just love them.

So 'Streetlife' gave me the taste, for sure. Once I'd resumed, like, orthodox coursework, I came straight here. It's possible that I'd simply got accustomed to making good money, of course – but there was something else, too. I wouldn't say I have addictive tendencies, but I'd have to admit to being drawn to the scene. I mean, it's deviant, yeah – this whole thing. This is where I've been headed since, fuck – since the night in Carlisle. Since the Patsy Kensit night opened up my eyes to, like, who I am.

And like I say, I was meeting a certain type of girl, girls whose thinking was honest and fresh and concurred with my own views on deviance and sex and gender and, I guess, power? I found *me*, yeah? This whole foo thing – it's, like, we've found it ourselves? It's so not a label? Or, yeah, it is – but we label ourselves. We define ourselves as good-looking chicks who dig other good-looking chicks. It's, like, *totally our own thing*. We love it that everybody thinks lesbian sex is all about butch dykes and rotund earth mommas. Like, I *can* half sort of dig what those chicks are into? I could easily go and pull a woman like that if that's the way I was feeling? Sometimes I do? I used to like guys. I might again one day. But right now, this is where I am. This is me. There isn't a man in this city who can get a whiff of any of this, let alone try to define it. If only Rick Knighton knew a fraction of it? He'd, like, freak?

And, not long before my twenty-first birthday, I was handed the chance to do something, to *do something* that reflected those values. I was put in charge here. It was, like, I was given free rein, more or less. So long as I made the numbers work for Mikey, I could pretty well do as I liked. And I did. I built something here. I made something up. And it's good. What I do here – it's good.

So I'm like *super*-wary of this new fella. I'm the manager of Ultimo. I'm the girl who's turned it around, transformed it from a sad backstreet wankers' gaff into like a thriving and much-loved *foo* house. That's, like, *way* simplistic, actually. Ultimo is *totally* a one-off. Certainly round here it is. There's nothing like it in, like, Manchester even? It's many things to many people, this place – but they all love it. They feel like they're *part* of it. That's one of the areas where I've drawn on my coursework yeah, used my degree to identify areas and sections of society I can cater for. And I'm doing it. I'm doing that, and I'm doing it with *amazing* success and fulfilment. I mean, it's like – I just don't want this new bastard stomping in and fucking everything up. My way *works?*

That said, there are *plenty* enough people ready to whisk me away from all this. There are, like, *dozens* of them, yeah, men, mostly – all too aware that I have a rare and immaculate First-Class Combined Honours degree in Sociology and Communications Studies. They're all after me – publishers, academics, media hawks – but what they see is not Jade Walker. They see a package. I mean, fuck it, I'm a good-looking girl, yeah – I *like* the way I look. I'm not one of these politicos that's always, like, grating on about how their looks have stopped them being taken seriously and how, like, they wish they'd been born dog-ugly. All these good-looking girls who decide they're gay and immediately put on three stone to get their own back on the men who've sexually objectified them for so long – fuck that! I'll take the eyes, the lips, the legs, the tits – I'll take the lot, thank you very much! I will not get strung out by the way I look?

What fucking irritates me about those academic shite-hawks though, is their fucking *dishonesty*. They don't say what they mean? Like, those people would say that I've wasted or am wasting that excellent qualification. All the research on the streets, all the profile and reputation that 'Streetlife' brought for me – not just here in Liverpool, but nationwide and beyond – they all assume that I should want to *use* that. They can't understand how I managed to live such a double life – such a *low* life. Fundamentally, they don't get how I went through all of that without some sort of pay-off at the end? They see all that as a noble sacrifice – something that I *went through*? And to square it in their minds they need for me to *use* what I went through? If they could really spit out what they *really* wanted to say, they'd be like: 'But, Jade, with your looks and your youth and your experience, you could *clean up*, yeah? You could be, like, the dark side of Naomi Wolf! Like, you've been through all *that* – there *has* to be a pay-off!'

And the answer would be, like so simple. There *was* no jeopardy. There was *no* sacrifice. I *wanted* to do it. I was the sociology student who took time out to work as a hooker. The module was all about Gender at Work. Where, please, where oh where is the fucking contradiction? Where is the controversy? I was *doing a course*! Why not get, like, right down to the bottom line, yeah, look it in the eye and *learn* something – something that the *textbooks* can never, never teach?

Of course, once they got hold of it, papers like the *Sun* and the *Sport* played right into my hands with their fucking uniquely salacious brand of reportage. That sort of publicity only helped. It, and they, provided me with a library of instant, hysterical and superbly quotable reaction. I was caricatured as 'Jezebel Jade' and 'The Student Strumpet'. And then, of course, they had, like, a *heyday* with my surname. But my supporters were stoic and grew in numbers exponentially. That's how I first encountered my good friend the city councillor, Shelagh Cormack. Shelagh has been a tower of strength over these last couple of years. She's one of the many who don't doubt for a moment the validity of my work.

I'm still not sure about Rick. Certainly, Professor Rick Knighton believed I should have gone on to big and important things, and for sure, the offers *were* there. No end of research grants, PhD invitations, proposals from publishers. You name it – Jade 'Street' Walker was in demand, yeah? And, like, *which* of those tempting opportunities did she opt for? Why, she decided to take up the offer of managing the lap-dance establishment she'd been working in for the last few months! And there we have it. That's me – that's where I am, thanks very much. It's *me* – and I'm *loving* it. It's, like, I've poured all my extensive and intimate knowledge of Queer Theory sociology into a real and stimulating career in the sex-service industries. That, for me, is *so* not selling myself! Fuck that! As a lap dancer, you're in control. As a media package? I don't think so. *That* would be prostitution.

Recurring Dreams 1

Moby

Fucking hate that one, by the way. Fucking does my swede in, that one. It's the same thingio more or less, every time. Comes into my dreams about once a month, once every six weeks or something – fucking horrible, it is. All's it is, is – right, I myself am a lad that's got a big cock. That's the God's honest truth, by the way. That's why they call me Moby – end of the day, I've got a fucking big chopper. Fucking whale of a thing, truth be known. Not in this fucking dream it ain't, man.

What happens is, I'm walking into the Aldi just off've Kenny. Prescot Road, to be fair – that one. It's always in there this dream, by the way – the one where the thingio happened. The tragedy and that. I never hardly go down Kenny these days. Hate to even walk past that Aldi, in fairness. Used to go to Vic's and that – used to do some circuit training down there and that, there and Tate's gaff, the proper gyms and that. Boxers' gyms, in fairness – just go on the bags, do a few circs, have a little go-around with one of the kiddies and what have you. But I haven't been near that Aldi in I don't know how many years. Don't even think about that Aldi no more.

But in this dream, right, I'm walking through the

sliding doors and I'm walking *dead* fucking slow, by the way, and I becomes so aroused that my trackies is slipping off've myself. And before I've even half had the chance to do a thing about it, I'm completely bollock-o. Oh yes – I'm walking around that Aldi, dead fucking slow, in the nack. Now, in the normal thingio of it, I myself would not have too much to be worrying about – big lad, big dick, end of. Not in this fucking movie, by the way. Oh no, kidder – in this filum I'm a lad that's got a *tiny* little dick and that, hardly no dick at all in fairness, and there's aul' ladies and mams with their kiddies and that and they're all standing back with their hands over their mouths and that, going:

'Fucking state of that fella's dick, Mam!'

'I know, Marie-Rochelle – it's sly, isn't it?'

'Is me dad's as small as that?'

'Fuck off, kidder! He's fucking *massive*, your da!'

Telling you, la, I do not like that dream. Gets myself off to a bad start, that does.

Clubland

Jade

Mikey had it right. He was happy just to use the place, use it as a front for whatever else he had going down. It was, like, money, money, money with Mikey. He was a dirty bastard – had see-through mirrors everywhere – but once you got the message across that, like, you weren't interested? He was wasting his valuable time? He'd let you get on with it. So long as the take roughly squared with his notions of what a backstreet joint should earn him, he was, like, *completely* cool with just letting me run things my own way. Like, everything from the door security (exclusively female, no matter what the occasion or day of the week) to the pricing policy was down to me. *Everything* – and that's exactly how it needs to stay. If this Moby has got his head screwed on, yeah, he'll just let me keep the whole show rolling, same as I've been doing for the past fifteen months. It works.

It's like, my Billies – and, I should say, overwhelmingly my Wilhelminas – come here from miles around. They come to me because I offer grown-up choices. In an adult world, I offer something that intrigues them and delivers the reality of that intrigue. The hundreds and thousands of straight women who want to come to a lap-dance bar, for example – *not* to see the fucking Chippendales, *not* for the Full fucking Monty, but to enjoy beautiful *women* dancing for them – they come to *me*. That's the situation here – they come to me because I fucking know. I know what they want. I provide the right experience for these people, the right atmosphere and the right environment. They come to FFF at Ultimo because we've got it *right*. They come here because *I'm* the manager now, and *I* know what they want and I'm giving them *exactly* what they want. I'm giving them a place where they can act upon those deviant impulses that, for all their lives, they've been blotting out. Just blotting out the way they really feel, because they feel it's *wrong*, yeah? That's so sad. A girl, who probably mainly likes men, wants to feel another woman's tits. What she finds herself thinking in school, in her place of work, in her dreams is that she would just like to neck with a girl – kiss her and feel her tits.

Maybe go down on her or maybe let the girl go down on her. She dreams about this and she also still dreams about Brad Pitt's firm stomach and she just shuts it all out. She thinks there can not be another sick fuck like her anywhere else in the world. Well, there are many, many of you here at Ultimo. Take off your coat and come inside.

That's where we're at right now. I'm the manager of a lap-dance joint who's got a first in sociology, which I'm using to cater for the sex industry. As manager, by the way, I don't even earn as much – in theory – as I did as a dancer. But I do, of course. I've got it right. I'm doing good for my Billies and I'm doing OK for myself. Ultimo works. So it's going to be interesting to see how this Moby shapes up.

Moby

Tell you what though, this fucking Jade one's superb. Fucking good job this one can't see inside my swede, by the way – if she'd've been able to look in on that fucking Aldi dream this morning she would *not* be looking at my good self with that same glad eye as what she is doing now. Oh yes – this Jade one is showing out for aul' Mr Moby, good style! Cracking on that that's her proper name, by the way, but I know where she's going with that. It's that 'don't show you're interested' one, isn't it? Don't put it on a plate. And I don't mind that, to be fair. Mr Moby does not half mind a challenge.

She's a fucking babe and all, too – pure lap dancer she is, straight blonde hair, green eyes, boss tits, boss arse, fucking brilliant legs – but she's one smart kiddie with it. Dead sharp, by the way. She's put us down a couple of times, to be fair. She talks like a wool, in fairness – Carlisle, she says she's from – but she's just like a Scouse girl. Can't say nothing to her or she'll just come back at you with knives. She's been looking after the gaff for a good few months and it looks as though she knows how to put arses on seats, know where I'm going. Looks like she could put a fucking show on herself, to be fair. She's shown us the books, which I make a big thing of studying closely and do not fucking understand one line of, in all fairness. She asks myself the usual things about Mikey and how I knew him and that. And she gives us this big, serious face and goes: 'Will you be looking to make any changes in policy or ideology', and I'm just going: 'What?' and giving her the big smile. Can see that she's into my good self straight away, to be fair. This could be the start of a *byootiful* friendship.

Jade

He's a dolt, but he seems manageable. Let's see.

'You'll appreciate, Mr Brennan . . .'

'Woah! Hang on! Slow it right down, love. It's Moby. Rule One. All the staff calls me Moby. OK?'

Like, hello! STAFF? Count to five, darling . . .

'OK, Moby, you're on – although I like to think of myself more as, like a partner, yeah? Not a member of staff?'

'You call yourself what the fuck you want, darling. Just so long as you're not expecting no more dough!'

He *completly* caves in at this. It's like the funniest thing the soft bastard has ever heard? So that's him, yeah? Laughs at his own jokes. Laughs *dementedly* at his own jokes. Calls me darling. And puts his hand on my thigh.

We'll have to put him straight on all of that of course, and pronto − otherwise, he seems fine. I can run rings around him.

'Moby, darling. It's like this. It's like − I'm hoping you and me'll be working together for a very long time, yeah? And the thing is . . . no, I *don't* expect profit share or a pay rise. Not yet!'

I follow his lead and crease up at this and laugh madly at my own cheeky parry. He *loves* it. The big, daft sod is grinning from ear to ear. Like, he's happy, because he's having a laugh with a good-looking girl. He's going to be easy?

'Maybe if I work hard enough and prove to you that I can make a difference, yeah? I'm, like, the difference between this establishment flourishing or withering on the stem like every other place in this neck of the woods, maybe then you'll be prepared to cut me in on the action. But I'm *so* not looking for that yet, yeah? I'm not long out of uni? I don't have a massive overhead? I'm fine for now, Moby. I'm twenty-two and I'm paying my rent. Money is not the thing with me . . .'

True enough − but equally I don't believe in generating stacks of wealth for others as a result of my own brilliance. No siree. FFF is now *so* successful that it runs Saturday and Sunday afternoons, too. It's notorious in the best possible sense. The Sundays are my favourites, actually − much more *foo* than the Fridays and Saturdays. Like, we make more on a Sunday than any other day of the week − quite remarkable.

'I can get by. But what I *do* need, Moby, is to be turned on . . .'

Moby

Happy days, well! I fucking knew it. Did Mr Moby know it or did auld Mr Moby get it fucking bang on – could tell right from the off. You don't get where auld Moby is today without knowing when chicks are into you. Don't get me wrong and that, no disrespect to the girl, but she's got it wrote all over her. She is fucking *dying* for it, by the way . . .

Jade

'. . . I need to come into work feeling empowered? I need to feel stimulated? You know what I mean by that, Moby – you're a man of the world. I need to know that I have a free hand to carry on running this place in the way I think works best.'

I hit him with my sternest but most dazzling green-eyed full beam.

'Yeah?'

Moby

Fuck! Thought she was getting thingio with myself there. Getting a little bit bored of all this rap, now. Wish to fuck the girl'd make her fucking point and shut the fuck up. When do all the Judies get here, by the way?

Jade

'So is that agreed, Moby? You don't call me "love" or "darling". You treat me exactly how you'd treat a man.'

Moby

What – fill you in when you're doing my head in?

'Seems fair enough to my good self, darling.'

I slumps back and lets her have a full hit of auld Moby's bulge. None of that Aldi thingio here, by the way, kidder – this lad is fucking full on, know where I'm going. I waits for her to clock it in all its glory, then holds her stare with my best grumble-melting grin. She knows who's the boss man, to be fair. And she fucking does not mind it one little bit.

Jade

Oh dear – a dolt that fancies himself. Bad combination! But we'll get by. We'll get by.

Moby

I sits up and switches into businessman mode, just like that.

'Does the gaff get full?'

Can see them lovely green eyes of hers flickering, trying to suss where I'm going with it.

'No. I'll be honest with you – it's only certain nights we're busy. We're like everyone, Moby. We're busier some days than others.'

Oh, and I know you are. Fuck that. I'll look into all of that later, the hows and whys of the dough. More interested in other things for now, in fairness. It's a fucking big joint, this. If it ain't doing the business as a venue, we could maybe use some of this space a bit better, in all fairness.

'What about next door?'

'The tanning studios?'

'Them.'

Got her on the run, here.

'They do OK. To be truthful, there's not too much passing trade in this part of town. A few of the local girls come in. A few lads – gays, students, bodybuilder types. But it's mainly our own girls that use the facility.'

'*Facility*? Not so sure as I likes the sound of that. Sounds like a freebie to YT, facility does. Put us straight on that one, will you – the girls do pay and that, don't they?'

She looks down again. 'No. They get tokens. It's, like – we figure that's one of the perks of the job?'

Fucking says everything like as though it's a question. My neck's half sore from nodding like a cunt whenever the girl tells myself the simplest little thing. I decides I'll give it her straight. Badly would like to bend her over and give it her straight up that tidy arse of hers to be fair, but that'll have to wait for another day. Talking ground rules, here. Talking about who's the boss.

'The perks of the job is they get paid. From now on, they pay for the sunbeds. That OK, my darling? They pay. And what I'm thinking, just so's you know, is that we might use some of that floor space better. Maybe we'll knock through into the tanning salon and put a few more high-power sunshower cubicles in. What d'you think?'

Jade

A dolt with ideas of his own – fuck. Now that *is* bad!

'I think that potentially that might be seen to be a good idea. But maybe what we want to do is see how the existing sunbeds go, once the girls know they're expected to pay for them, yeah? I do think you're right. They'll probably still carry on using them, but I'd suggest that maybe we take like a month to sit back and watch how the pattern pans out, yeah?'

Poor bastard's nodding away like a buffoon – he's *so* buying that crap. You can give this one a load of sticky toffee so long as you do it with a smile. But this might be a tricky balancing act. On the one hand, I don't want him tumbling to the fact that there's *foo* action – *any* kind of action, actually. I just don't want him down here, period. His mere presence will kill the whole thing stone dead. Yet, by the same token, if I carry on trying to convince him there's *nothing* going on down here yeah, he might just take matters into his own hands. Tricky. Very tricky. The one thing I *do* know is that if a man has the option of postponing a decision, he'll put it off. Not much, but I can buy some time.

'Let's give it like a month, yeah, darling? We'll sit back and see how it all pans out on the sunbed front – and in the meantime you also sit back and let *me* get on with trying to make this place work as a business, yeah? Agreed? And if I make you rich into the bargain, maybe *then* you'll want to give me a bonus.'

Moby

I'll give you a fucking bonus! To be fair, though, got to admit it, she is a class act, this Jade one. Jade or no Jade, she does seem to know the score. She's more than confident she can turn this thing round if I gives her a free hand. And that's what's getting myself thinking. It's all very well myself getting on to a easy graft and that, just lie down and take the readies and what have you, but I don't know that I can have a tart telling myself what's what, in all fairness. At the end of the day, she's saying that what I do is I turns up of a Monday and she gives us the readies. That's it – that's my part in the fucking story. Don't know if I'm having that, to be fair. Do not know as I can just stand back and let this one run the show. The lads'd give us loads if they ever found out I was working for a Judy, by the way. I'll ask our Ged about it later, in all fairness. End of the day, though, maybe I needs to get my own man in there.

Jade

He's bought it. It's written all over his stupid face. Fundamentally, I've said to him: 'Come here once a week. Have a drink, have a little look at the girlies and I'll hand you two grand on your way out.'

He's *well* pleased. Well pleased – he's over the moon! I don't know what he was expecting out of this place. Maybe I'm giving him too much, but it's a fraction of what we take down here at weekends. And it keeps him away – it keeps the big dobber out of our hair.

The Rules 3

Margueritte

I should love him for it. I should embrace him, but I know that what I'm going to do is kill him for his sentimentality.

Ged

One thing I couldn't square up with aul' butch kecks was how come they was freezing Margo out. Whichever way you looks at it, that's not right. Even if you're just looking at it on a business level, she's the one that knows this project inside out. Seems crazy to want rid of the girl. And in any case, I wouldn't do that to no one. Not her fault she was with that cunt, is it? She probably never knew what he was like. Fucking nice girl, Margo. Hates it that I still calls her that, by the way, but old habits die hard. She was one bird that every cunt was after when we was all young bucks. Part of it was that she was that classy, know where I'm going. She always had this thing about her. That's how come I always called her Margo, half to wind her up and that about the way she talked. Wouldn't've thought that she was from the barrio to hear the girl talk, mind you – she was like thingio from off've that show. No two ways about it man, the girl was fucking posh. That bit too young for myself, to be fair, but fuck was she a boss-looking girl! Another thing that stood out about her was she could *walk*, Margo. She walked like a lady. Always looked as though she knew she was going places. Would not be right to fuck her off from the Village now. Cormack's said to us, fair enough, Ged, it's your shout at the end of the day, but Margo Lascalles can not be seen to be fronting up this project in any way, shape or form. She's strictly below stairs if she's involved at all. She seemed all right with that, Margo, in fairness. Seemed made up just to stay on board.

Marguerite

The point is, you get one chance in life. That's one of the Rules. I nearly lost my chance and now I've got it back. I know exactly what I'm going to do and how I'm going to do it.

Re-start Schemes 3

Cormack

We take nothing for granted. By any standards at all we're thorough. We research, we lobby, we test and probe and feel our way ahead. But perhaps we've rested on our laurels with Ultimo – we've taken Ms Walker's ongoing involvement completely for granted. Ultimo is one of the key sites just behind Duke Street. It's a *big* club, quite under-utilised just now but definitely one of the gateways to The Loin. (We shudder with joy sometimes when we hear other people, people who in the past have opposed or doubted the scheme, mention The Loin by name. It reverberates. It's immediately mythic, like the Bowery or the Left Bank or Las Ramblas. *The Loin.*) The Loin is going to join the Chinatown tip of the South Village development with Ultimo and Duke Street. West of Duke Street and you're in clubland. Cream, Concert Square, the Wood Street lofts. Duke Street itself has been the front line for so long – or the last line. There's only really the Monro now that's managed to keep on going.

Yet, once upon a time Duke Street *was* clubland. Uglies. Hollywood. The Gazebo. The Exec. When we first arrived in this city, Duke Street was the frontierland that separated town from the mysterious depths of Liverpool 8. There were dozens and dozens of night-clubs, casinos, gay joints, drinking dens – open all hours, every day of the week. We loved that. It was a real city. We'd never known anything like that in Stranraer. It all seemed to fizzle out, though. First with Thatcher. The clubs stopped opening Mondays, then Tuesdays, Wednesdays. Then some of them closed for good. After the riots, they started all the promotions – Mad Mondays, Student Night, 60s Night, Doctors & Nurses. Where did it all go? Natural wastage, of course. Displacement. But Duke Street was where it was at. And it will be again. We'll be keeping a close eye on Ultimo from here on in.

Doable 1

Ged

Margo seems made up, to be fair. I'm made up myself. I wouldn't want to say that we never got on that well, we just never seen that much of one another. But it's like we're proper rellies, now. Better than that. We're getting on sound. We're like mates.

It's a weird one for myself. I've never, ever got up in the morning and gone into a office. But that's what I've been doing these last few days. Margo's been showing us the blueprints and explaining how it's all going to take shape. The last phase of the Village, this Stables and what have you, is just mind-bending. They've uncovered a whole street, almost exactly how it used to be in the olden days. We're looking to preserve it as far as possible, but bringing the houses into commercial use in some way. Fuck knows how, to be fair – we're waiting on the findings of one of these council think-tank efforts to get back to us on what the options might be, what's doable and what's not. But the bottom line is that the little street and the stables at the end stays exactly how they are. My two'll be made up with that. Bang into all this conservation, they are. Can't wait to tell them all about it. They'll be made up with us. Can't wait to tell them all about it.

We've already got tenants for a lot of the First Phase. I know I can get Johnny Halloran to take up a lease on the Acoustic Café. He'd love that and all, Johnny. He's got places in town, clubs and what have you, but he fucking *loves* music. He does, he's always going to watch bands and that. Fucking names he comes out with – he's worse than our two. He'd fucking love a place that's half a café but bands come and do a low-key set, acoustic or what have you. Bit like Kirklands, how it used to be. Bit of scran downstairs, bottle of wine, jug of sangria or whatever, then upstairs for a boogie. He'll go for that, Johnny. He'll double go for it.

Just Business

Moby

I've had a quick word with our Gerrard, but, in all fairness to the lad, he never sounded like he was taking in what I was saying to him. Fobbed us off a bit, to be completely fair. I just wanted to have a quick word with him about that other thing. I've never been like this over work before. I don't fucking *like* work. But that little gaff and that, that Ultimo – I don't know what it is. I fancy it. I do. It might be fuck all to a lot of people, but I fancy making a go of it. My own little place and that. Have the lads round to watch the girls, maybe get a bit of a thing going with them every now and then – not when we're busy and that, obviously. At the end of the day, it's a business and the business comes first. But I could see a nice little thingio going, all the lads coming down of a Tuesday or Wednesday afternoon before the European games, put a big pan of scouse on – fucking like the sound of that, by the way. All's I wanted was to ask our Gerrard what he thought and that – whether I could make a go of it. Weren't really listening to us, in fairness. Not proper, he weren't.

It is hard for the lad, to be fair to him. People are on his case the whole time for this and that. You couldn't blame him if he just switched that fucking mobie off.

Could not say a word about it if he went and done that, in fairness. Said he'd see us in Dool's for brekkie, but he'll be up the wall still, pound to a penny. Did say one thing, mind you. Didn't say fuck all about whether he thinks the place is a goer or nothing like that. But he did say that if I wanted a right-hand man and that, why not think about Steady? Which is fair comment at the end of the day. Fucking good lad, Steady is. Fucking solid. And he's out soon. Could do a lot worse than Mr Steadman, to be fair. Give that some serious thought, I will. Don't know where that leaves little Jade, by the way. I do like the girl. I do – I think she's quality. Fucking nice girl and all, too. But most of the lads has got places or businesses and what have you, and I do half fancy having this gaff for myself. I fancy having my own place where all hands are, know where I'm going, 'Here y'are, that's Moby's gaff, that.' Would be a shame to fuck her off, in all fairness. But at the end of the day, that's what I might have to do. Business is business, to be fair.

Family Fortunes 1

Ged

Pair a little tigers, they are. If they both end up being lawyers, which is what they're saying at the minute, then God help the poor cunts that comes up against them. Leave me standing sometimes, they do. Some of the fucking stuff they come out with and all, too. I don't mind the binlids making a cunt out of myself, by the way. I'm made up when they come out with some of the things they do – I don't even know what half the things they say *mean*. It's her I'm upset with. She's no different from myself. She knows fuck all. She certainly don't know fuck all about listed buildings or none of that, so I do not know what the fuck *she* was fucking laughing at.

All's it was, was – I'm telling them all about this stables and that and at first our Stephen's bang into it, asking us loads of questions and that and I'm coming back with all the right answers. I'm reaming some of it, to be fair, just spoofing up the answers. Like, he asks us if the street was kind of like this E. Chambre Hardman's gaff in Rodney Street. Did not know what the fuck the lad was on about, in all fairness, but I reams it with him and I starts to get a flavour of what it's all about. This aul' photographer's gaff in town, still pretty much preserved as it was when the fella was living there fucking years ago. Bit like that Anne Frank's yard, but loads of aul' photographs and all, too.

Then Cheyenne starts chipping in. With Shy, you never can tell whether she's taking the piss. Stony-faced, she is. Only cracks up once she's made a cunt out of you. She's asking us all about the tiles on this little street of houses. Are they some fucking kind of slate or are they fucking Cheshire rose clay or what? Have not got a fucking *clue*, by the way. I hasn't even been down to this site, yet. Only just got told about it all, in fairness. But the girl does genuinely seem to want to know all about it and I'm bang into it myself, the three of us all buzzing off've the same thingio – well, four if we're counting her. From what I remember the tiles was black or black-*ish*, slate grey and that. So I goes to her – I says to Shy: 'Think they was Afghani black, girl.'

Don't know why. Do not for the life of myself know

where the fuck that came from. I half think it come from the way tiles look in the rain. Slick and what have you. Afghani black though, by the way. Haven't even heard of it for twenty-odd fucking years. Must've just been lodged in there, wedged in the back of my head and that. Cheyenne looks at us. Like I say, she's stony-faced. Can not get a reading from off've her. Fucking Jesus, help the poor cunt that comes up against her in a courtroom, by the way. Make mincemeat of the cunt, she will. Make a fucking balloon out of any cunt. She looks at us.

'What was that, Daddy?'

Sweet little girlie voice, mind you. Should've known I was getting it when she called us Daddy. Always means there's something around the corner when she calls us that. Pocket money or sleepovers or something – something I'm not going to like. Did I fucking take the hint, though? Did I fuck.

'Pretty sure on that, babe. I've been looking over the gen thisavvy. Afghani black is what the tiles are, girl. Deffo. Afghani black.'

I'm looking at her, nodding my stupid head like I knows what I'm on about. She looks back. Almost looks spiteful at times, our Cheyenne does. In fairness, she does have that bit of hardness about her, half like she fucking despises you. Our Stephen looks like he's going to burst, the little cunt. Cunt's looking dead ahead at the table, mouth clamped shut and you can see he's fucking pissing hisself. And she is and all, too. Fucking Deborah. What the fuck she's got to laugh about is any cunt's fucking guess, because she's had exactly fuck all to contribute to this conversation. Fucking thick as shite, she is.

'Afghani black?'

I just nods, now. I feel a cunt.

To be fair, she's fucking merciless. Is not going to give myself a inch, here. Then they all looks at each other and fucking explodes. The three of them, all laughing their bollocks off. They've left us no choice in the matter. I just gets up and leaves the table.

Lunch

Cormack

A presentation to City Focus that will take all morning, then lunch with the exquisite Jade. Whenever there is tiresome work to be done, we try to alleviate it with some manner of treat. Jade Walker is one of the things of joy in our life. At one time not so long ago the scene makers might have classed her as a Lipstick Lesbian. That would have been a mistake. That would have been to wage war upon the tenacious Ms Walker.

She is one person we always look forward to seeing. For one thing, she's relentless. She thinks about every single question before answering. Even with a bland 'How are you?', she wants to give you a fair and accurate appraisal. We enjoy the intellectual rough and tumble of a date with Jade Walker – although we wish she'd apply more rigour to her modish speech rhythms. She talks like someone from *Hollyoaks* – and we find it rather irritating.

But that is to be *most* ungenerous. Jade is as yet a mere child. She works in a young environment and she has not learnt to sieve the inflections and pretensions of youth. And her youth is not without its compensations

– our Jade is, and one can not, *need* not overlook this, breathtakingly easy on the eye. She is a rare and stunning beauty. We could gaze on her for hours on end. It is not without the most stupendous guilt that we allow the pleasures she brings with such ease. This heaven she dispenses with purity and generosity. She thinks nothing of it. Why, then should we? We can not help that. And yet, with the joy comes also the pain. As much as I have often wanted it, wanted just some little sign that she feels anything more than a meticulous grace and satisfaction in her skill, she will never, has never bestowed a kiss. Jade will not kiss me. We have come to accept that as part and parcel of a strangely remote and thrilling girl who brings so many things to our life.

And there's a third thing. With her hard-nosed confidence and her sassy, almost self-righteous conviction in her own scheme of things, she greatly reminds us of ourselves when we first came to this city as students. Many, many years ago, alas. But we're still here, still in love with the old whore Liverpool and all her voluptuous legacies. And we're about to do some good for the old girl, too. We're going to bring some ideas to this city that might make a difference. Too late for us of course – we are old. But we think we might finally make a difference. And that would be good.

Moby

One thing that I do love is that *Sport*. Tell you la – it's not the photies, it ain't the stories, it's the fucking other thing. The fucking adverts, la. Fucking telling you man, I cannot wait for her to fuck off out the house so's I can get into some of them little adverts and pull the fucking head off it. Look at this one, man. Fucking better, it is. Fucking vintage, la.

'*Mature Lady, large breasts, curvaceous figure, out of practice since death of husband needs dominant male to pleasure her. Can entertain. S. Manchester.*'

What? That is fucking gorgeous, that is. Aul' lady with big tits, going up the wall 'cos she's not getting no quality in her life, knowmean. I can fucking see the aul' mare now – fucking *dying* for some cunt to just pin her down and ram her. Fucking noises you'd get out of her, by the way. What? That has got Mr Moby rock hard, that has. That's got myself ready to rock. South Manchester? Is right.

Ged

Margo's taking myself to one of these new gaffs in town for lunch. *Lunch*, by the way! She's saying we need to zap some of their interior design ideas for the Acoustic Café, but she says she's had a little something from off've the grapevine and all, too. It's to do with ourselves, she reckons, just some possible recommendations from them planners about this last phase of the Village. The Stables and that.

Cormack

This is the aspect of the job that we relish least. We've never really taken to public speaking, though it undoubtedly is one of those things we simply nail with practice. We're constantly in the public eye, on the television, in the newspapers, so it's as well to make our point as powerfully and concisely and as simply as possible. Simplicity is a good thing.

But presentations – presentations are another matter

altogether. Here, we are addressing our foes, our allies, those who potentially are both. On this occasion, it's a routine debrief to City Focus. But we all know it's so much more than that. City Focus are policy formers. City Focus have more ultimate sway on matters of architecture and planning than we do ourselves. But we have one small advantage – at least in theory. It was we, after all, who recommended the council hire Marc Kelman and, in reality, Marc is more friend than foe. And yet he's scrupulous. He's almost *too* rigorous. He needs to know *everything* and he calls us in for reports and update sessions constantly.

The other reality is that, whereas it has widespread support and the right *sort* of support, The Loin does have its detractors. Our local constabulary, for example, are far from impressed with our liberal stance on drugs. They *understand* the argument – they just don't *agree* with it. Other elements of the council, too, have maintained a watching brief that's more a watchful silence. That happens, of course. If we're a success, they'll want in. But they're happy to bide their time. Bottom line is this. The Loin will happen, is happening – but it still needs to be rubber-stamped. There's a substantial grant element we need to bring on line if Ged Brennan is going to continue pushing on with his end. That's where Marc is indispensable. It's City Focus, fundamentally, who gets us that rubber stamp.

On this occasion, he's requested a bald policy debrief for a guy from Brussels. He's told us the guy is *not* crucial to the future of The Loin – he's from a separate architectural commission – but he's well aware of the work we're doing. He's interested in the ways in which town planning and social inclusion can collide, so this presentation will be more than just window-dressing. When Marc Kelman informs us it's procedural, he knows that we know precisely what he means by that. But it *matters*. No matter who the messenger, we need to ensure that the message back to Brussels is a positive one. We need to keep the guy smiling. And if we do that, if we make Liverpool look good in front of him, then we do the growing international reputation of City Focus no harm at all. They are independent consultants. They are in business. By a perversity of logic, if we are on form this morning, we please the agency whose services we pay handsomely to retain.

It's all going fine. They're both doing a lot of nodding and smiling. Intriguingly, though, the man from Brussels sits up intently now we've got to the meat of the subject – the notion of a council-regulated permissive zone. His primary interest is the waterfront – supposedly. So what's his brief? What's he after? Is this something Europe is looking at across the board? We hope so, of course – but we hope that Liverpool is seen to have piloted and pioneered the initiative. Pot has already been downgraded nationwide, of course, and there was a *big* lobby at the NHS conference in favour of prescription methadone on the health service. This is good, mainly. These are good conditions for pushing right on with The Loin. And we *are* streets ahead of the game. We need to get this right, though – all of it. We're pointing at a big and basic map as we address them – river, town, docks, clubland.

'Ultimo is just behind Duke Street, on the corner of Henry Street. The South Village extends as far as Grenville Street, at its closest to the city centre. The Stables, still wonderfully archaic, even after several attempted bombings and even worse from a succession of Tory councils . . . .'

Pause for chuckling. None forthcoming. Head down and on with it.

'. . . The Stables represent the counterpoint to Ultimo. They're two absolutely vital – in every sense, but mainly in the purest sense – sites for us. They bring this project to life. They're not just gateways, they're focal points. They set the tone, the ambience – they're the landmarks that tell visitors they're entering a separate zone, and as such they have to be integrated perfectly into the soul and rhythm of The Loin. If Ultimo, is, we trust, the first leisure venue you hit when you penetrate The Loin from the city centre, the Stables will form the heart of the warren. It's a totally pedestrianised concept, encouraging not just appointment visitors and hedonists but also the casual, the curious, those straying off the beaten path. The Loin will welcome voyeurs, but a measure of its integration into the city's inscape will come from the numbers who drift up from the South Village when it's fully operational. The traffic of visitors should be multi-directional, and as far as the South Village is concerned it should travel in both directions. The two communities need to coexist, to complement each other and, ultimately, to blend their boundaries into one bohemian swathe.'

Margueritte

Time for phase one of the new plan. Poor Ged. He's quite a honey. I could easily get to like him if I didn't have to use him so badly. But that's one of my Rules. There *is* no bad in business. And this is business. Forget all the other rubbish, the Uptones and the piecemeal developments we've got going here, there and every-where. The South Village is what I want. It's mine. That's all there is to it. It's *mine*. Black is black – I want my baby back.

Cormack

We won't have a problem with City Focus. Marc has guided the meeting in just the right way. The Brussels wallah has raised one or two practical queries. In actual fact, his are the sorts of question that bode well – this we know from much and varied prior experience. Which buildings, if necessary, could the council target for CPO if their owners resist the city's vision for development – things like that. But he's with us. He's *so* with us that he's bringing a working party back next month to show off this model for inner-city regeneration. The Loin is going to happen.

But now we've appeased the politicos, we have to get back on track with the fabric. We've made some extremely bold predictions today. We have to ensure they come to pass. From our side, the South Village aspect now seems to be back in production. Ged Brennan is behaving. We can work with him, and the South Village will work – with him.

So we now need to get back to young Jade and make certain she's fully cognisant of and prepared for all eventualities vis-à-vis the rather bizarre news that Anthony Brennan is to assume ownership of Ultimo. There wasn't a problem while Mr Green was still with us. He would gladly have offloaded the place at first reasonable offer. Our assumption was always that Jade would quietly build up the business, expand her customer base as effortlessly and elegantly as always, in a way that, as soon as the money comes on line for The Loin, Ultimo can receive full and immediate benefit. Jade, with a team of designers, will ensure that aesthetically, thematically and spiritually Ultimo announces itself as the gateway to Liverpool's throbbing new Loin barrio. But now, suddenly, we have Moby Brennan on the scene.

Jade, of course, has been a consultant to our steering committee almost from the outset. It's incredible the impact a passionate, intelligent and beautiful prostitute can have on the hearts and groins of local politicians. We're confident she will eat this dullest of the Brennan boys for breakfast. But it is important now that we get her report on the new owner as soon as possible. Or perhaps we could make that leaseholder, if necessary.

Ged

North-American restaurant, by the way. State of the menu. Here's one:

> Arkansas Goulash: a rich and aromatic melange of maize-fed Texarkana chicken fillet diced and doused in a stew of turnip, mild chillis, corn and vine tomatoes.

Chicken and turnip stew. Sounds all right that does, as it goes. Never will understand why these gaffs make a big thing of how unfresh the gear must be, mind you. Fucking Martha's Vineyard lobster and Vancouver sea bream and what have you. How fucking fresh can that be at the end of the day? You can park your dinghy off've Hilbre Island and catch sea bass right now if you want fresh. Does not have to say 'From Dead Far Away' on it, in my book. Nearer the better, if you're asking my good self.

I'm not a one for big mad dinners, myself. I don't want to be a aul' arse over it, but it's just not for myself. I can't help it – I just think the soonest it's out again the better it must be for you. I hardly even used to make dinner when I was in the house. She'd be out most days, aerobics or shopping or what have you. Myself, I just couldn't be arsed. I'd skip brekkie and just have a early dinner about half eleven. Usually, I'd just put a pan of beans on, tip a tin of tuna in and stir it up. Just heat it through, know where I'm going – I wouldn't let it get to the boil. Then I'd stand there in the kitchen with that Sky Sports news on, hoping for a blimp of that Georgie Thompson. Everyone goes on about Kenny's girl and that Kirsty Gallagher one, the one that married the rugby fella, but Georgie's different class. I'd eat it straight out the pan.

In fairness, the scran in this place looks all right. Simple enough clobber it is, not too silly. They could get away with lobbing my own tuna and beans special on the menu, here. What'd they'd call that one, then? 'Cape Cod Beanpot'? Is right.

Margueritte

For a big, tough fella he's awfully unsure of himself. All his actions, everything about him tell you he doesn't feel comfortable. He doesn't belong here. No, I can refine that. He doesn't feel as though he *deserves* to be here. If he'd only look up instead of gluing his eyes to the menu, he'd see he's in company. None of the wretches in here *belong*. With minimal strain, I can see a very young soap starlet lunching with a writer who's comfortably old enough to be her father – doubtless telling her he's devised a character specifically with her in mind. I bet he has. There's a retired villain with his despicable brief, Jonathan Hunting, two tables away – and making up the numbers, if I'm not very much mistaken, is a very senior Granada TV producer. There's one of the Liverpool FC board sitting with the buyer and the head of PR of one of the fashion stores. I can never remember names, but I never forget a face. Shelagh Cormack, though. There's a name I'll never forget. Who's *that* she's with? She's absolutely stunning, whoever she is. Credit where it's due – that is a very good-looking girl she's landed herself. Looking around the room, actually, it's a tale of the beauties and the beasts. And the beasts have all the power, the ugly bastards.

All of which brings me back to Ged. He could be such a player in this world. He's quite dry, quite droll and with his physique and his George Clooney looks he could clean up if he decided to play the game. But he can't. He's hidebound – totally straight. He doesn't even flirt. I mean, I'm not being anything more than factual here – this is reportage, that's all. And the news is, most men would kill to fuck me. I'm obviously quite used to being me, but every now and then I see how a new man looks at me. They're staggered by what they see. Women, too. It's nothing more than the plain truth – I'm an astonishing-looking girl. Iman, is what people always say, but I honestly don't see that. I'm much better looking than Iman and nowhere near as black. And what's more, I'm a good six inches taller than her and I would never resort to fucking David Bowie unless he could get the South Village back for me. Right here, right now, I'm getting a faint buzz from the reaction as I walk back from the Ladies, but from Ged – nothing. He's dead to me, dead to his surroundings. I'm wearing a Prada blouse, three buttons elegantly, beguilingly undone to give no more than a suggestion of honey-brown cleavage, and he's completely immune to it. Not a flicker.

I can't even imagine him having sex. I'm certain I'm not the only one who does this, but one of the first things I drift into when I'm with someone new, is to wonder about their sexual side. I can be sitting there talking to them, but a part of me is wondering to myself: do they *do it*? Does she fellate him? Does she *like* it? Debbi Brennan, yes. She's an alleycat. Pure white trash Debs is. In actual fact, she's more orange trash these days, the amount of time she spends on the sunbeds. But she's alive, at least. She still reeks of the street. If Debbi had to fuck you to keep hold of her home and her Mosquito card she would do just that. One hundred per cent – she'd screw the arse off you. And she'd enjoy it, by the looks of her. That toned and fanatically buffed and waxed body of hers is just honed for hard action. But her hubby? It's going to have to be more than feminism fatale to get old Gedders out of the road. Fortunately, I do have a Plan B.

Ged

Strange how the memories start filtering back. I hadn't really thought about her for years, other than what to get her for Chrimbo and that, whether to invite them round for kiddies' parties or what have you. Driving back now, I can remember them first coming to the barrio. I remember the *rumour* of them, anyway. We'd all heard about Margo before we seen her, heard about this fucking gorgeous black girl that was six foot tall and had eyes like Bambi. Did we fuck, by the way. All's we had was Franner half having a coronary, going on about her tits and her legs and her arse. He was the first lad I ever knew who was into birds' arses – probably because his own was so fucking fat and horrible. Got a lot of time for the lad, I have.

There was other Haitian families round by ours, but not that many of them, and nothing like Margo's clan. They was dead religious, for starters. Serious – they all used to go off to church, the whole lot of them. Their Henri was the nearest to myself in age and he was all right. Boss footballer he was, *dead* skilful and everything, and he could have a fight and all, too. He never used to get involved if he could help it, but if he had to the lad knew how to have a proper go-around.

But their aul' fella still made him go to Mass. There was loads of them, or it seemed like that because they was all so fucking tall. That's what I remember about Margo. We'd all line up on the corner of Admiral Street, waiting to give them loads. Their church was up just off've Prinny and they'd come down Windsor Street almost in single file, old Pere Lascalles at the front. Margo always, always used to wear these white knee-length socks and she had her hair scraped into bunches with this mad wax to make it shiny. She looked like a fucking orphan. Antwacky clothes, bunches, white socks – proper virgin, she were. But when she seen us lot waiting on the corner, suddenly she'd put all this attitude into her walk. And I remember it, now. It weren't, like, I may be wearing this clobber but underneath it I can *rock*. It was: stare at us all's you like, you gang of no-marks, because not one of youse is ever getting within a inch of this piece of fanny. I'm cut out for better. I remember that look. Fucking scary, by the way. Fuck knows what she seen in Him.

Jade

It's, like – I'm always pleased to see Councillor Cormack? I don't know whether you could properly describe us as *friends*, although I don't know why not, either. It's like, the things we've been through together since we've known each other, we'd certainly pass muster. But it's *so* not just about that with the councillor and I. I mean, there's no way I could've done all of this without her guidance and support – and that support has *so* gone beyond like just sound advice.

Like, one of the odd things about me was that I *loved* my course. Most kids tolerated theirs, did the bare minimum to make their grades, but me – I used to wake up excited. I wanted to *know* more. And I developed, like, a fascination for female sexual politics. Not *feminism* per se – at least not the feminism that was the given understanding of so many of my fellow students. That particular school of thought seemed to have an inherent understanding that men were in and of themselves The Enemy. Their credo, as told by the Dworkins of this world (who I don't disregard, I hasten to add), had it that if we could forsake men in every way, we could go forward and plan for success and happiness. All female misery was and is generated by masculine dominance. They even argued, yeah, that in sexual congress, a woman satisfying herself by taking what part of a man she needed – going on top, restraining him with bindings, punishing him or having him lavish her with cunnilingus – was only deluding herself. To acquiesce to any sex act with a male was to be complicit in one's own abuse.

But I *so* did not, and do not, go along with all of that. At first, I found difficulty articulating my theory, but I felt its truth lay in a more honest appraisal of the multiplicity and complexity of, like, female sexual need. Being simplistic, I was looking to investigate the way our needs and desires change? How our sexuality can be fluid? And I kept on going back to the Patsy Kensit night – I knew that bound up in all the things I let loose that night were the same basic truths that confront a lot of women. To be blunt, I just could not work out why women could not cut themselves the exact same deal that men seemed to take for granted, yeah? Why, for example, should a sexually frustrated woman trapped within the constraints of a loveless and sexless marriage not avail herself of the services of a prostitute? Or, why could she not let off steam in a lap-dance bar in the same, relatively harmless way that men do? These seemed to me to be aspects of the sex industry that helped to, like, *relieve* some of society's pressure situations. Violence, depression, all manner of anti-social behaviour can often be traced back to a lack of sexual outlet – yet the sex industries were services predominantly only available for men. These were just like two of the areas I felt intrinsically could lead me to some truth, and they were areas I was determined to know more about.

And after the furore surrounding 'Streetlife', yeah, Rick Knighton introduced me to Councillor Cormack – at her request. She was fairly, like, guarded at first? But over a period of time she confided in me about her working party's vision for a Permissive Zone in the city centre. I would have, like, *so* readily got involved in that anyway? I would joyously and enthusiastically have helped in whatever ways she wanted, but Shelagh Cormack immediately commissioned me on to the advisory panel as a consultant. The money isn't amazing, but that has never been the overriding issue with me. Money is a bonus and it only becomes a big thing with me if I feel as though I'm being exploited. I *so* will not line someone else's pockets, yeah? But The Loin development, as Shelagh calls it – that fills me with the same thrill of possibility that my degree course did for so many years. I want to see it come to life? I believe in it absolutely? I can't believe that anyone should want to oppose it – but oppose it they do, of course. It gives me *such* a rush, though. It's a pure and powerful thrill, and the thing that thrills me more than anything is that it feels *possible*. It's within our grasp. It *is* going to happen. I think The Loin is going to happen. But as I'm telling Shelagh here, this Moby is going to be trouble.

Ged

Can't believe what the girl is telling us here. We're not even a month into the thing and Margo's telling us what fucking Manhead is planning for Duke Street. I fucking knew there'd be weirdness, to be fair. Fucking woman with sidies, in a suit. Button-down shirt, fucking cigar, fucking no fucking make-up! Can not for the life of myself think now how I never smelt a rat. That's if what Margo's telling us is right, by the way, and there's no reason to think she's lying.

By the sounds of it, old Millie Tant is wanting to create a fucking druggie's paradise, with all kinds of knocking shops and bars for benders and cokeheads and all sorts. I know from the *Echo* that she's got some fucking weird ideas, that Cormack, but to be totally fair I'd have to say I turns straight to the footy pages. I haven't really bothered with it, in fairness. End of the day I should've read up on it – bit embarrassing, it were. Margo seemed surprised that I never knew more about it. Says it's been all over the papers. I know there's been bits and bobs, but there hasn't really been no meaty story about it. If there has, *I* haven't seen none of it.

That's wrecked my head, that has. Kids was made up when I told them all that about them Stables the other day. They might have had a laugh and a joke with myself about the tiles and what have you, but bottom line is they're made up with us. Afghani black or not, they was made up that myself is involved in a conservation project. Now I've got to go home and tell them all bets are off, their aul' fella's a fucking pimp and a dealer. Fuck that, by the way.

I was ready just to do one when Margo told myself one very important thing, mind you. Don't know what I'd've done without the girl, to be fair. Probably would've done one already, by now. But she's right. Girl is a fucking top brief, by the way, fucking double sharp, she is. And she's told us: who, by the way, is the fucking developer here? Only Yours Truly. I myself am the fucking developer here. The council can advise and they can stand in the way and veto no end of ideas from us. They can go to appeal and they can carp and moan and slap no end of conditions and orders on us. But what they can not do is they can't, won't, *can not* make us go ahead with that fucking rat's nest they're wanting to build. No wonder she never told us nothing, aul'

Manhead. She was biding her time, weren't she? She was waiting till it was all too late for my good self to do fuck all about it? Well, I've got news for her. She can forget it. Her perverts' fucking paradise is not even getting off've the starting block if GB has got anything to do with it.

Margueritte

Mission accomplished. If that doesn't set the cat among the pigeons, then I don't know what will. Whoever thought that this girl was dead and buried had better think again. We've only just begun.

On Monsters

Moby

I'll admit it. I like Monsters. I don't mind saying so. You know exactly where the fuck you are with a Monster. Chicks like that Jade one today, they're all well and good to look at and wank over. If you're lucky, you'll find one that likes fucking you even more than what she likes looking at herself in the mirror. But by and large, girls like that Jade is a waste of a time. I mean it. Go for a horror, any fucking day of the week.

And it's not just fucking law of averages, by the way, neither. It's not even that aul' one of, knowmean, they'll half be desperate and that. Be grateful for it. It's not that. I just go for them, end of. At the end of the day, I like skates.

Got it down to a fine art I have and all, too. That Internet, la, I was like that when it first come in. All hands started going on about it. Like, all the European games with the Redmen, the lads was website this, website that, blah blah Ryanair, £32 from Stansted, Go will fucking pay *you* to fly with them. Like a gang of tarts, they was. But it was on one of them trips that old Paul the Hom told us about *Scat*.

Now, this'll disgust a lot of people but I for one do not mind a bird taking a dump right on my chest. Fucking love it, I do. And there's plenty enough birds that love it and all too, by the way. Oh yes. Golden Showers, Disabled Gentlemen, Toothless and Fifty – there's a chat room for each and every one of them. Serious. If your particular thingio is that you want to get gobbled off by a aul' granny with no teeth, just log on to *Mabel's List*. Veiny tits, destroyed nipples, collapsed arses – get fucking paid! Aul' Paul put us on to all of that.

He's all right, by the way, Paul the Hom. Some of the lads are still that bit thingio with him, but I've got a lot of time for the lad. Never really knew him all that well before the Rome trip – well, the fucking Ancona trip, the amount of time we ended up having in the eternal fucking city. But it's times like that that you get talking to people, really get to know them and that. Tell you what, he knows some fucking things, that Paul! Telling us all sorts, he was. *The Art of War*, that was one thing he was going on about. He was shitting himself that little bit, in fairness, worried that the Roma clan was going to moody it like they done in '84.

To be fair, he's never said he's hard, Paul – but he *is* a bit of a shithouse. First time I really ever seen his grid he was shitting hisself. Chelsea away, fourth round of the Cup, 1978 – what a fucking season that was. Chelsea were whacking big time in them days, whacking all comers they was. The Shite had had them first game of the season. No excuses, they took loads and that, but Chelsea hopped on them at Kenny High, didn't they? Didn't so much hop on them, in fairness, they annihilated them – threw all kinds at them, pure wiped them out. The lads I know that was there, they're half going back on that now, saying how it weren't that bad. If that's right, how comes they asked all us lot to give them a hand when Chelsea come up here that October? And they *did* come and all, too. Loads of punks and skins and that, silver DMs and donkey jackets. Fuck all that palaver about how they was all in Lois and trainies – were they fuck. I was one of the ones that lured them into Gerrard Gardens after the game. I weren't at the match and that, fuck that – but I was there after. I seen the cunts. And I fucking heard them and all, too. One all, by the way.

So when we went down there in the Cup we was all singing: 'We won't be like Everton, we won't die at Kensington!'

Tell you what though, la, fuckinell! Fucking *thousands* of the cunts, there was. We had a tidy crew ourselves and that, all good lads, by the way, all lads that knew each other. But tell you what, kidder, after that match . . . We all gets split up and that. I'm on the tube, just trying to keep my head down and blend in. There's all kinds of Chelsea on the train, all talking about where Liverpool are going to be and how they'll have to mingle in and what have you. Telling you, la, that's a fucking nightmare, that is. You're on a tube train, you've got about another six stops to go and you're right in the thick of Chelsea's fucking boys. The one thing that was saving me was that I was about the only lad in our mob that never had a wedge. Still a bit of a skin, I was. I was wearing a Harrington and Samba but I was into that Sham 69 and that – like say, half still a bonehead, in all fairness. That's when I first seen Paul the Hom.

He was stood on the other side of the compartment, holding on to one of them handrails. I just suddenly become thingio – suddenly could feel him looking at myself. And what I seen was a lad pure fucking gone white. His fucking face, la – it's the end of January and he's got sweat fucking *pouring* down his face. How the Chelsea skins never seen him I still do not know. Maybe they wouldn't've seen him, neither – but he's trying to tell myself something with his eyes. He's making this big mad eye contact with myself, and what he's nodding at is my wrist. My forearm, if you will – he's nodding at it and making big angry eyes. And then I twigs – he's telling myself that my tattoo is starting to show. The sleeve of my Harrington has slipped down that little bit and you can see the claws of the Liver Bird and the LFC. I'll never know if someone would've clocked it sooner or later – the carriage was packed out, so probably not, in fairness. But suddenly one of their little rats susses Paul, follows his eyeline and that's that.

Know what was the worst part of what happened? He never done nothing mad. That was what was fucking horrible. He looked myself in the eye, half done a little grin then whispers something to the lad next to him. And I can see the word getting passed round. All's I can say is that I made it better for myself by not trying to run. I knew right away that that would've made it worse – and we couldn't've gotten away anyway, in fairness. Fucking panned us, they did. Weren't one of them horror stories you hear, one of them where a lad

68

gets his eyelid sliced off or they put ciggies out on his face. They never fucking tortured us or nothing. Fucking Paul, though – crying his eyes out, he were. Made a cunt of himself, in fairness. After that one, he started trying to do mad things and that, half trying to get a little bit of rep back for his self. But I never really got to know the lad till Ancona.

He was telling us about this little book from the Middle Ages wrote by a Chinese fella about how, if you followed some basic rules, you could never get beat in a tear-up. Mind you, one of them basic rules was Don't Fight If There's More Of Them Than You, so it wasn't like the fella was telling you nothing you didn't know.

Scat, though. I never knew nothing about that. And it's not like you have to drive to fucking Milton Keynes to find some monster that wants you to piss on her. Oh no. You types in your area, keeps it as general as you feel like, and they'll come back with ten or fifteen names of absolute fucking dogs you can go and see within a hour. Fucking superb, it is. I'm gorging my good self on it, I am. Fucking *gorging* myself.

Some of it's a bit thingio, in fairness. I mean to say, it's not thingio in that sense, just, like, they'll want you to wank yourself off over the webcam and all of that. I can't be doing with webcams. How the fuck does all that work, by the way? Just give Mr Moby a name, a place and a time, and I will be there. Make no mistake. I will be there and I will roast your dimpled fat arse.

I can always tell the ones that's wanting a good go-around. I don't leave no margin for error, by the way. You can't afford to be too genteel, know where I'm going. Paul told us that. Give us some good tips, he did.

So I know my way around all that now. I'll just ask some very basic questions.

Please answer the following as honestly as possible. I am a man in his 30s, bald, muscular physique, big cock. I'm interested in large ladies that likes it rough. Other turn-ons include GS, F and S/M. Which of the following best describes you?

1) Body: ample, fat, obese
2) Looks: unusual, ugly, hideous
3) Nipples: coarse, bulbous, lacerated
4) Downstairs: bushy, trimmed, bald
5) Belly: round, flabby, overhanging

Any other special information – e.g. stretch marks, varicose veins, specialist needs and desires.

That was Paul's bit and all, too – he wasn't trying to say I'd be into that, just like it's that much better to know what you might be dealing with. Didn't feel like telling the lad that the more fucked they are the more I'm into them. Oh yes. Oh yes indeed.

Two interesting things about them last two on the list, by the way. One is that I can not bring myself to mention the downstairs to a stranger and that, someone that I don't even know. And the belly. The belly is the thing. If I can get a reply from a Judy that's fifty-odd, shaven and her belly's so loose it's folded over, then old Moby's in clover. That's a dream ticket, that is, by the way. That is heaven. And they're there. They *are* there, these birds. Fucking going up the wall for lads like myself, they are. It fucking amazed me at first how many of them come back describing theirselves as 'hideous' and 'obese'. They was the ones that knew how it worked, they were. Knew the whole fucking score, they did. And they was the ones I couldn't wait to see. Could not fucking wait, by the way.

Home

Cormack

The majority of folk who live on their own have acclimatised themselves to it. They've become accustomed. We, on the other hand, *adore* living the solitary life. We'd have it no other way. From a convenience point of view, the fact of having nobody else to answer to or take into consideration is a wonderful thing. And the tranquillity, the solitude, the ability to be absolutely flexible and spontaneous one day, programmed and predictable the next – these are things of joy. Mostly, we end the day sat on this gorgeous balcony. We don't dispute that we were fortunate to be in the right place at a time when these apartments in the Colonnades were unknown, unusual and affordable. Who on earth wanted to live in a cavernous former warehouse? Worse, in this combative and militant city, a warehouse once concerned in the business of holding slaves prior to shipment and misery overseas? Who'd want to make their home here? Not many folk. Not then. But we knew as soon as we stumbled upon the place that it was Home.

Sitting right here, gazing out beyond the ink-black bay, way out to the gas rigs and supply craft, is the most sumptuous and restful thing. We're happy. We're relatively happy. We have peace of mind and we have things to look forward to. This seems to be a useful definition of a life that still has purpose. We have things to look forward to. And first among those is a visit from the uniquely gifted Jade. What it is that makes her so good, so free and so very willing to challenge conventional wisdom, we no longer question. It is enough that she is a free spirit and she will freely come here and soothe our weary flesh.

Patsy Kensit

Jade

Do I fancy Shelagh Cormack? I wouldn't say so, not *fancy* her *per se* but there is undeniably some trigger that gets pulled when I'm in the company of women like her. What I mean by women like her and for want of any better way of explaining it is, like, *manly* women? Women who, if we all followed the rules, would not even allow themselves to *wank* over a girl like me? But I go for them. I go with them. What it is, is – I turn them into *girls*? I make them go weak over me? And then I fuck them. I fuck them, I get dressed, I leave them. Shelagh's the only one I have ever had any kind of consideration for. With her, at times, I stay the night. I don't feel anything for her? But I like her? I can do something for her, so I do it. The only time it gets messy is when she herself gets soppy. She'll want to hold me. She's tried to kiss me. That has never, can never be any part of anything that takes place between Shelagh and I.

My first came a matter of days after Daddo's funeral. I still don't truly understand what happened or where it came from, but the indelible effect of it was that I came here and did a degree in sociology. I might have stayed with Mum and just put all those ambitions to one side – but I became me instead? To that extent, at least, there was a chain of events.

I'd gone to this pub in the centre of town on the most ridiculous of pretexts. A lad I quite liked on the basis that he did a little bit of dealing and had quite a good sense of humour and, well, all the other girls fancied him and he seemed to like me – this lad, Darren Power, told me that I needed 'cheering up'. Seriously, my dad's just died of a rapid and ravenous cancer and this bland, blond boy persuades me to come into town to be cheered up – and I accepted. I went.

I sat around pretending I'd seen the episodes of, like, *The Simpsons* that they were all laughing about. Even then, even at that age, I also picked up on the body language, the inter-male signs and signals that said that Darren, when he'd concluded being the life and soul of the Public Saloon, was probably going to fuck me. He was going to cheer me up.

I was washing my hands in the Ladies when a voice made me look in the mirror.

'You look like Patsy Kensit.'

In the mirror, I see a woman of about forty-five. Tough face, big bags under her eyes, yet she's not quite ugly. She has short grey hair and is wearing a tight white blouse tucked into grey men's slacks. I turn around. Her fingers, every one of her fingers, is covered with gold rings, sovereigns mainly, and she has at least two gold chains around her neck. Her blouse is undone.

'You're prettier, though. You're fucking gorgeous.

73

But you know that, don't you? You're fucking gorgeous.'

And a fire ignited between my legs. Fuck knows where that came from – I really don't recall wanting women before that night, certainly not old, grey, masculine women – but I wanted her to push me into a cubicle and drag down my jeans and bury those sovereign encrusted fingers in my cunt. I don't think I'd ever been so wet. The way the woman was looking at me was soaking me through.

That was Babs. I only ever saw her and Susan that one time – but it was enough. We played pool. Susan was quiet and almost pretty – pretty in a plain, sweet sort of way. She reminded me of Deirdre Barlow off *Corrie*. They both told me I was gorgeous, both let me win at pool. Babs bought us all Jack Daniel's. I remember her scowling at Susan when she got tipsy and told me I had beautiful breasts, but the argument was over in a second. They took me back to their house and, within a second of seating me on the couch, Babs was kissing me aggressively and Susan was feeling my tits. They had my top off. Both of them were fondling my tits, both at them at once, greedily mauling at my tits, kissing them, sucking them – and I loved it. I loved it so much. They took all my clothes off and Susan stood back, out of the picture while Babs kneeled down and licked my cunt. She said such disgusting things to me. She told me I was a pretty little bitch and she was going to chew my cunt up and make me come like thunder – and I just lay there. When I opened my eyes Susan was lying on the floor, in tears. But when I sat up, she smiled at me. It was a beautiful smile, one I'll never forget. It seemed to say: 'Me too.'

That night changed everything.

Numbers and that

Paul

Normal morning for Paulie: up at five fifty-five and out the house at six o-six. Don't like even numbers, me, but what can you do? There are going to be times when you've got to work with even numbers. I've been cutting out at six o-six for years now and nothing too bad's happened. It's just one of them things, isn't it – I can't hardly wait for seven o-seven or I'd be well behind. That'd totally fuck me up, that would.

I cut up Maria and Helena and across Rice Lane and into the park. I do at least three complete circuits, right around Wally Hall Park then back to ours for seven thirty-seven. I love that start to the day. No matter what the weather, I will always always put the work in, in the park. Can't really explain how fantastic it sets you up. It just does. You're sharp, you're fit, you're ready for whatever.

When I get back to ours, I always always always wake my aul' fella up with a cuppa, but that's as far as any conversation goes. Neither of us is a big one for chit-chat, we just go about our own thing. He's still quite a handy lad, old Brian. If it weren't for the ale he could've gone all the way. Certainly could've had his own team of lads, maybe could've moved a bit of gear, who knows. Had one hell of a dig on him in his day. I know. But he's all right with me now. I know I give him good rent and that, and it's me puts the food on the table, but I think he's got used to me now, too. I think, in his own way, he likes things the way they are.

Once I've give him his cuppa, I make myself either porridge in the winter or just a bowl of cereal in the warmer months. Maybe something like bran flakes with some sliced apple and strawberry on top. I love that. I do. I'm not really one for the gym. I mean, I am, I love to work out, but people that know me take it that I'm there for the wrong reasons. I can handle that – but I don't want to *have* to handle that. And besides, I've got everything I need out in the back shed. There's weights, a pull-up bar – I'm not looking to put on muscle mass, it's more a general tone and strength programme I try to stick to. I'll do maybe half an hour in there, then it's change into my civvies and out.

I'm always always out by nine o-nine. Come what may, even if I haven't got work on, I'll get off and out by then. I'll sit and watch the digital clock go from nine o-eight and that'll be me, soon as it changes over to nine I'm out. With Ratter off the scene I need to keep my eyes out for something half regular, but, truth be known, I'm not exactly struggling. I've got enough contacts of my own to carry on moving gear round here – and I was never so stupid as to just specialise in one thing, anyway.

Truth be known, I do more on the Frankies than I do on the gear. Telling you man, the Frankie Vaughan and the Viagra is worth more to me these days than a few keys of smack. Serious. I can't really be doing with bagheads, neither. Like, I'm the last fella in the world who'd pretend to have any morals whatsoever, but I just don't like dealing with the little b's. I don't *like* them. I hate the way they talk, I hate what they do to their bodies – and their language is shocking. I don't see the need for the constant effing and blinding those kids get up to – for me, it shows a basic lack of self-respect. I hate dealing with them, end of. I'd much rather bang one big bag out to one relatively reliable kid and concentrate on my other interests.

Take today. Aside from a swift but necessary detour to Soldier of Fortune for this *savage* lock knife I've ordered, I'm on the road non-stop. This little Shogun I've bought is my pride and joy, just now. It's not the showy model that all the boys in town are driving, mind you. Mine's the Pinin. Little runt Shogun, it is – a sort of a sawn-off Shogun. Ouch! Terrible, that! *Mea culpa*, but you've got to laugh. Sawn-off Shogun! I'm terrible for gags. I'm known for it. But I do, I love my little sawn-off Shogun. She's just the ticket for what I have to get up to on a day-by-day basis.

On any given day you're going to find me picking up, dropping off, dashing down the South End, back up to Bootle, Norris Green, Huyton, Crokky. Truth be known, I cover more miles in a day than a cabbie. Take today. I goes into my lock-up and I loads up the mags, the videos and the tablets. The Viagra's doing me a bomb, truth be known. One thousand and one for Billy Murphy in Vauxy, another 1,001 for Lloydy, 505 for Foy in Soho Street – moody bastard he is, you'll get your money but you half have to plead for it as though it's a bonus to get weighed in. Fair enough, this is Speke Viagra – but everyone knows that. It's not like I've been telling them it's kosher NHS swag they're getting. All they need to know is that it makes your cock hard. And it does. It's got all the right proportions of all the whatnot that you need for a working woody pill.

Sildenafil and what have you. Lad from the John Moores is the one knocking them out. It's good swag, but that Foy, tell you, la – he's a wrong'un. Bad fella. Pure does not like handing the dosh over and that's that. Not like I'm asking for Pfizer prices, either. It's three grand a grand, seventeen hundred the five. Won't sell less than five hundred – not worth my while at the end of the day. These fellas are knocking them out for a tenner a pop so it's happy days all round, isn't it? Don't know what the fella's griping about.

Last port of call will be a nice cuppa in Co-Zee's with old softarse. Big Moby. I shouldn't be horrible about him. He's all right, Moby. What I've got for the big grock today is a really vile dog-sex movie and a full-on batch of fatty mags. *Real* horrors these are, really, really horrible, disgusting women with no shame. But he likes all that. At least he's honest about it, Moby – I'll say that for the big halfwit. He's not just *admitting* that he's turned on by all these creatures, but *glorying* in it, truth be told.

But I can't say that I warm to Moby at all. He's typical of so many big, hard roidheads in this city. He's ignorant. He's a thug. But if that's not bad enough, he has no concept at all of his own power. I don't mean physically – and he is a big, strong lad, to be fair. I mean that he underperforms. That's unforgivable in my book. If I had a half of his standing in town, I'd clean up. I'd be top man. I would – aul' Paulie would be *numero uno*, no two ways about it. But Moby – he just wants it easy. He'll do what he's told, make a few quid, friends with one and all. Everyone loves the big galoot. I don't.

He can't hold a candle to Ratter. Now Ratter, I had the utmost and ultimate respect for. He was clever, sly, manipulative, strategically immaculate. He was clever. He let his brains, and other people, do all the work for him. I would've done anything for Ratter. Anything. Moby – it just really really depresses me to have to associate with him, man. But I have to. I have no choice. I can't make an enemy of him – yet – so I tolerate him.

He does make me cringe, though. He's cottoned on to the fact that I read, I've read a few books and that, and Moby always always goes out of his way to quiz me about this or that – what's the difference between a Hindu and a Moslem? How come Buddha's a fat lad when he does all that kung fu? In his own crude way he's probably trying to show that he's cool with me. He has the opposite effect. By making an issue of his 'tolerant' stance, he's only patronising me more. At least the others are obvious about it. Moby – he's an idiot. But I can use him.

Becoming Hardened 1

Moby

Ah, for fuck's sake! Last thing I need. Little cunt's out there, night and day. I've heard of footballers having stalkers and soap stars and what have you. The royal family has stalkers. Lads like myself don't *get* fucking stalkers. My own stupid fault, by the way. Fucking emptyhead, letting on to all kinds. He's just a young lad and that – not even that big a lad, to be fair. Must be fourteen, if he's that. Soft little cunt fucking *idolises* doormen. He's fourteen and he's dressed like one. Fucking Mini Me, he is – no hair, Schott jacket, black jeans, black shoes on. As if I'd have no fucking hair by choice, mind you! The little cunt's got his head polished like the pink ball and he just hangs around outside of ours for hours on end hoping to catch sight of yours truly. And when he does, half the time he just fucking *stares* with his dozy gob wide open, like I'm Michael Owen or something. He just . . . *looks*. And if I'm going the shops and that, going on foot, he'll follow. He's only ever said about two things to us. I mean to say, he quite often opens his fucking mouth but all's he says is either:

'You doing the doors tonight, Moby?'

Or:

'You been doing the doors then, Moby?'

If I'd've told him straight the first time maybe we'd be getting none of this weird carry-on. If I'd've just said to the lad, look, I don't do the doors, kidder. Maybe that would've been a end to that. But I never. I stops and goes to the kid: 'That what you want to be, then? When you leave school?'

I was half going to give him a big talking-to, tell him how it's a mug's game and how he should get on with his studies and all of that. But then I've gone to myself, there's worse things a lad can do in life than the doors. There's a lot worse. And it's not like as if I ever done my homework myself, by the way, so I can't say that to no one. So in a way, I've got myself to blame. I've raised the lad's hopes. I've spoke with him for one, so he half thinks I'm his mate, now. And I've also half said that I'm a doorman myself and, even if I'm not, I've showed interest in the lad and he's took that as something more than what it is. Little cunt's out there now, just sat on the wall. There's nothing can be done

80

about it. I'll have to just walk out to the car and blank the little nuisance. Late enough as it is.

Sexism 1

Ged

I'm a fucking wretch. Worse than that. Just for even thinking them thoughts, I deserve to get something done to me. Fuck knows what's got into me, doing what I just done there. But I know this – I am sick with myself.

One thing I am not is a lecherous fella. Knowmean, I could do all that, no doubt about it. There's birds left, right and fucking centre that's *dying* to get into Ged Brennan. Don't even have to be told, in fairness, you know when birds are into you. I'm not being thingio, it's just what it is. I'm a prize scalp, if you will. Birds like me.

But I don't go for it. All of that caper, I can leave well alone, know where I'm going. For one thing, I'm married. No matter what I might think about her – and she does, she pure does my head in most of the time – she is my girl at the end of the day. She's stood by us, in spite of some of the things what I've done. *Had* to do, in fairness. But more than that, the main thing why I don't go chasing fanny like some of the lads do is that it's so fucking *easy*. There's nothing to it. Giving in to that, la, it's just *weakness*. I can't be doing with it. It's harder to say no. By blanking it, you're being more of a man to yourself than if you just goes for it like every other cunt, and sits around telling all hands what you've been up to and what a tidy shagger you are. Not for myself, all that.

I don't even think like that no more. I'm not trying to make out like I'm some dead principled fella and what have you. Obviously I'm not. I'm a twat, most of the time. But fellas that sit round in the Revolution and that, the Living Room and what have you, letting on to a couple of nice birds then turning round to the lads and going:

'See her. Wouldn't think it to look at her. Me and our Billy took her back to ours and she sucked him off while I was giving her one up the arse.'

Well, maybe she did. But that's what they wanted, isn't it? And that's what she done. So how come it's something they can all have a laugh and a joke about now? I hate all that. Know where I'm going, I'm *not* that nice a fella. But I don't look at a bird and the first thing I'm thinking on is that. That's not on, that isn't. That's a cunt's trick.

So I'm chocker with myself. I haven't been able to get her off've my mind, in fairness. Hasn't even buried her husband two months and I'm thinking about her like that. Can't help myself. Could not stop what I done. I did, I tried to throw myself back into work when we got back from that American gaff, but all's I could think of was Margo. To be fair – and only to get it all out and that, just confess all of what I've been thinking and what have you – it's not even Margo I've had on my mind. It's her blouse. The way her blouse was open. I'll say it, right – then it's said. Her thingios, la – they're fucking perfect. They was two fucking feet away, cupped together in this lacy bra and she never even knew I could see nothing. I tried not to perv on it knowmean, but fucking hell, man, them two shiny, beautiful you-know-whats pushing out of her blouse. I didn't know what to do. Pure did not know what to do with myself. Good job she told us all about the other carry-on with Millie Cormack and all of that, because I would, I would've made a cunt of myself in that place if I never had nothing to take my mind from off've her. I could feel myself starting to get dead hot in there, anyway. I probably would've been like some *Looney Toons* knobhead with my eyeballs zooming out on springs every time I had to look at her, to be fair.

Soon as I got back here I locked myself in the bog and thought about her. That's exactly what I done, by the way. I thought about her while I done the other thing. Fucking sick, I am. Don't know what's gotten into myself. But one thing I do know – it won't be fucking happening again. And I'm going to fight this perv's yard all the way. The Loin and that? No fucking way. Not while YT is around to stop it.

Sexy Beasts

Moby

Here he comes. He's getting bolder these days, Mini Me. Never used to say fuck all.

'You off to do the doors now, Moby?'

I tries to get in the car, as though I haven't heard the kid. I gets the door open. I can feel him staring after us, just wanting a answer, *any* answer just so long as it's from myself. Just so's he can tell his mates he's been knocking about with Moby again, can tell them all what I've been saying and that. I can see him, right there in the wing mirror. Fuck it!

'That's right, lad. Just off into town now. Got one or two little messages to do, first.'

Fucking lights up, he does. The little lad is fucking made up. He's half gone red, but he wants more. He comes up towards the car. I'm thinking it won't hurt if I just slides the window down while I'm reversing out the path, but then I just think fuck it. I've let on to the little twat. What more does he want?

Soon as I'm out of ours and heading down Park Road I'm all right again. Not just all right, to be fair. I'm *fucking* all right. I've got a club of my own, a nice little sunbed business and I'm just off to pick up a whole stack of wank mags from PTH. Hates getting called that, Paul. And he is fucking mental, by the way. You wouldn't want to get the wrong side of him – boom-boom! Hates that aul' one, too. Paul the Hom – you wouldn't want to get the wrong side of him. Terrible. Paulie, that's what he calls himself. That's even worse. Says it, like, all the time, as though that's what the lads call him. Like as though that's what he's used to getting called. Paulie, by the way. Nice lad and that, but there's no way he's getting called Paulie. Not by me, he's not.

He's told us all about this stack of magazines he's managed to get hold of, and they do sound boss. He knows what I like, Paul does. Other lads that know us are used to seeing myself in town with this one or that one and, to be fair, Mr Moby can land himself a class Judy when he needs one. The lap-dance girls – I can have my pick of them and it's all quality fanny. Fucking lining up for it and all too, they are. To be fair, my reputation has exceeded me where lap-dance Judies is concerned.

But I don't really go for them, in fairness. I don't. I

like the ropy bints, they're the ones. Always has been for myself, in fairness. Give us the fucking beasts, la, give us the dogs any fucking time. Telling you, la – I go for them. I do. Goes back to when I first had my hole. First proper goose and that, the full monty. We was at summer camp, at Barnston Dales. They never used to call it Correctional or whatever back then. It was mainly run by the Christian Brothers in them days. There was a bit of thingio involved, bit of Bible class and Thought of the Day and all of that carry-on, and it was all the worst lads from by ours went. We never *had* to go or nothing, but our mams was always the first to put us down for it. All the suckholes and Holy Joes, they went and all, too, but there was some fucking brilliant lads come along. Micky and Tony Anciano, their Dominic, Sean Gilhilley, Ronnie Mooney – to be fair, all the Mooneys was there at one time or another. Them and the Salgados, they seemed like they run the place.

But it weren't that sort of place. There was rules and that, but it weren't like DC or nothing. There was wide games, blocko, British bulldog – things that you never would've done round by ours. You would've felt a cunt if you'd've done any of that round the Holylands. What sort of a cunt wants to play hide-and-seek when you can rob cars and what have you? But when you was at Barnston, you felt different. It was like everyone was in the same boat. There weren't that same pressure to act hard. It was like a unwritten thing that it was all right to do normal things and that, play games and what have you. I was thirteen when it happened.

I done it willingly. What I mean is, I weren't surprised when what happened, happened. In fairness, I volunteered for the kitchens mainly to be near her. Her tits was fucking enormous. I couldn't get them out of my mind, la. She must've been close on sixty, even then. Maybe not that old – maybe she just seemed dead old to myself, with being so young and what have you. But I had to be near her, just so's I could get a blimp of them massive big tits.

Mrs Moir, the head cook and that, she fascinated me. There was one other girl there, Heather, and all hands reckoned they'd shagged her. She did look you in the eye, to be fair. She stood dead straight, even when she was peeling the potatoes. Upright, she were, half as though she was proving a point to you. But I weren't interested. There was no two ways about it – Mrs Moir was all I was interested in. Mrs Moir and her big, pink tits. Heather was straight, upright and that but Mrs Moir was always bending over. Fuck, what a sight! For starters, her tits must've weighed a stone each. They was fucking gigantic, la at least a double-G cup. And she always had this starched, navy-blue, button-through, all-in-one kitchen pinafore on. Now, in all fairness, it was fucking warm in there. There was loads and loads of big fuck-off pans, *really* big pans full to the brim of boiling vegetables, steam fucking everywhere, by the way, and it was fucking *hot* in there. But Mrs Moir, tell you what la, she had a good three or four buttons on that dress undone. I could not take my eyes from off've her big, wobbling tits. She'd be down on her knees, pulling the roast out the oven or checking to see how the spotted dick was coming along and they'd just *be* there, these huge, flushed tits.

She weren't ugly, neither. I mean, she weren't Miss New Brighton, in all fairness – she weren't even a Glamorous Granny. But she had, not, like a *nice* face, but you could see yourself necking her. Nah, tell you what, man, she was fucking horrible but there was something about her, knowmean. She had a big mole on her cheek and, instead of that making you sick, it was quite fucking thingio. Serious. It give my good self the horn. I must've been stood there, looking down her cleavage because I never seen her stand up. One minute she's on her knees, basting the lamb, next thing she's looking at myself and she's got this look about her – I only realise this in whatsit, after the event – she's got a certain look in her eyes. She does a quick look around the kitchen, twigs that there's no cunt else there and she goes: 'I need the big, black frying pan out of the scullery. And I need a big, strong man to fetch it in for me.'

That was myself, obviously. So I've been in that scullery for ten seconds when suddenly she's come in herself and she's there, next to us. It's a bit dark, but you can make out the outline of her face, and her bust. She doesn't sound like herself. Again, after the event I'd have to say she was just as thingio as I was, and I was shitting myself, in fairness. She comes up next to us and half bumps into us and she goes: 'Oh! Sorry! I was wondering where you'd got to.'

I hadn't even been gone a fucking minute, mind you. Then she reaches out a hand, which is soft and dry at the same time, and is trembling a bit and she holds my hand for a second, then she feels down between my legs. That's what she's done, by the way. She's come in and put her hands on my cock. She goes: 'Come here.'

She's put her arm behind myself and she's pulling me up close. I'm hard. My cock is twitching and lurching and there's fuck all I can do about it. I'm thinking she's

87

going to report us, have us thrown out the camp. But she says fuck all. She is breathing quite heavy, to be fair – I half think I can hear her heart thumping like fuck – but she always breathes heavy. For what seems like a long fucking time, she's just pushing her thigh against my cock and seems to like the feel of it. She's just breathing. I can feel the swell of her tits and she breathes in and out. I want to feel them, but I'm still not sure. Then she starts feeling the shape of my dick through my kecks. She goes: well, I couldn't do the noise, but she's breathing fast and she mutters under her breath. Then she pulls myself right into her groin, so's my knob is jammed tight up against her and I can hear her now, she's going: 'Dear boy, dear boy,' which makes myself want to laugh but I don't. I stands dead still. She carries on feeling me, pushing the flat of her hand against the full hardness of my dick, and then she takes my hand and puts it inside the folds of her tits. It's heaven. It is – I feel like as though I'm going to spreck up there and then. I'm half getting used to the light and I can see she's trying to look at us, look into my eyes and that, but I don't want to. I'm looking down. Looking at them tits, pale white in this light. She's not breathing so heavy now, but I am. I'm racing. I feels this mad surge come over myself, I want to do everything to her all at once. I starts to feel her through her dress. Fuck, la – that is one thing I will never, ever forget. The feel of that woman through the starch of her dress and her girdle. I'm feeling her hard, squeezing her quite rough and starting to push her backwards.

'Take them out,' she goes, or at least that's what's I've thought she's said because when I'm trying to prise them out of them fucking gigantic cups, she just stands back and with one snap she's unhooked her girdle and she's stood in front of us with her dress wide open and her grey girdle hanging down and I can't believe that them tits and them big fat nipples are right here, in front of myself, waiting for Yours Truly to maul them. It's better than anything I've seen in a wank mag. The smell of her, the feel of her, it's all too much for myself. I must start getting that bit too thingio with her, because she eases us back and, half with a bit of a grin in her voice, half amused she is, she goes: 'Wait. Take him out.'

And it dawns on myself that's what she's said before. She's been tugging at the zip but my cock's got so hard and so big that it ain't easy for her, getting the fly down. I stands back and pulls the lad out, but I don't really know what to do next. That's all right. She just holds my dick in her hand and she's really trying to look in my eyes now, going: 'Oh, son, son. Oh, you beautiful boy.'

Then she lies down and holds her hand out for myself to lie on top of her. I can't stop myself from putting my hand there and the feeling is immense. Even now I can feel it. Girls by ours I've fingered, they've all had hairy motts. Even the younger ones, they've half had a trace of hair. This aul' girl's almost bald. Smooth as her belly. What hair there is, is like a baby's. It's silky. My fingers just slide all around her, she's *fucking* wet – can smell her – to be fair, and she clamps her hand on top of mine and holds it hard, grunting and pushing them huge thighs up. I'm lying there, rigid, never had nothing like that and she's like a out-of-control spin-dryer in the baggy, jerking my hand like she's on the electric chair. Then, somehow, she's taken my knob in her hand and guided us down there and she is so fucking wet that it half just slips in. Fuck! That is another feeling I will never fucking forget. In fairness, I come straight away, but I think that's a blessing in disguise. If I'd've roasted her for a bit the poor aul' girl'd've had a heart attack. She was fucking glowing after. Dead fucking made up, she were. There was none of that 'this is our secret' carry-on that you hear about. She never abused no one. I fucking loved her. We done it about three or four times after that and then aul' fucking emptyhead here goes and fucks it all up by telling Dom Anciano, and that was that. It was all round the camp. In fairness, though, I had to tell some cunt. I'd had my hole, at the end of the day. Never seen Mrs Moir again after that, to be fair. Never forget the girl, neither.

Becoming Hardened 2

Jade

I don't often stay the night at Shelagh's, and when I do it's rarely for sexual reasons? I'll be specific, yeah – she likes me to massage her and, if that leads us into like an orgasm scenario, I'm quite comfortable with that? She, on the other hand, is *so* not comfortable with it. She feels terribly badly afterwards, feels as though she, a masculine and unattractive woman, has, like, in some way defiled a pure and innocent beauty. I can usually talk her out of that. If either one of us can claim any innocence any more, it certainly isn't Jade 'Street' Walker.

But the times I will end up staying the night are those

evenings when our meandering debates and conversations take us way, way off into the smallest hours of the morning. For this, Shelagh has no equal. Quite simply, there is nobody who *knows* as much as she does. There is no subject on which she can't give an opinion or an explanation? I've been telling her about my new boss. Moby. Or, to be precise, she's been *asking* me about him. About the *type* of man he is.

Through Shelagh, I've learnt to like distinguish between the various types of men. Moby's hardened, yeah – he is a hardened, aggressive–submissive heterosexual. The most interesting aspect of that generalisation – because all categorising involves an element of generalisation, yeah – is the 'hardened' part. We have a theory about people, men in particular, becoming hardened. It's an inevitability – it's, like, a product of their environment?

From like an early age they're exposed to brutish and cynical behaviour that, by turn, makes them brutish and cynical themselves. But we maintain that if the right influences – teachers, parents, social workers – get to a child while something of his innocence still exists, then that process of cynicism and vicious self-assertion can be, like, delayed? Or softened? It doesn't have to be a given that males from hard places become hardened of themselves?

We see children of seven and eight who are already lost – they believe in nothing other than the efficacy of the gang, and their own efficacy within that framework. They *so* do not believe that the images they receive via the television and the outside world can apply to them. They think the mythical and idealised good life they see on the telly is for others? This is the crucial part. They are already like justifying their anti-social behaviour, justifying it to themselves and to their peer group. There's an unspoken agreement, yeah, a common bond that society has let them down – therefore they can be forgiven for taking from it whatever they can: making society work for themselves, on and in their own terms.

It's very sad. We know that people want and need love. But for these kids, to show that, is to show weakness? We see young boys affect disinterest in their teenage girlfriends. We agree that there, somehow, lies the way – or one of the ways – to staving off the hardening process. For all their swagger and bravado, yeah, we see signs of humanity and well-being, of well *meaning* among those youths who have sexual partners. We know that nothing is simple and there are no universally applicable truths – but we are desperate to see sex encouraged and promoted in schools, not thwarted.

I tell Shelagh that Moby displays, like, *all* the signs, yeah, of one who's been hardened by his environment from an early age. I think I'm right.

Machiavelli 1

Paul

Men who are anxious to win the favour of a prince nearly always follow the custom of presenting themselves to him with the possessions they value most or with the things they know especially please him. Thus we often see princes receive gifts of horses, weapons, cloth of gold, precious stones and similar ornaments worthy of the highest position.

Don't know about the horses or the precious stones, but I have brought old softarse a little gem today. He is going to *love* it. I think I know his taste in Frankies pretty well by now, and the rule of the thumb with Moby seems to be the more repulsive, the more he goes for it. So here, tucked away in this Farmfoods bag, we have a ripe little number called *Anal Pitbull*. Think it's from Turkey. It's horrible. Really – it's disgusting. He'll absolutely *love* it. He'll love *me*. He'll think I'm his friend.

Machiavelli 2

Margueritte

In a life that's short on thrills, I do extract maximum satisfaction from a morning like this. To lie here, away from the action, knowing *exactly* how it's all going to pan out – it's a wonderful infusion of so many good feelings: power, superiority, fulfilment – I feel all of these things and more.

Perhaps I'd feel differently if I still had the ability to thrill, to truly *thrill* in the purest, most childlike sense. But I can't. I don't. I haven't known that giddy excitement since Christmas 1977. I can be this precise because that was the only Christmas on record and recall when I knew I'd be getting a *real* present. Not some carved, hideous Haitian doll. Not a fucking *book*. In 1977, Uncle Serge from New York was coming to stay. He knew what children wanted. He'd written to tell me I could have whatever I wanted for Christmas. Whatever his little princess wanted, he could get it in America. He was a big man now in the USA and he was

93

coming home for Christmas. I knew straight away what I wanted, and I wrote back in funny, almost hieroglyphic hand that what I wanted was a Tiny Tears. A *plastic* doll, not a carved one – with big, baby blue eyes instead of mournful brown. I was five years old and all my heart desired, a Tiny Tears, was going to be delivered to me by the Santa Claus of Port-au-Prince in the form of Uncle Serge. The giddy skip of my heart in the days leading up to Christmas is a thrill I've never known since. Every beat of my heart is slow and calculated now, lest I trip myself up in my excitement. I never got the Tiny Tears. Santa Claus got drunk. He was knifed in a fight.

Perhaps I'd feel differently if I had children of my own, children I could treat properly, as children deserve to be treated – with boundless, selfless, unconditional love. But I know that's not me. I can't deliver that. I'm still delivering myself. So, on mornings like this, I come closest to a state of grace.

I've programmed poor Ged. I've sucked him in. I know exactly what he's going to do and say, and I know what the outcome will be. The outcome will be that I'll only get what's mine. I'll get what was coming to me.

Recurring Nightmare 1

Moby

Fuckinell! Do I not like that! To be fair, it's not often that Mr Moby gets bad dreams, but that was a pure fucking shocker. Still shaking from it now, in fairness. The bed sheets are fucking wringing wet. Good job she's gone straight into town from dropping the binlids

94

off – she'd think I'd been having a thingio – watching that Kirsty Gallagher in bed and that.

I gets myself up – got to meet our Gerrard at Dool's for ten bells. But the dream was that fucking weird, it still feels real. It's that fucking mad video Paul give us that's done it, in all fairness. It's stayed with myself during my sleep and fuck, what a weird one! Dreams are fucking weird enough without having to piece them together. There wasn't no, knowmean, *pattern* to it. One minute I'm in the Ultimo with that Jade and the next thing she's going, here y'are, Moby, and she's thingioing, she's on the pole dance then she's bending herself over, looking at myself through her legs and she's, 'Come 'ead, lad.' So I'm just about to give her one when her little, suntanned arse is suddenly this big, flabby one, dimples and welts and all sorts and I'm, 'Now then!' And it's that Mrs Moir. I'm made up, by the way. In this dream, I can feel how made up I am that I'm about to goose Mrs Moir again. In the dream I'm half in love with the aul' rip – I am. I can feel it – I fucking *love* the girl! So I'm getting stuck into her and the big, daft Allie that was always asleep in the kitchens at Barnston Dales is suddenly watching us. And he's got a hard-on. This is where it gets fucking thingio.

In Paul's fucking Frankie, that *Anal Pit Bull*, the dog starts boning this pregnant bird. Fucking tidy she is and all, too. You'd well get into her yourself. Fucking nine months pregnant she is, about to drop. Her tits are *all* fucking nipple, knowmean, it's like they've been dipped in melted chocolate. Big swollen tits and this pit bull is ramming her and she's crying out and you're half thinking, 'Fuckinell, is she liking that!' when this horrible Turkish grock comes in and pulls the dog from off've her. Her back's covered in scratches. I mean, she is scratched to bits, by the way. That's why she's sobbing. Next thing, the dog comes back and it's wearing *socks*, la! Not messing – the fucking canine is wearing fucking socks! Tell you, man, I nearly wet myself.

But then, in my dream, while I'm sorting Mrs Moir – and it does feel boss, by the way, *dead* fucking lifelike, at the end of the day – this dog starts wanking itself off with two paws. It's watching us, tongue out, panting like fuck and rubbing its horrible red dick with its paws – paws that, by the way, have only got socks on. Then, if that isn't enough, next thing is it's backing itself into myself. Serious, kidder. The Allie is now a pit bull, and it's got a thingio, a horizontal erection that it is pointing at the arsehole of my good self. But this hard-on is coming out backwards. It's pointing out between its back legs, but *behind* its fucking arse, and it's backing itself up towards M'sieur Moby's ringpiece. That's when I wakes up. Fucking horrible, by the way. Don't know as a full Dooley's growler is the thing for myself, just now.

The Art of War 1 – The Use of Spies 1

The first type of spy is a local spy. A local spy is in the employ of the enemy, or resident in his realm.

Ged
She's right and all, that fucking too. Doing the right thing doesn't always have to be complicated. It's a bit exciting at the end of the day, all of this. It's half sort of

like going into battle and that. Strategic. Like, what Shelagh Cormack needs, what she really *has to have* for this Brasslands carry-on to get going is two things. She needs for myself to play ball over them Stables. No chance. Not on, by the way – not a fucking chance of it.

But the other thing she needs by the sounds of it is Moby's new gaff. I never knew that that was meant to be a part of it. In fairness, I never knew nothing – but I'm fucking learning, and fast. Oh yes. Our Anthony's been wanting to have a word about all of that, and I know exactly what I'm going to be telling the lad. The girl he's got in there is a snitch. Serious. This Jade one is on the fucking payroll. She's getting paid by the council to make sure that Moby's gaff is sewn up. That's all's I'll need to tell the lad at the end of the day. He'll do the rest. Get Steady in, work the gaff proper, keep the fucking weirdo crew out and that'll be that. Game over. Happy days.

Sexism 2

Margueritte

Poor Thom. He's in love with me. He's been in love with me since university days – or at least he thinks he has. He's just not my type, though. I've tried telling him, in the nicest and nastiest possible ways. I've told him there are a million girls out there who'd walk through forests of fire to have him for a partner. He's well spoken, well connected, he's now a partner in the land and property division of a *very* respectable firm – and he's got a great body. If you like that sort of thing,

Thom Harries has got a terrific physique. For me, though, he's far too clean. He's *safe*.

I've let him fuck me a couple of times these past few weeks, but fuck knows why. He does nothing for me, sexually. I think I quite like hurting him. Not physically, I don't mean that. I haven't properly analysed it, but I think I enjoy offering him a chink of light, a beam of sunshine, then tugging the drapes tight shut again, shutting him out resolutely.

I *do* quite like him in some ways. He *idolises* me, and you could see that his fucking father did, too. But I saw right through all that shit. Thom would have idolised me for as long as he couldn't have me. The moment I let him possess me, the moment I gave up my allure is the moment the first 'nigger' would have come. I knew it then, I know it now. I see it clearly. It'd be over something pathetic, a wrong choice of meal when he's had a bad day, or a careless remark about the rugby match he's watching. I'd put his food out and it'd be:

'What's *this*, you black bitch?'

I see it. It's how he defines me. It's what he wants from me. He wants – he *thinks* he wants – that which makes me outstanding. He's drawn to my difference, my otherness, my blackness. The poor bastard is hypnotised by my sleek, my beautiful, my so-brown skin. But as long as I turn him down, as long as I toy with him and tease him and palm him off, his ardour, his respect, his *love* for me seems to grow and grow.

At least his father was honest. He couldn't keep it off his face. He'd have *loved* to have me on the side. He wouldn't even dream of going public with a girl like me, no matter that I was the sharpest and brightest light in law school and would undoubtedly have been an asset and a source of pride and joy to any man. And you could see that he despised his son for it, for believing himself to want to make a wife of me. But he was charming with it, Thom's father. I would've done it. For all that it went against everything I thought I stood for, I knew it inside. *I* was fascinated, too. I would have fucked the old man, if he'd wanted. He used to look at me from under those wild, shaggy eyebrows with mean and beady eyes and his thin, always-moist lips would say: 'Come 'ere, m'dearie. Come and sit a while and make an old man happy.'

And we'd sit and make fun of Thom. One time I got drunk and said I hated the way Thom spells his name. I thought it was silly and pretentious, and old man Harries laughed along and added in a few more of his own, people with silly affectations that he knew. But I wasn't invited around again, after that. Thom continued to bombard me with flowers and requests for dates, but I'd already fallen for Ratter by then. I can only guess at why the phone calls and the flowers stopped coming – I've never seen the need to have those suspicions confirmed. It'd only make me love John-Paul even more than I still do now, three months since I buried the boy. But it's no coincidence that poor Thom has suddenly turned up on the scene now, claiming his firm has been instructed on land next to the South Village. He forgets that I know everything that goes on down there.

'When will I see you again?' he asks.

I've already forgotten he was here. I'm wondering how well Ged's doing with his cousin. It ought to be simple. Ged advises Moby not to cooperate with The Loin. Moby concurs. Ultimo is suddenly off the map. The South Village and Ultimo, the twin peaks are starting to look shaky – very shaky indeed. I present myself to Shelagh Cormack and cut her a deal. I put it to her that, within a month, I can get both projects back on line for her. But she's going to have to wear the consequences. I want in. I want to be reinstalled as Chief Executive, responsible and rewarded for all aspects of the development of the South Village. That is non-negotiable. End of story. I feel good about this. I feel fine.

'I don't know. There's quite a bit going on. I'll call you.'

I'm aware that he hasn't moved, but I don't look up.

'Is that it? I'll call you?'

I crane my head around and look at him with mild confusion, as though I truly do not know what else he might imagine there could be. And I know that I look exquisite. No make-up, no lipstick, no nothing. I'm splayed out on the bed wearing nothing but a silk slip that has ridden up above my bottom, which is perfect and firm and small. I know that he is looking at my brown bottom, looking at the two supple indents at the base of my delicate spine, and he is fallen. Whatever he had wanted to say, he is speechless. Poor Thom is speechless with love.

Prejudice

Ged

Don't know what I think about that, in fairness. One thing I am not is thingio – no way in the world am I prejudiced – but I've never had much time for homs and that. Fair enough, by the way, times has changed, but it don't mean you have to like it at the end of the day. Does not mean you're all over one another, by the way, not in my book it don't. He looks cake and all too, that Paul. Bit of a roidhead, he is – half looks like he's on the steggies and that, bit of a gymhead. He *is* all right and that, I've half known the lad on and off for years – seen him around, at the match and what have you. Got a weird walk, he has. Cunt walks like as though he's got extra muscles, knowmean. Dead fucking bouncy he is, like his calves has been pumped up and he's got a extra spring in his step. Bit of a muscle walk, know where I'm going.

And the other thing is, he was Ratter's right-hand man. Now, Moby swears that Paul is a good lad, but the thing about Moby is he thinks every cunt's a good lad. He's telling myself that Paul's sound, he's honest, you can rely on the lad and he knows a bit about business and what have you. Fair enough, but at the end of the day how far can you trust a fella that does that, know where I'm going.

On the other hand, there isn't exactly a lot to choose from. I myself would've gone for Steady, no two ways about it, but he's not out for a while. I'll bring him in on the taxis when he gets out. What with all the work I'm going to be putting into the South Village and that, even with Margo by my side I won't be able to keep tabs on all the other shite. Steady I can trust. He'll do a boss job looking after the cabs for us. Is right.

I've thrown another few names in the hat, but Moby's sold on that Paul the Hom. Fair dos. It's his gaff at the end of the day, he's the lad that's got to make all the loose ends tie together. All's I want to know is that he's not going to let the council turn his gaff into a glorified knocking shop. I'll have a little word with that Paul and all, too.

Soul 1

Cormack

No matter how crowded my schedule seems, whatever the weather, regardless of any other concerns, I make it up here every week. She's in my thoughts constantly. She is the flame that lights my path. And it's beautiful up here, too. There's the city, the teeming, chaotic city way down there below, but here, here is peace and quiet. One so seldom has true quiet. And no matter how bad, how futile, how wretched my life might sometimes seem, she makes me know that I must carry on. I come here and I remember and I draw strength, for I know that it's a good thing that I'm doing. I always return renewed, and ready to fight on.

Lists 1

Fat Francis

Always a treat to hear from the boy. Things is changing up there. With all the deaths and that, things is starting to get out of control again. But Gedders, he's a fucking one-off. Love the bones of the boy, I do. The thing what we done for him before Christmas – that was the least I could do. Fuck, things he's done for myself – I could live three lifetimes and still be in debt to him. I was made up to hear from him. Coming down soon, he is. Says he'll fuck everything off and just come down for a weekend, just me and him like the old days. This Paul he's on about, he's nothing. Don't know what he's getting so worked up about, but that's old Ged for you. Thorough. Can't wait to see him.

The Art of War 2 – Tactical Dispositions

Paul

One who seeks to conquer only by sheer strength is liable on occasion to be vanquished; whereas he who can look into the future and discern conditions that are not yet manifest will never make a blunder and will therefore invariably win.

If someone calls me in for a meeting, I always always want to try and cover all my bases. I try to see it from their point of view. What does he *want*? What's the worst that can happen? How is it *likely* to happen? If he's going to come at me, *how* will he come at me?

But this is Ged Brennan. I'm honoured. A real player, at last.

Ged

Take it back. The lad's as good as gold. I'd had it on good authority that he was in deep with the other fella, moving the beak and the smack and what have you. Franner's gone, yeah, he'll do a bit of this, bit of that, but he's fuck all. He is zero on the map. He'd like to be took serious and that, thinks he's got a lot to offer, he does. That's why he took to fucking Ratman so strong. Ratter was prepared to give him his head and, fair dos to the lad, he repaid him with his loyalty and his graft.

But he's nothing. What he does mainly is sex work. Serious. Franner's checked it all out. He moves jarg Viagra pills and fucking porn. Blue pills, blue movies. Always reminds myself of that fucking Milo when the lads start going on about the Frankie Vaughno. Coming back from Norwich or Ipswich or something one time and our Anthony's going on about how he got this bird to watch a blue movie with him. Fucking Milo gets up, the way he does, like as though he's the Pope and he's addressing the masses and that. He goes: 'That's tommyrot!'

Tommyrot, by the way!

'Forget this blue movie nonsense. Myself, I prefer to take a filly back to Sanderson Acres and treat her to a *red* movie! That soon gets the juices flowing, I can tell you! 1986 double-winning video, King Kenny at Chelsea, Rushie at Wem-ber-lee . . . oh yes! Oh yes! She will be mine!'

Lads was in bulk with him. Fucking one-off, that Milo. Would love to see that fucking cunt again, telling you kidder.

But this Paul one, the funny lad, he's just a bit of a run-around. And that's what's got myself thinking. The Viagra and that, they're not banned far as I know myself. My own take on it is that they're half legal. So what I've gone and said to Paul and that is, here y'are, you've got a captive audience here. Fellas that's in a lap-dance gaff in the first place are probably the same cunts that's going to be wanting tablets. Is right. So why don't him and Moby nail it in? Fucking nail it in, lad! Is right. Aul' Paul half wants to be a gangster at the end of the day, doesn't he? So here's his fucking chance. Fuck the council off with their brasses and bagheads and what have you. Get the lads in, nuff funny pills and Robert Bernard Fowler's your uncle, by the way.

And he was having it, in all fairness to the lad. He did seem to be that little bit overawed by my good self at the end of the day, but he was having it. Made up with myself, he was. Give us the video of that *A Beautiful Mind* one.

Machiavelli 3

Paul

A prince is always compelled to injure those who have made him the new ruler.

Just as I feared, I really, really liked him. You hear so much about lads like Ged and you're almost half expecting a cartoon character to walk in. You half expect them to be seven foot tall with fists like cannonballs. But he wasn't like that. He's just like a normal fella, dead down to earth. There's no airs and graces about him. He made no pretence of trying to 'interview' me. We just talked. I'd have hated it if the lad had made a big thing of who he was. Don't know what I would've done, in fairness, if he'd've started scrutinising me like some of them kind of fellas do, like as though they have a higher intelligence and they can see right through you. I *hate* that. I would've sunk my teeth into his cheek if he'd've looked at me like that. But he didn't. He looked at the table a lot, and stirred his tea constantly. And he didn't pretend to be my friend. I like that. I like him a lot. I'll have to watch him double close.

On Moments in Time

Cormack

In politics, as with so many things, it all boils down to our Big Days. These are not always good days – far from it. We spend our political lives planning for that in which we believe, planning and paving the way to do good, to do the best we can. But we are always mindful that anything can happen, anything can change. These are the Big Days. It can be the day that we get the call we hoped for – that our application for funding has been approved and we can move on to Stage Two or Three or Four. But, equally, it can be the day that we are called in to see the Chief Whip and we're coolly informed that our tenure is over. That's what happened with dear old Councillor Bennett, the old rascal. And not before time too, if we're completely frank about it. The timing could have better, though. We can understand our colleagues wanting to come into the New Year fresh and poised and ready in every sense – but to do him in over the Christmas break was a bit callous. So nothing but nothing surprises us in politics, and we're intrigued to hear from the Bishop. This, indeed, could be a Big Day.

Medi-Tan 1

Jade

This is *so* not a good thing. I'm like – *what*? I'm not at all sure what I can do about this. It's like *hello*? I *know* about this stuff? His abject bad manners I can learn to live with, yeah, but his plans for this club are cause for mild concern.

Firstly, I'll have to try and establish who Paul is, and what role Moby envisages for him. The two of them have like barely acknowledged me since they let themselves in, unannounced. Moby's just been walking this Paul around the club, showing him where everything is? Telling him what goes on? Usual stuff, yeah – usual stuff when you're appointing a new manager. Even if he's bringing in an under-manager – which now looks like a very desperate best-case scenario – it's *so* not a good thing that he hasn't, like, even *consulted* me? There's no other way of looking at it? It's bad?

I've been following them around the club at a distance, listening in. The acoustics of an empty club aren't as reverberating as one might imagine? But it's not as though these two are keeping their voices down. Their plans are, like, *crystal* clear. They're going to gut the sunbed salon. Instead of the four lie-down sunbeds, they're going to install, like, eight sunshower cubicles. That side makes sense, in all fairness to them – I'd have to admit it. It's a good business move. It'll give us like twice the capacity for starters, and without encroaching into the club proper. Plus they're right – the girls (and lads, in all truth) seem to prefer the high-power sunshowers to the lie-downs. They complain about lying in someone else's body sweat? And with the shower, they can move around and tan their sides and under their arms and so on. So on that basis, I *am* in favour. If you're just looking at this as like a *business*, then yes – it makes sense. If they'd have sat me down properly and enlightened me as to their budget and like their business aspirations, I would've come to the same conclusion?

It's the next bit that's so worrying, though. From what I can like glean from this Paul, he's au fait with the theme and ethos of FFF. I prefer the raw initials to Foo-Femme Fatale. That all seems soooo last millennium, now – but call me a sentimental old fool yeah, the name still makes me smile. FFF it is, and Moby's new man seems to know all about it. I didn't get a full transcript, but I don't need it – I know enough. It's bad. They're going to kill the *foo* nights – kill the vibe and the atmosphere I've spent a year and a half building up. It's, like – they want to kill the customer base, the loyal and devoted following (whose full potential we're only now starting get a feel of) – they want to kill Ultimo, basically. The club that so many Billy Bunters – actually, no. *No.* The thing about my customers, yeah, is that they're *not* Billies. *They* found *us* – they cultivated us, they chose us because they're *not* Joe fucking Public. They want something else? They want something *more*, yeah – and whatever it is that we've given them here, our new mine hosts are about to take it all away. That much is crystal. They're bringing in more girls, and more from outside the area. They're going to encourage the girls to allow touching. *That's* going to be their unique selling point. It won't be Touch and Go. It'll be

Touch and Come. I should be the last girl to gripe about that – but it's breaking my heart. This is so not the way to run Ultimo, yeah – and that's just the half of it. It's bad, bad, *bad* news all round.

Touching Cloth

Cormack

We're not entirely certain whether support from this particular Bishop is A Good Thing. He's certainly very eloquent, and he's charming company. Lunch was divine. We went to the new seafood place on the dock and ate pan-fried crawfish (question: in what might we fry if not a pan?), bass steaks with sour-cream potatoes, and summer pudding – in March! – and we drank a zesty Muscadet and half a bottle of shamefully expensive pudding wine. The Church may be abstemious in matters of the flesh, but only when it's human. The Bishop was in no sense reticent, not least in his support for The Loin.

This is not straightforward, however. Firstly, the Bishop has little direct impact on our own immediate city centre. Secondly, he is a notoriously political beast. His profile is substantial. He is often to be seen and heard on television and radio, and his articles proliferate in a whole slew of journals. And he rarely speaks with any great evidence of forethought or tact. We could not claim he's unintelligent – he knows a great deal about wine, Corsica and the poetry of Gerard Manley Hopkins, and he can name every Men's Singles champion since Fred Perry. But he's controversial. Worse, he *enjoys* the controversy. He revels in fighting his unpopular corner, playing devil's advocate, throwing the question back at the inquisitor. After the 11 September attacks, he made some astounding remarks about the nature of God and justice. The Church was quick to distance itself from his views, while the Bishop was quick to appear on breakfast television in spite of all the flight cancellations.

Even this afternoon, we noted his tendency to raise his voice to an unavoidable boom whenever he wished to express an unorthodox point of view. Viewed from all sides, his support is not unequivocally A Good Thing. We shall satisfy ourselves with the following. He is not going to whip up a storm *against* us – which he could, easily. But we will not be looking to him to spearhead the publicity either, as and when we hit that stage. This chap is a potential loose cannon.

On Letting Her Go

Moby

Did not enjoy that, by the way. Did not like having to do that one little bit. There's lads that half get a thingio out of sacking some cunt, but not myself. Not aul' Moby. I've gotten to quite like the girl, in all fairness. Bit of a smart arse she is, thinks she's running rings around my good self, but at the end of the day she's only a young girl. Done my head in to have to do that to her. To be fair to the kid, she's took it quite well. She's shook my hand and she's gone: 'Good luck,' and that.

Jade

Fuck. This is, like, *serious*, now. This is a crisis. Whatever I was expecting, yeah, I wasn't expecting this. I feel very, very silly. I should've seen it coming? I'll see Shelagh, but to be honest, I don't even know what *she* can do.

Family Fortunes 2

Ged

We've sat down to watch that *A Beautiful Mind*, but it ain't all that at the end of the day. And not only is it fucking boring, about every three fucking minutes this thingio comes up on the screen. 'Viewing for Academy Purposes Only'. That's what it says, mind you. They're trying to get you to thingio, and they goes and puts that all over the screen. So we jibs it and waits for *Millionaire*. One thing I love is that *Who Wants to Be a Millionaire*? I like him, by the way. Always seems to have a nice way about him. And he appeals to all kinds of ages and all, too. The binlids love him, just as much as the ones that can remember him from off've that *TISWAS*. That'd be a boss question that would, by the way. You can just see that Chris Tarrant with that funny little grin of his going: 'Here y'are, then. What's this stand for? TISWAS.'

That'd get them. But it'd be one that Mister Gerrard Brennan'd get. Oh yes. Answer *that* one if you can, Cheyenne. She wouldn't have a fucking scooby, by the way. But it's one thing we can all watch together. I look forward to it, in fairness.

We're up to the one for a grand. They're always fucking rock, these ones. I tend to find that the ones later on, the ones where they're starting to flap and that, they're not half as bad as these ones for a grand. Here y'are.

'*What is the chemical symbol for lead? Is it a) Ti b) Pb c) L or d) Ld?*'

Fuck. I think I know this. When we was first starting out we used to zap the lead from off've the church roofs. Cunt's trick and that I know, but at the end of the end it was *there*. It was easy. We used to take it round to this mate of Freddie Woan's. Funny cunt, he were. He weren't like none of the other shady bastards we'd come across, he was half sort of *jolly*. Mean it, la, that's exactly how he were. We used to call him Redhead – he had this big mad red face and he always come across like he was half-bevvied. What the fuck did he used to call the lead? Had a fucking mad name for it, he did. We used to bring it round in handcarts and he'd be half dancing a jig, going: 'Ah! The bum-bum! Bring it in, boys! Bring in the bum-bum!'

That's what he called it, Redhead. *Bum-bum*. Funny cunt, in fairness.

Our Stephen's half having a nark with Shy. They're going for different ones.

'Duh! That's a red herring, dick-brain! There *is* no Ld! It's L!'

I gives Debbi a quick look to see if she's having that. I don't like them using language, to be fair – certainly not on one another. She's just staring at the TV. She never answers none of the quezzies herself, just sits there stroking our Cheyenne's hair. Sometimes she gives her a little kiss when she gets one right. In fairness to Debs, she fucking loves them kiddies. Can see it in the way she looks at them. Sometimes I catches her having a sly mosey at little Shy, and the look on her face, la – it's pure adoration. She can't believe they're hers. We've done all right with these two, at the end of the day. People can say what the fuck they want about myself and what I do and that, but they can't say nothing against the binlids. They are two boss little fellas, them two.

'*Is that your final answer?*'

'*Final answer, Chris. Ti.*'

'Nooooo!' I goes, before I can do fuck all about it. The kiddies both looks at myself. They half look astonished, in fairness. I can feel myself going that bit beetroot. Half turning into that Redhead myself, I am.

'All's I'm saying is, I know this one. And it ain't Ti.'

'What *is* it, then?'

Now I *am* going fucking red. I'm boiling up, here. What the fuck was it? *Bum-bum.* But I'm too late.

'If you'd have said Pb, you'd have been giving the Latin for lead which is *plumbum* and would have won you a thousand pounds.'

Everyone sighs, but I can't let it go.

'I *knew* that!'

They're all looking at us.

'I *did*! I *knew* that one'

Our Cheyenne comes and cuddles up to us.

'Never mind, Daddy. You'll get another one. Like, next year or something?'

I know she's only having a laugh and a joke, but she doesn't half do me in sometimes, our Shy. The next game gets going, but I'm half not taking it in. I'm thinking about them two. Her and all too, in a way. I love the bones of them all. I do. I fucking love them. I don't give a fuck what they think of myself. I'd do fucking anything for them. Shy's still snuggled up to us and I can tell she knows she's hurt us. She's being extra snuggly. She can do that, when she feels like. Most of the time she's dressed up like a hooker, in fairness. There's all sorts of clubs and discos for teenagers now, just Pepsis and hotdogs and what have you, but tell you what though la, some of the girls that goes in there of a Friday night, the one in New Brighton – fucking dressed to kill, they are. Thank fuck it's not myself that has to run *that* door. I'd rather face a big load of grocks than have to deal with all them fucking Lolitas. That's a fact, by the way. I would.

'For a hundred and twenty-five THOUSAND pounds . . .'

Love the way he says that, I do. You just don't hear that these days, do you? 'Thousand pounds' and that. No cunt says – 'a thousand pounds' and that. Should've done that when we was doing the blags, in fairness. Maybe put on a thingio, a Prince Philip mask and what have you. 'Hand myself one thousand pounds, you fucking cunt!' Is right.

'. . . tell me which of the following films starred Robert Duvall: was it a) The Godfather . . .'

I'm about to jump up and shout: 'Yiss!' When it dawns on myself that I should take my time over this one, string it out that little bit.

'. . . b) Carlito's Way c) Scarface or d) Donnie Brasco? Take your time . . . there's one hundred and twenty-five THOUSAND pounds riding on this.'

I turns to my two and goes: 'It's long time since I seen it and that, but I'm pretty sure he played Tom Higgins in that Godfather.'

Our two looks at me, then they looks at one another.

I know there's something snide coming. Our Cheyenne doesn't let us down. She's forgot she's snuggling up to her aul' fella and that. She's forgot all of that and she's back to being a boss snide. In her best snotty voice, she goes: 'You're probably thinking of a different film, Daddy. He said *The Godfather*, not *that Godfather*.'

Our Stephen chips in.

'Maybe it's *That The Godfather!*'

I can see her smirking in the corner there, the aul' dog. Fucking grinning to herself, she is. Hasn't got a fucking clue, by the way. Has not ever even half tried to answer one of these. Smirking she is, behind her hand.

'*That The Godfather II!*'

Pair a cunts, they are. Pair a little aul' arses, kicking off on myself like that. It's not on, by the way. I'm not rising to it, mind you. Oh no. No way in the world am I rising to their fucking Laurel and Hardy act.

'And *Godfather II An' All Too*, if I'm not mistaken.'

'Is that the *National Lampoon* version, Daddy? *Godfather II An' All Too?*'

To be fair, I am now half having to keep a lid on it. These two, they're taking the piss at the end of the day. They're sat there on leather sofas provided by yours truly by way of honest graft, watching a fucking boss flat screen also courtesy YT and they're giggling in my fucking face. That's what they're doing, by the way. They're fucking laughing at me. And she's no better. She hasn't said a fucking word to them. Well, I'm not having it. I'm not giving them the fucking satisfaction. Pair a fucking aul' arses.

'Why don't you ask your mother. She'll know.'

Ha! That's fucking got them. She's suddenly sat up from her fucking stupor looking half panicked. They all looks at each other. Them two gives their ma a little sort of half-questioning look. She shrugs back. Makes no bones about it, Debbi. She knows fuck all. Does not give a fuck who knows neither, by the way. She just shrugs at the pair of them as though to go: 'Don't fucking ask me! *I* don't fucking know!'

Shy pulls herself up now and goes all serious and looks us in the eye.

'You're bluffing, aren't you, Daddy? You do not really know the real answer to that question, do you?'

I've got them now. Let's see who's fucking sniggering in a minute, shall we? I pulls a amused face and shrugs at her. Let's see, and that.

'*Daniel, you phoned a friend who thinks – who is not SURE, he says, but who THINKS Robert Duvall played Tom Higgins in* The Godfather *films. But he might have been a priest in something else. He wouldn't like to bet on it. Do you want to stay with that?*'

'*Yes, Chris. I'm sticking with that.*'

'Good lad.'

I'm made up now, by the way. I am. I'm buzzing, here. They're all looking at myself, Debs too and all, and they're trying to make out whether I know this or whether I'm bluffing them.

'*Final answer?*'

The lad thinks on it. The wait is fucking horrible. The camera's gone right into his sweating grid. Half can see up the poor lad's nostrils, mind you. Lad's in fucking bits, in fairness. Losing it big time, he is.

'*No, Chris. I'm just not sure. Can I take a few seconds?*'

'Ay, you soft cunt! You're right! You've got it fucking right!'

I've forgotten that they're there for a second and I've

jumped up out my seat, thingioing. The others are looking at us like as though I've gone mental. I'm a little bit like that, and I sits down again. I waves my hand at the telly. I've fucking lost it, now. I don't care what no cunt thinks – I know the fucking answer to this. I know it.

'He's right, the soppy fucking cunt!'

'Aye-aye, Gerrard. Language!'

She nods at the nippers, who are both just staring at the TV now. They half look morbid, they do – like this is suddenly a very horrible experiment gone thingio. Do not give a fuck about their aul' fella's verbals, by the way, they just want to know one thing. Is he right? Is our aul' man a fucking genius or what?

The lad on the telly's shaking his stupid head. Tarrant's doing his soothing voice, trying to calm the cunt down. Mad kite on Tarrant, by the way. Money the cunt's on and all, too – you'd think the lad'd sort that golfball out on the side of his grid. Looks like as though his fucking cheekbone's slipped, he does – looks like he's had half a facelift and that. Crazy, crazy grid on the lad.

'Take as long as you need, Daniel. If you get it right you win a hundred and twenty-five thousand quid. Not much if you say it fast!'

The whole audience is in bulk. That's nerves, that is. Every cunt's nervous for the lad. Tarrant's just loving it, smiling that fucking pervy grin of his, the gobshite. Would think he'd give the lad a bit of a hand at the end of the day. Can see he's shitting hisself.

'Get it wrong and you still walk away with thirty-two thousand pounds. Or you can quit now and leave with sixty-four thousand crisp smackeroonies. I have the cheque here now

with your name on. Take your time, Daniel.'

Can't stand it. Can not stand this, by the way. The lad's got it right but his arse has gone. He looks up and swallows and you can see his fucking Adam's apple bulging with the disappointment he's feeling. I know what's coming.

'I'm going to take the money, Chris.'

'You're taking the sixty-four thousand?'

'I am, Chris. I think it might be The Godfather *but I just can't risk that amount of money. I'm sorry.'*

'You BLERT! You fucking soft cunt! It IS *The Godfather!'*

And it were. That was the right answer. And know what? The kiddies was fucking made up with myself. Made. Up – by the way. All that nasty business from before, that's all forgotten. They've seen myself in a different light now, in fairness. At the end of the show, Shy makes us a coffee and our Stephen's going: 'Here y'are, Dad – I'll phone the number and get you on the show.' Debbi gives us a lovely little smile. Know what I'm in for tonight, mind you. Is right.

Superhighways

Moby

Happy days. Paul's looking after the refitment of the tanning salon while I'm going to be auditioning a few girls later on. Is right. The club'll be closed just for a few days and that – maybe a couple of weeks, in fairness – but we'll open again soon, bigger, better and bosser. Once the word goes round about what this new Ultimo is all about, we're going to have queues right around the block. And that's just for the tablets, by the way. Paul's talked us through the whole thing. Every cunt's after the fucking Viaggies and guess what? It's fucking legal. There is not a fucking thing any cunt can do about us selling legal swag in our gaff. We're not being thingio, mind you – we're not trying to make out like we're whiter than white or nothing. Not as though we're going, here y'are – you can't drink ale in here, it's bad for you. We're in business at the end of the day and if a lad wants a bit of boot or whatever to give his night a bump, then he's come to the right place. But if he wants a Viaggy, he's double come to the right place. That's where the dough is these days, to be fair. Forget the other caper. Maybes that we're only selling these ones for tens, but they cost fuck all to produce. Fuck. All – by the way. We're going to be broosted.

But with these lazy mares, the fucking pole-dance crew, first audition's not till three o'clock thisavvy. Fucking shite, that is. Three o'clock, by the way. Must take them till then to get their tans put on, pump their threepennies up, shave the beaver and what have you. Lash the Big Hair spray on. Whatever, it leaves Mr Moby with a bit of time on his mitts, end of the day. Time he will now spend revisiting the unbelievable *Scat* pages of that fucking Internet.

Down

Jade
This morning reminds me of one of those dog days when I first arrived here from Cumbria. Fuck, but I hated those days! The sky seemed low and bleak and,

like, unrelentingly grey. It wouldn't even rain. It wouldn't do anything, yeah – no wind, no sun, just this low, low, overhanging deadly dull grey sky.

I so knew I was where I wanted to be, though? This was the course, this was the course I'd set my heart on? And this was the city I'd visited in the flesh and in my dreams, yeah – time and time and time again. Basically, I'd fallen in love with Liverpool?

I knew I was a toughie. Out of anyone, anyone my age, I would have backed myself as the born survivor? Yet I was going under. After a week here, barely more, I was getting weighed down by some intangible, debilitating low and the sky was dull grey and I just, like, wanted to go home? Yet I had no home. Not any more. It was enough that my Daddo, my bedrock, was gone and lost for ever, but on top of that there'd been the night with Babs and Susan. Patsy Kensit night. What would they make of that back home? To be so unloved and so alone – I'd never felt so lost. I couldn't motivate myself to do anything.

And yet that time was the making of me. Looking back on it now, those were the days when I could have crumbled. I so could have got on the first train back to Carlisle and been a decent daughter and put everyone, everyone else first for the rest of my life, yeah?

But I so didn't do that – instead I dug deep and found me. Those low, claustrophobic feelings left me just as quickly as they'd descended. I was down and then, quite suddenly, I was on top of the world again. I was liberated.

Not now I'm not. This morning I'm stricken again with, like, that same nauseous low. Shelagh has gone into work, but me, I have no work to go to. I can't stand the idea of going back to my flat – for what? To water the plants? To sit in that room instead of this?

Meanwhile, up the road there – quite realistically five minutes up the road, gangs of men are ripping the guts out of my baby. Those same men will probably be enticed to work harder, take less breaks, less liberties, yeah – with the promise of free entry to Liverpool's Latest Table Dance Sensation. Stunning Girls! (all new!) Reasonable Prices! Happy Hour! Bastards!

I drag myself to the vast casement window, looking out beyond the dock. Once again, I see only low grey, sullen skies. Shelagh Cormack has provided little in the way of hope and inspiration this time. She's put her arm around me, but she knows – she knows that *I* know – there's little she can say, less still that she can do. How could this have happened? How could we, like, stand *back* and *let* it happen?

And then, a chink of light. An idea, at last.

Lust

Paul

I'm quite an upbeat guy most of the time. I am. I always always have a smile on my face. I'm a terrible one for gags. I've always got a joke up my sleeve. Everyone groans and runs for it when Paulie's about to tell a joke, but it's the bad ones that's funny, isn't it? Today I can't see the funny side. I'm reeling, I am. I've just seen perfection in the form of a little scally labourer that's working on the refit. Can't get him off've my mind. I can't. It's as much as I can do to stay away from there. I'd be down there asking them if they want mugs of tea every five minutes, just so's I can get another little look at him. Can't be much older than sixteen. He's only a young lad. He's the usual scally sort, looks just like any lad from off've the street: shaved head, toned but not built, absolutely *gorgeous* little arse. But it's his face that's the thing. His beautiful face has done me. It's that angels with dirty faces thing – it gets me every time. His eyes are just gigantic. They are the biggest, bluest eyes you'll ever, ever see. You'd think he was wearing lenses but he's got no class, this little lad. He's trash. He's got a nasty jagged scar right under the socket of his eye, where he's been glassed. It's not a big scar. Maybe he only got done with a Coke glass! Terrible. But he's got this frown as well, he seems to always be looking down and concentrating, deep in thought.

'Shall-I-use-the-lump-hammer-or-is-this-a-job-for-a-power-tool?'

I wish. He looks like a young version of that footballer. Kevin Phillips. Him. I'm going to have to go down there and see if they want anything. That's what's getting me down. The older workies, they'll see it right away. They'll give the little lad hell over it. They'll completely *slaughter* the poor kid. That's what does me in. Everyone's so nice to you, so polite to your face. We all like to pretend that times have changed and nobody's really arsed about what goes on behind closed doors any more. But it's still the same. I'm sorry la, but it is. It's just as bad as ever. I know full well that as soon as my back's turned they're going to be calling me all sorts. The city's backward. Forget all this Capital of Culture carry-on, by the way we're still in the Stone Age. When it comes to the ordinary men of this city I tell you, the times they are *not* a-changing! I have to let them call me *that*, just so's I can work. I'm just not in a position to go it alone, yet. So I have to grin and bear it and make out like I think it's *funny* being Paul the Hom. I can't say it doesn't hurt. It does. And what hurts more than anything is that I can't so much as look at that lad because, even if he *did* want me to, he'd be too terrified to do anything about it. He'd be shit-scared of what people'd say. That gets to me. It really really does my head in when a good-looking young lad can't just be himself. It makes me unhappy.

Obscenity

Moby

Tell you what, la, that was fucking *better*! Fucking bestial that, man. That is one little lady aul' Moby is going to be seeing more of. Not that she's that little, by the way. Not that there's more of her that you *could* see, know where I'm going. This one is fucking *grotesque*, man. I nearly come when I seen her, and that was only some shady photie on the website.

Just shows how right aul' Paulie is about these things. Tell you what, he knows the fucking score when it comes to obscenity. Got to hand it to the lad. He is one sick fucking cunt! I done exactly what he told us. I just went for it. I got on the site and I went: 'Shit on me.'

That brought them tumbling out the woodwork, by the way. Oh yes. Fucking dozens of the fucked-up aul' mares. *Hundreds* of them. That time when *Brookie* had a audition and no cunt turned up – all's they needed to do was say: 'And by the way. Youse can all dump on Maxie once youse are done.'

That would've brought them out. Telling you. Form a orderly queue, if you will.

I had to narrow down the search a bit. All the ones going: 'Let's have a quick blimp of this legendary fucking dobber then' – they was off, and pronto. Can not be doing with them webcams, me. For myself and that, it spoils the romance of it all. Spoils the intrigue, know where I'm going. Want to have something to look forwards to at the end of the day.

Then I lashed all the ones that lived miles off, and all the ones that was trying to hint that they was gorgeous. Maybe they was, in fairness. Good luck to them, and that – but what I types in next is: 'Any fatties?'

To be perfectly fair, it all went that bit quiet for a moment or two. But three come back. And one of them, like I say, she tacked a shitty picture of herself on. Made the Readers' Wives pickies look like that David Bailey done them, but fuckinell, kidder! Fucking obscene, she were. No two ways about it, man, she was just *fat*! She was your ma's mate, done up in a nightie that never even went close to covering them tits of hers and she had *loads* of make-up on, mad red lippy and rouge and that and she'd just wrote these words: 'I am *extra* large and I love to wallow in mud. Come and cover me in shit. Yours and mine. You don't know what you're missing. Love, Hilda the Hippo.'

Mr Moby read that and he was out the door. Fuck knows what we all done before that Internet, la.

Buttons

Ged

Was a bit chocker at first when she never invited myself along to the lunch. Quite getting into all that, in fairness – lunch and what have you. Do not mind that whole carry-on. End of the day, though, I need to get my head together. Margo is, or was, the bird of my dead stepbrother. She's my business partner. She is gorgeous, she is sexy as fuck and she always has a silk blouse on with buttons undone. She wears perfume that gives my good self a hard-on. But that's as far as it goes. Have not even thingioed about her since that one time. I haven't even been tempted to. Not right to think about the girl in that way, at the end of the day.

But I am, I'm made up she never asked us along to that Heathcote's, by the way. Why? Because it's woke us up. It's made myself realise that I'm turning into a soft arse. It's good having Margo around the place, end of. We'll make a fucking good go of all this, but not if I'm moping every time she walks out the room. My own set-up is sound, mind you. It's as good as it gets. I've got a boss bird, two lovely binlids and I won a hundred and twenty-five grand on that *Millionaire*. Everything's sound as a pound.

The Use of Spies 2

A converted spy is a former agent of the enemy . . . it is impossible to obtain trustworthy spies unless they are properly paid for their services.

Cormack

In light of everything that's happened, we're not surprised Margueritte's called a meeting so soon. We're just wondering when she's going to come to the point.

'Gerrard's wife's a very interesting woman, you know, Shelagh. Have you met her? She might be the key to all of this, you know.'

'Really? How so?'

She toys with a forkful of kedgeree. She looks up playfully.

'I've known them all for years, you know. Known them nearly all my life.'

'Continue.'

'If you'd have only taken me into your confidence, I could have told you *exactly* how Ged Brennan would behave.'

'We had very good information to the contrary. That is, we genuinely believed he'd cooperate.'

She teases the kedgeree until there's just a flake of fish on her fork, which she eases into her mouth. If this is eating, there's an art to it. She meets our gaze.

'Can you not just take the entire project back from him?'

We can't avoid smiling. This is not a meek and innocent suggestion from a well-wisher. It's clear and basic espionage. It's Margueritte Lascalles saying out loud: 'I think I've got you, and I think you know that, too. But I'm just checking.'

We continue smiling and say nothing. She smiles with her eyes. It's devastating. She's about to come out with it. We can feel it coming.

'Let me in, Shelagh. Bring me back on board. It's the only way this fucking thing is going to fly now.'

We attempt to look as restrained and as dignified as possible, in keeping with the standards one would expect of a high-ranking officer of the local government. We look down, all gravitas. There can be no ambiguity. There is no room for misinterpretation.

'We've explained why that is not possible, Ms Lascalles. It can't happen. It won't happen. The Loin, however, *will* happen. With or without your assistance.'

Just like that, the eyes switch off. They lose their sparkle, their wit, their power. She looks at her plate, biting her lower lip. We're tempted, so tempted to reach across and cover her hands with our own. We attempt to sound as conciliatory as possible.

'The wife? How do you think she may be useful?'

Margueritte thinks long and hard about this. Her face is the most transparent window to her thoughts. She changes her mind several times. But then she speaks up, at length.

'Ged's wife, Deborah – she's not so different to any of us. A little more naked in her ambition, but she wants the same things, more or less. More than anything, she wants money. This is a woman who loves *things*. I doubt Gerrard has even a hint of the extent of her obsession. That's what it is, Shelagh. She loves to buy *things*.'

She sits right back in her seat. She throws her head back. She has the most luxurious throat we have ever seen. She's stunning.

'D'you know, when I was studying for my A levels, I often used to see her around and about. She was the real breadwinner, you know? Ged'd be doing this and that – God knows *what* Ged was doing, actually. But Deborah brought in good, steady income. She had literally hundreds of customers.'

We smile and encourage her.

'She was a mobile hairdresser. She had a little Fiesta van with her gear, and no one ever went near it. She never had to lock it, no matter where she was parked. Guess what her little business was called?'

We shake our head. Margueritte giggles. That's exactly what the noise is that she makes. It's a little girl's giggle.

'*Deb On Hair*. Think about it.'

She pauses and smiles the most radiant smile.

'But not for too long.'

She's just – irresistible. We smile back at her.

'And you suspect that the wife's love of the material might be channelled towards turning the husband around?'

She nods. She's Halle Berry turned Julia Roberts. It's the combination of the smile, the vulnerability, the wanting to be liked, loved, taken seriously.

'Forget it. That's a complete non-starter.'

'May I know why?'

'Of course you may. It's risk. Too much risk. For all that she *might* bend her husband to our will, she is so much more likely to bend his ear, instead. In effect, she'd provide a direct conduit to him. Whatever we'd be thinking, he'd know it immediately.'

'What if you didn't tell her the truth?'

We like her. We really do wish we could work with her.

'No. Sorry.'

She seems to accept it with grace. She seems disappointed, disillusioned even. But she seems to take it as final. She doesn't attempt to debate the point. But then she speaks up. And this *is* exciting.

'I understand. I understand more than you think. I know that, in politics, there always has to be one side that tells the truth. It can't all be chicanery and second-guessing. I know now that you're the good guys. Or, at least, I'll qualify that. I acknowledge that you're doing what you think is right, and you're doing it within the rules. You're doing it honestly. So, in a spirit of transparency, let me tell you where I'm coming from.'

She tells us. She tells us she believes the South Village is hers. She tells us why. She tells us about her life, her upbringing, her father, her uncles. She tells us how and why she feels we could be allies. She tells us once more why it is that the South Village matters to her, and she is *very* compelling. She asks for nothing. She gets up to leave but before she goes, she says: 'I hope you pull it off. I mean that. I'd rather see my vision realised in *some* way, than see it turned into a shopping mall. Heaven forbid. But, Shelagh . . .'

Our heart misses a beat.

'. . . I *can* deliver this for you. I promise. Probability is that you won't like the way I go about it, but the end will justify the means. It will. I'll deliver you your two gateways to The Loin, just as you want them, just as they appear on your architects' blueprints. I can bring it all back for you. You can be absolutely sure of that.'

Now she's fixing those unbelievable eyes on us. It's almost impossible to meet her gaze, but we can not show discomfort. We lock on to her, and we do not flinch. We are weak inside.

'If you ever want to go down that route, don't think twice. Just pick up the phone.'

Then she's gone.

Moby

To be fair, I'm not sure as a audition for all kinds of tasty grumble is the best way for my good self to recuperate after all that. Driving back into town I still had a mad fucking stalker on, just thinking about alls that'd went on. Could fucking smell it and all too, to be fair. That's one cunt of a smell to get off've yourself, the shite is. Telling you, la. Even if you've been wiping your arse that bit too hard and you get more of it on your hand than on the bog roll, it's a cunt's job getting the stench from off've you. Every time you scratch your nose that fucking stink is there. And it's not as though I could've showered it off, by the way.

Fuck knows what the hotel girl's going to make of all that, mind you – the chambermaid and what have you. It was bad enough where the fucking room they give us was. Right by the fucking reception it were. No fucking wonder they'd fucked off by the time we come out. They wouldn't've known where to fucking look. Fucking *howling*, she were. Screaming. She fucking loved it.

It was only a little aul' Travel Lodge thingio, just off've the motorway. The bird and that, the Hippo, she was only from Rainhill. Happy days – I was there in half a hour. She'd already booked in and that. Room number 2, by the way – right next to the fucking reception and the walls is made of plywood. Fuck that. They think aul' Moby's going on mute? Not even a fucking chance of it, by the way.

And when I seen the girl, fucking Hilda and that – fuckinell, though! What a monster! Sixty if she's a day, been a looker in her time and with all the fucking mascara and the bright red lippy she just looks like a aul' brass. A fucking enormous one though, in fairness – this aul' girl's fucking immense. Makes Mrs Moir look like a whippet. But she is one horny, pervy aul' girl, to be fair to her. There's no messing around with her. She puts a plazzy sheet down and squats.

'I'm going to go first because I'm dying for one. I hope you've got one too, have you, luvvy?'

I'm staggered. Takes a lot to get my good self speechless, but I just shut the fuck up and watch. Tell you what la, that is gorgeous what she done. Just curled it out right in front of us. Don't think I've seen nothing more gorgeous in ages. She's wearing the same caper as what she's got on in the photie. No knickers, no nothing, just this way-too-small teddy that makes a fucking poor job of holding in her knockers. She squats down, big, white, blubbery belly shaking with the movement, hikes up the bottom of the teddy so's it's not in the way and out it comes. It's a bit fucking runny, by the way, doesn't look as though the girl's been eating her bran flakes and what have you, but it all comes in nice and handy – as I soon finds out.

It takes myself a good few minutes, but I gets my own one out on to the plazzy sheet and all, too. Say so myself, but that is a quality dump, that is. There isn't a doctor in the land that'd be able to resist having a little poke through that pile, to be fair: 'Ah, now look here and that, here's a nice little bit of sweetcorn, by the way.'

What she does next – well, she's talking to us the whole time, talking to my good self as though aul' Moby's a virgin and he needs soothing and relaxing and what have you, which is all making my cock *extremely* hard, in fairness. But what she does is, she folds over the sheet and presses the two piles of shite together then, dead careful and that, she goes off into the bathroom with it. I can't help myself, by the way. I half have to have a look where the girl's going with it, but I can't keep my hands off her neither. I grabs her from behind and gives one of them big fat breasts a good squeeze, and with the other hand I'm going down there, having a little delve into the aul' honeypot. And she fucking loves it, by the way.

But she gets loose and teases myself a little bit about what I've got coming to me. Tell you what though, la, the voice on her. You'd blow your fuse just to hear her talk. Fucking quality, she is. Could get that Prince Edward spanking off over the phone, she could. Then she goes and does a amazing thing. Just stand there and does it, she does. She unscrews the jet filter from off've the shower head and she scoops handful after handful of shite in there. She fills up the shower head, she stuffs it inside the fucking faucet, and with what's left – which is a fucking lot by the way – she fills two plazzy shower caps. She gives us mine. I don't need no second bidding. I steps into the empty bathtub with her.

We've got the fucking cack all over ourselves. I've got it smeared on my chest and all down my gut and I'm pressed up against her, rubbing my chest and belly and bollocks all over her back, spreading shite all over the girl. I've got shite in my hands and all too, and I'm holding her tits from behind, rubbing them and caressing cack around her nipples. Fuck, that feels good, feeling them big nipples slipping through my finger and thumb as I tweaks them, getting shite on them. Noise from out of her, by the way! Fuckinell, was half ashamed at first, but then I was bang into it, ramming her doggy-style in that bathtub, but standy-up and that.

Then the best bit. She starts coming right away, to be perfectly fair to the girl, but she's not stopping at that. Fact of it is, she's putting aul' Moby through his paces, she is. My fucking thighs is only half standing up to the job, at the end of the day. I has to bend her down that little bit so's I can thrust more downwards, which is that bit easier on the old French fries. She's getting louder and louder and I'm half starting to chuckle, just thinking on what them two on the reception is going to be making of it all when it happens. She just backs into myself to make us stop banging her for a second, and she reaches up and turns the tap on and for five, ten seconds there is nothing but pure shite cascading down. We're fucking covered. *Covered,* by the way. After a second, the water starts to run clear and that, but the two of us is completely fucking chocolate. I mean it, man, it's fucking demented. Best bit of nonsense Mr Moby has ever had. Telling you.

Desperate Measures

Jade

I should've known it. To think that after all I've done with the club this last year or so, I could just walk back in here as a dancer again – well, I should've known better, is all. I don't even get past the Monro. No way in the world am I dancing for Moby Brennan. That big, bald dolt is so *not* feasting his eyes on *me*. I stop by the hairdresser's, totally gutted, totally undecided what to do next. I feel empty, totally, totally lost. I know now what people mean when they say they're gutted? Without that, like, *core* – without the people, the purpose, the *life* it gave me, I just do not know what to do. I don't know what I *do* do. I catch the eye of a bored, very good-looking girl in the empty salon. This area really has not, like, taken off, as yet. Duke Street, Ropewalks, the Digital Quarter – it just hasn't happened in the way or at the pace that everyone envisaged. The city *needs* people like me. It needs *me*. It needs The Loin.

I cruise the girl without even thinking about it. Great bone structure. Lovely, neat cropped hair, as naturally white as peroxide can take you. And that's how it comes to me. If I get my hair done like hers – like, *exactly* the same? No variance whatsoever? If I do that, fucking dickhead can look at me all he wants. Because, like, he won't be looking at *me*. He won't *know* it's me – so it's not as bad? I'll have to say cheerio to my luscious eyebrows for now but what the heck. It gets me in, yeah – it gets me behind the lines.

Family Fortunes 3

Ged

Aye-aye! What's our Stephen doing out at this time? Fucking half six it is, and he's walking along Barnston Road. Barnston Road, by the way – at this time of day! Road's fucking treacherous at the best of times, but in this light – he's lucky he hasn't got knocked down.

I pulls over and beeps him. He half looks embarrassed

at first, but he soon hops over. He looks fucking done in.

'What's up, lad? How comes you never got the bus?'

He don't answer at first. So I know straight away what the answer is. I mean to say, I don't know the *detail* and that, but I *do* know that something's went on.

'Dunno. Just felt like walking.'

I says nothing about it for a minute or two. Partly, I'm trying to keep a hold of myself, but as well as that, I want to give the lad the benefit of the doubt. I gives him a little smile.

'Lady problems, is it?'

He looks chocker, in fairness. Does not want to discuss *that* with his aul' fella. He looks down. Takes a big deep breath. Fuck. Lad's going to give it up. Has never told myself fuck all, by the way, never had a peep out of the kid. Smashing little lad, he is. Not at all like myself. He's a good kid.

'It's just — ah, it's nothing. I'd rather . . .'

And then the waterworks start. Just like that. There weren't no hint of it, even. One minute he's all charmed up. Next thing his fucking lip's quivering like it's got a electric shock and he's crying his eyes out. Bit embarrassed for the lad, to be fair. I looks out the window so's he doesn't feel too last about myself seeing him like that.

He pulls hisself together pretty fast, in fairness. Now it's him looking out the window. He takes a few deep breaths, like he's about to launch into something, but he don't say nothing to us. He's biting down on his bottom lip and getting his breathing back as regular as he can. Always was a emotional lad, our Stephen. Wears his heart on his sleeve, he does. He looks at us and gives us a little grin.

'Sorry about that, Dad.'

He's laughing now.

'Look, it's nothing. It was just all sorts of things building up, right. I can take care of it. I can handle it my own way, yeah?'

I must look not very convinced. He puts his hand on my shoulder. I'm made up about that, by the way. He's never really done that. Never gives us no hugs or nothing, our Stephen. Too old for all of that carry-on now, to be fair.

'Dad. I know what you're thinking. I know *exactly* what you're thinking. But I want to work out my problems a different way. Fighting your way through your enemies hasn't exactly helped the Middle East situation, has it?'

Things the lad comes out with, by the way. Says 'situation' and that more often than big Ron Atkinson, he does.

'Want to know what my ambition is, Dad?'

I don't mind saying so – my heart thumps like fuck when I hears him call myself Dad.

'Go 'ead, lad. What is it?'

He thinks on it for a mo. Half changes his mind. Then he goes: 'I want to never, ever have a fight. That's all. I don't mean anything disrespectful to you, Dad. I know how it works, and I know you only do things the way you think best. But that's not my way. D'you know what I'm saying? I don't *want* that to be my way.'

Filling up, I am. I don't say nothing, though. I love the bones of the little shithouse. End of.

Horribleness

Moby

Don't know what I think about what I done, in fairness. Way I see it, a girl that's shaving her borders and doesn't stop when you walk in is half putting a little show on for you. Is right. And if she's putting a show on for you, she's half saying – here y'are. And that's all's I've done. I've come up behind the girl, still half thingio from the mudbath this afternoon and what's struck us is two things – things that I've never really took much time over, in fairness. One is that, because this one's got her back to myself, I notice that she's got a beautiful, beautiful back. She's very pale, she is, and because she's sitting forward to trim her beaver, her spine is that bit more noticeable. Tell you what, la, it's one fucking beautiful sight, that spine and that long neck that looks even longer and more thingio because of how short her hair is. She's half a skinhead, this one. The other thing I notice is her eyes, half watching myself through the mirror. Them eyes of hers, man – she's fucking beautiful.

Forget the skates, la – this one here is in a league of her own. You're half into the whole thing of boning a pig while you're doing it. It's all the thingio in your head, the madness and the fucking *horribleness* of it, la. Telling you, man, you get *right* into it. But this one here – she's different fucking class. You'd feel every inch of it, no fucking messing. And I'm fucking ready for another little go around by now and all, too. Would not half mind bending the girl over that make-up table and letting her know. But I don't. Because this one here, she don't even have to say nothing to us. It's wrote all over her. Either she's a dyke or a fridge, but whatever it is, la, she don't want to know. End of. She's just sat there with that fucking strimmer in her hand looking at myself, and the look is pure fucking lethal, man. Half looks like the girl wants to kill myself.

I can't think of nothing to say, so I've just done one at the end of the day. It's got past the point where we can have a laugh and a joke about it, so I don't say nothing and I gets out of there. No way in the world can I give this one a job, by the way. I takes one last look at them beautiful eyes of hers. Stunning. Unforgettable eyes, them.

Becoming Hardened 3

Jade

Bastard didn't even recognise me – that's the good news. But no way am I going back in there, now. That's the bad. My plans of going Fifth Column have not even like got off the starting block. What that bastard just did back there – it was worse than rape. I'm not one for hysteria, yeah, but that disgusting big bastard just fundamentally like *possessed* me? That's exactly what he did? He stood there and he made it excruciatingly plain. He takes what he wants. If you want to say something about that, take him on, yeah? If you can't, then shut the fuck up. I don't know whether I despise him for it or whether I pity the big brute. Both, really. But mainly I despise him. I hate him and I will bring him down. I can't do it from the inside now, but there'll be a way. There will be a way.

Right

Cormack

If ever we doubted that the tide, slowly, inevitably, irresistibly was turning our way, we know now that we were right all along. Our instinct, the instinct that has driven our political animus from the very start, has got it right. It's simple as that, as always it was. We're *right*. If we think that this is a good thing, if we think this is the right thing, then others will agree. For we are propelled by – and *only* by – what is good, and right, and beneficial for and justifiable to the people. Doesn't have to be the *majority* indeed, just enough of a quorum for the change to matter. And if we ever faltered on that basic principle – most specially where The Loin is concerned – then today's newspapers have brought us right back on line, focused and determined to see this big thing through to the end. It's right here in black and white. People want this. People *want* what we're doing here.

Almost half the population of the UK does not see any harm in paying for sex, while one in every 20 Britons has actually paid for a night of passion (sic!), a survey revealed today. The findings, from online banking company Egg, showed that of those surveyed, 9 per cent of men and 1 per cent of women have paid for sex, while more than 20 per cent said that they knew somebody who had. Forty-eight per cent said there was nothing wrong with buying sex if that was what someone wanted. Meanwhile, 42 per cent of women said that they would hire an escort for the night, against 36 per cent of men.

Hallelujah. If those Brennan savages think they're going to put a spanner in the works, they can think again. This *has* to happen. This is going to happen.

Peeping

Paul

I need to be careful that I don't make it too obvious. If anything, I think I'm overcompensating. I hardly ever go down there when the men are working. Just occasionally I'll walk past like as though I've got like a thousand things to do and I'm really, really distracted and I haven't even noticed them, but there's no way they'd get on to that. I know his name, anyway. Gavin. And I get the impression he's a Taurus. No one's said nothing or anything, it's just a bit of a vibe that I get off the lad. He just *acts* like a Taurus, know what I mean. I just know it. I know he's a Taurus. He is. I'm sure of it. Little Gavin is a Taurus. That'd be perfect. A stubborn little bull. Little Gavin the bull – you are fucking beautiful. I can't show it, though. I need to be careful I'm not making it too obvious.

Soul 2

Margueritte

In my heart of hearts I never expected her to call. I don't know why – it was one of those intuitive things. I just seemed to have a deep and ultimate understanding that, much as Shelagh Cormack sympathises with me – *admires* me, I'd go so far as to say – there was in all reality no way she could reach out to me. It couldn't happen. There was no way of changing that basic reality – or so it seemed to me. I was laying my fires, but I had no real hope for a flame of change. At best, I expected my conflagration to bring everything down with it – me and all.

But I was wrong. Shelagh has telephoned. She wants a meeting. Wants it soon.

Class

Ged

I'd go First if I was taking her and the kiddies down to London. Or if I was with the lads. But for myself – I don't see no difference, in fairness. Better class of knobhead in First Class, couple a free drinks and that, Ritz cracker and a bit of Cheddar – but the journey time's the same wherever the fuck you sit. To be fair, the ordinary seats are all right. They are. Can't hardly tell the difference now between First Class and ordinary. Sometimes you'll see aul' Jimmy anyway. Been doing the trains since we was all going the aways years ago. Sound he is, Jimmy. Always have a laugh and a joke with him. Think he's half shitting hisself at the end of the day, thinks he has to keep on the right side of us and that but, in all fairness, we'd never do nothing to the likes of aul' Jimmy. Always waves myself through into First anyway, whenever he sees us.

'Here y'are, Ged lad, there's all kinds of wine and that through there. Gegg in, lad – there's no cunt in there!'

But he ain't on today. I'm just sat here watching the

sun slat through the Runcorn bridge and I'm more mixed up than ever. It's not Margo. I've got my head together over all of that, by the way. Fucking stupid, that were. She's a good-looking girl and that, no two ways about it – but at the end of the day, that's all's it boils down to. She's a Judy. Margo's a good-looking Judy with a little bit about her, knowmean, bit of class and that.

Only said I'd come down and see Franner, half to get a break from it all, smooth myself out, knowmean, just take it all nice and easy for a change. But, in fairness, I was also looking forward to bending his ear about all the shite that's going on and all, too. If any cunt knows what to do or what's going to happen before it fucking happens, it's fucking Franner. Fucking Go-Inhead. Knows every cunt, he does. Knows the fucking Taliban, by the way. Serious. Go-In knows the fucking Taliban. You'd think he was having a laugh and a joke and that, but I for one can remember the fat cunt telling us about some of his mad trips and what have you, bringing in the other gear and that, and he definitely told us about this one time when he got lost in Afghanistan and a goatherd took him back, no messing, he took him back to a mud fucking hut or something and made him smoke a fucking bong with him then tried to suck him off when he took the knock. Anyway, the Taliban was involved. That's the God's honest truth.

But looking out on that river with the sunlight all gold and yellow, I don't half feel moody. I feel restless. Something ain't right with myself, and I do not for the life of me know what the fuck it is. I'm going to find out, though. Oh yes.

On Power

Jade

This is, like, as bad as I've been for a long time. I've got a bit of an insight into how these depressions can come and go. It's no more than a layman's knowledge, an understanding of the symptoms and so on – and it *so* doesn't help at the time. The knowledge that it will pass and I will inevitably come to wonder how I could ever feel such *despair* has never in and of itself made that despair go away.

Today it's worse than despair. Not only do I feel hopeless, I feel worthless. I don't *stand* for anything. What am I? I'm fuck all. I'm a person who wants a certain sort of club in Liverpool. A person who wants great-looking women to get off with other great-looking women, lesbian or not. I'm, like, a person who wants to bring the party to the people who'll love it most fanatically? I *know* those people and I know that they are legion and I know that I can give them what they want. What does that amount to? Fuck all.

That's how I'm feeling now. I'm nothing. I'm nobody. I just let that fucking oaf come in and look at my tits and I did fuck all about it. I just, like, *sat* there? Something told me that that was the right way, the only way to respond – by not responding? But now it feels different again. I feel as though I endured it because, in some way, I *had* to. I don't want to say I *deserved* it – I'm so not going down that route. Like, that's simplistic, and it's not that anyway. It's a hard one – the closest I can come to that sensation is that it felt like it was *meant* to be happening like that, at *that* point, yeah, in *that* way. I was dead to it? I just let it happen? I could've covered up, could've told him to fuck off, but I knew it was futile.

Like, he'd already done his worst. Just by standing there, by caring less what the fuck I was thinking or feeling, by taking, taking, taking what he wanted, just by *looking* – he'd *so* already done the damage. I can't justify it, but I know what I felt. I felt that by just sitting there, by taking it, by saying fuck all that somehow I was winning. I felt I had the power. I was overcome, yeah, I was imbued with like this *sureness* that what I should do is just sit there, sit there, sit there. I don't feel that now. I fucking hate the bastard, hated him then, hate him now – but I sat there and let him take what he wanted of me. It was him that had the power, not me.

And I sit here now. I sit and follow the weak sun's trail upriver and I see the distant gentle drift of the poison winds from the chemical plants of Widnes and Runcorn and Ellesmere Port and I think of Daddo, as I do whenever these moods descend.

Would he still love me if he knew how I'd turned out? The thing he always used to drum into me – no, he didn't ever *drum* anything into me, he didn't do it like that. But what he always used to tell me was, don't be easy. Don't get a reputation with boys. You can have all the fun in the world and there's plenty enough time to find it – but get a bad name with the boys when you're young and it's with you for life. It'll follow you everywhere. It'll kill you. What he was telling me was that it's a man's world.

Would he still love me now? Would he love *me*? Of course he would.

Back to Basics

Moby

The cleaning girl in this place, she looks like that aul' one from off've that Freeserve advert. The one with the nudist camp on, the naturalists and what have you. Them. They're all playing tennis in the nack and there's this aul' saucy one that's posting a letter, then she's just stood there, letting you see how boss her legs are for her age – which they are, by the way. You'd well rag her, in all fairness. And this one here – she'd give you a good go-around, no two ways about it, she'd bang the arse off've you given half a chance. Way she's looking at my good self, by the way. Wants it right here, right now, truth be known. That's fucking Paul, that is. Truth be known. What cunt says that, by the way, 'truth be known'. Homs and teds is who. But the fact of it, this cleaning girl wants sorting. Mr Moby's got a bit of important busy-ness to take care of right now, but she's definitely one over the pocket, this aul' fox. Fucking tasty, she is – game as and all, too. Bit of a ale gut and that, but she's fucking all right.

Medi-Tan 2

Paul

I need to be really really careful here. Like, Moby's got to feel as though *he's* chose the name for the new tanning salon, but, truth be known, he'll come up with something horrible. He hasn't got a clue, really. He's concentrating too hard on the actual end product, know what I mean, the *tan* itself. Can't hardly believe some of the names he's come up with already. 'Toptanz' is one. 'Boss-Bronzie', 'Golden Globes'.

His ideas are all to do with the tan itself, which isn't what makes people come inside. Like, if he's going to go down that strasse, he might as well go the whole hog. Why not just call it: 'Brown as Fuck'. Or: 'I Can't Believe That's Not Natural, Girl'.

Your Billy Bunters don't want that at the end the day, that's why. They're more seduced by the idea of, like, a calming environment, know what I mean. They want to half believe they're stepping inside an oasis – they're half on holiday already. That's why I need to be careful. I have to subtly steer the big galoot away from 'Supatan' and more towards a sort of upmarket-sounding destination type place. 'Lanzarote'. Or, I know – 'Costa Dorada'.

That'd work.

On Teds

Ged

These fucking rugby divvies are doing my head in. They're not even proper rugby ponces, neither. I wouldn't mind that so much, by the way. I've watched a couple of them internationals with our Stephen – England against France and what have you, England against Wales, and it's not as bad as people might think. Bit slow at the end of the day, bit too much stopping and starting for my own good self but it's not a bad game, in fairness. These teds though – pure wool, they are. Fucking pricks they are, no two ways about it. Don't know whether they're Wigan or Widnes or Saint fucking Helens or what, but they're bad wools, dead loud, doing my head in badly, they are.

They got on at Runcorn, bladdered by the way, fucking *steaming* drunk already they are, and straight away they're starting all this: 'Hey, Donny – it's the Liverpool train. Check your wallet.'

Fucking hilarious, by the way. Pass us that needle and cotton while I stitch my sides back together. There's about fucking twenty of the cunts and they will not shut the fuck up. Fucking bad nuisances they are, bothering aul' fellas for their papers and what have you, letting every cunt know they're there. Big cunts and all, too. Don't see that many petite woollies at the end of the day, mind you.

'Err, mert! 'Ave you got a job?'

That fucking slays them, that does. In bits, they are. Poor auld lad's sat there minding his business and this fucking grock is leant over, giving him a hard time. Not for long, though, he's not. I gives the cunt a look and he can feel me looking and he half tries to look back, then he makes a big thing of getting distracted by his mates. Pure shithouse, he is. Making a big thing of concentrating on his mate who's telling another shite joke and who this prick suddenly finds fascinating.

'The CIA have located three of the four Liverpool men they're seeking in connection with al-Qaida terrorist cells. Bin Fightin, Bin Stealin and Bin Onda Sick are all in custody, though the whereabouts of bin Workin is still unknown.'

Fuck – that kills them. Joke's older than fucking Gary Mac, but it does them in good style. Fucking all over the place, they are. It's the funniest thing they've ever heard. More cans come out, more ale's spilt but the

Widnes wool posse don't give a fuck. Do not give a fuck about nothing, these cunts. They will do, though. Oh aye.

I'm just waiting for one of them to get up and go the bog. They'll have to in a minute, by the way. They may well be big fucking hard cases, but no cunt can drink six, seven cans and not need the fucking toilet. One of them's going to go in a minute. And when he does, Uncle Ged's going with him – all the way. I'm going right inside that cubicle with him and we're going to have a little word. We're going to introduce the lad to Bin Fucked.

But just as one of them's going, here y'are, let's get past while I go the bog, this fella walking down the carriage slows and catches my eye.

'Gerrard? Bloody hell – good to see you, man!'

Coley, isn't it – it's only Ray fucking Cole. Fuckinell though, la, amazed that he's let on to us, there. Would've give anyone a pound to a penny he'd blank us, Coley. Just goes to show you.

'What takes you to Londinium then, Gerrard?'

Love the way he always calls myself by my full name. Hate the question, though. Can feel myself going beetroot, in fairness. Half feels like the teacher in class asking who's robbed the Lourdes box and even though it's not you, you cherry up anyway. I'm going to see fucking Franner, aren't I? That's enough to make any cunt feel guilty-as.

'Quick in-and-out, Ray. See a couple of rellies and that, bite to eat, back tomorrow night. You?'

Tell you what, la, wish I'd never asked the cunt. Fuh-kin-ell, man! Did not realise the cunt could be that fucking boring. He goes on and on and on . . . What it is, is – there's this aul' hotel near where he lives. Victorian or something, Georgian, I think he said – and some developers are looking to knock it down and build flats there. Sounds all right to myself, by the way. Hotel's not getting used at the end of the day, what good is it just stood there? But Coley's not happy. Is not happy one little bit, by the way – he's only off to London with a little posse to front a MP and some fellas from The English Heritage.

And it's all starting to come back now, in fairness. I remember it, now. As well as the golf club and the Rotary and all the other charities Coley sits on – kiddies' things and cancer and what have you – he always was very big on the auld conservation, wasn't he? Fucking *always* going on about it, mind you. Half lived in the olden days, he did. That was how come he always used to drink in that Wheatsheaf by the way, the aul' thatched one up at Raby Mere. Still does and all too, most likely. It's just myself doesn't go there no more. I miss that, at times. I do. I miss having a pint with the likes of Ray Cole in that Wheatsheaf. I don't mind saying so. End of the day what's happened has happened though, hasn't it?

I'm half about to tell Ray that I've got a conservation thingio of my own going on when some fella's trying to get past him one way and there's a woman with a kiddie coming the other way. There's no room for him to sit down next to myself, neither – not that he'd want to, mind you. But, in all fairness to the lad, he shakes hands like as though he means it and he wishes us well and all of that and then he's on his way.

'Come and lend a hand sometime, if you're of a mind,' he goes, and he gives us a leaflet saying why this hotel has got to be protected. 'If you're of a mind', by the way. Things the cunt comes out with. As if he wants the likes of myself coming down there going, 'Here y'are, lad. Turn the fucking bulldozer round, know what I'm saying?'

Thinking on it, though, he did stop. I never had to pull him up or nothing. It was him spotted me and, to be fair to him, he could've just blanked us and I wouldn't've known nothing different. But he never. He stopped. Means a lot to myself, that does. Means a lot when the likes of Ray Cole give you the time of day.

Wrong

Cormack

It's not too often that we can look back and say we got it wrong, but maybe we were wrong about young Margueritte. Sometimes the culture of spin can have a negative cumulative effect. We still feel somewhat sensitive to the potential for media attack. She is beautiful, she is female, she is black. She wishes to be a major player at the forefront of a development the mainstream will describe as wicked, subversive, immoral, sleazy, unjustifiable. Wrong. They'll say The Loin is Wrong, yet she wants to be its champion. They could flay her alive. Or could they? Not on the evidence of her performance last night – no they could not. Margueritte would win, and with some ease. She's cool, she's clever, she's utterly in control. We could see her running rings round Paxman, if it came to that. We could see Paxman running rings around himself, befuddled with lust for the girl. Seldom have we known a woman to channel her sexuality so subtly and yet so powerfully into her professional, her political persona. Thatcher, one has to admit it, did this beautifully. Margueritte is forty years younger and infinitely more exquisite. She's got it. She knows it. We're with her. This time, and finally, we're with the girl.

I Love the 80s

Margueritte

OK, I'm back on track, I feel better, there's now a way ahead – but in no way have I been vindicated here. Fundamentally, all that's changed is that Ged and Moby have backed that old dyke into a corner. She has, really, no room for manoeuvre. So, in effect, she hasn't so much called me up in some belated admission of guilt – she's got no fucking choice. It's as simple as that. But it feels – it feels *not bad*. I can't deny that I feel the control coming back, and that was the biggest loss of all.

And *she* has called me, after all. She's called me in – and I have a clear run at this now. I'm not doing this for anybody but *moi*. What Cormack's told me is that if I can derail the Brennans, whatever it takes, however I do it – if I can get The Loin back on track, then Byzantium gets the contract. That's how it was, how it always should have stayed, but at least, now, that's how it's going to be. We've lost some time, and we *need* some time to bamboozle those two halfwits. But we're back in business.

That feels *very* not bad, incidentally. When they tried to take this thing away from me, it almost broke me. Only for a moment, but it very nearly did me in. This was *mine*, this thing. Others saw it too, but I was one of the first fucking wave. Me and John-Paul Brennan. We fucking *lived* through those riots and we were the ones who learnt the most from that whole thing. We had our eyes opened by it, and by what came next – Tarzan Heseltine, the Garden Festival, the Mersey Development Corporation, Albert Dock, regeneration. Regen – we almost started that sacred fucking cow. I saw it. *I* saw it all coming.

It's true to say that pre-John-Paul I had a worrisome altruistic period when I set up a pratice, helping the helpless women of Liverpool 8. But I saw all this coming. From the detritus of the riots rose new cathedrals to consumerism, to opportunity. Literally – we turned churches and schools into fitness centres. That was just the start of it. Everywhere I turned, everywhere I looked, I saw opportunity. Every burnt-out library and dance hall and bank and post-office building looked like paradise to me. I could see it, I could see the new manifestation – the bars, the restaurants, the holistic treatment centres, the MIDI suites, the post-production facilities, the coffee shops, the lofts, the lo-fi office suites. That was all me. That was *my* baby. I *saw* – saw it before any fucking councillor or city planner – how this city would make an industry of its heritage and its soul. I saw Cream coming. I saw that Liverpool could become the biggest urban pleasuredrome in Europe, bigger than Amsterdam if we got the basics right. And we were starting to. We were starting to do it right.

So I've got to face up to it. It does feel pretty good to be back on course again, albeit by this backhanded route. Me, that is – it's me that's back on course again.

Old Cormack talks as though we're all on some joint mission, bless. Like all the other cunts who come to live here, she's fallen head over heels for our beat-up city. She thinks this place is wonderful. She thinks Liverpool is special — most romantics do. Shelagh Cormack really believes we're doing something great here, something historic. Maybe she is, maybe we are. Me — I really don't care. I don't give a fuck how Liverpool comes out of all this. This is the big one I saw all those years ago. So I'll be doing my bit, all right. I'll do the job, get paid and fuck right off. Just watch me.

Recurring Nightmare 2

Moby

Tell you what though, la, that felt fucking horrible, that did. Was only dreaming, by the way — just nodded off in my chair there, fuck all to do, feet up on that fucking desk wondering where the fuck Paul's fucked off to and thinking on the cheek of the cunt saying as how Medi-Tan sounds like a abrasion cream. Fucking cheeky cunt, by the way — stood there he was, like that fucking Graham Norton with his hand on his hip and he just goes: 'Call it what you want, Moby. But try and remember it's a tanning salon, lad — not a BUPA ward!'

Thinks he's running the show, by the way — fucking arse bandit! Well, I weren't letting that go, to be fair. I just looks at the cunt and goes: 'Ay — Medi-Tan's a boss fucking name. The Judies'll love that, man. You've only just been saying how it's got to half remind them of their holidays and that. So where do they go for their fucking holidays then, softarse? It's fucking Medi-Tan, all right?'

And he's stood there, twitching and that, face flickering and pulsing like as though he's on a Charlie comedown. Bit of a roidhead he is, Paul the Hom. Stood there twitching like a fucking cunt, but I'm not that surprised and that all the shite he's putting in his body. Cunt's fucking *ballooned*, by the way. Since he's been here with myself, the cunt must've been caning the steggies 'cos his fucking shoulders, la – fucking untold, they are. Big mad chest, crazy big shoulders and that – and a tiny little head. Looks a cunt, in all fairness. He's stood there with that little fucking tiny head of his pulsing away. His temples are doing spasms like as though he's short-circuited. Half wants to say something to myself, but the lad knows the score. And just in case he don't, I goes: 'And leave us a couple of them Viaggies, lad.'

Not that I need them and that, but I have been caning it on the grumble front in fairness and, at the end of the day, you want to have a little dabble, don't you? You'd be a liar if you said that you didn't want to try that Viagra. End of the day, I just wanted to tell the lad to do something. Not bully him – I wouldn't do that to no one. I weren't making a cunt of the cunt or nothing, know where I'm going. Just – he had to be told at the end of the day. He had to know he weren't the boss around here.

He give us two Viaggies – well, he never, in fairness. He just put them down on the desk – *slapped* them down on the desk, in all fairness – and done his funny little half-run out the office. Done that mad gay muscle-run of his. Makes me laugh, he does – cake as fuck.

He'll be all right. Good lad, he is. Bit high-strung and that. Always was that bit liable to go off on a mad one, Paul. Was always the one trying to make a name for hisself at the match and that. He weren't hard, to be fair. He weren't making out he was hard, neither. He just wanted the lads to think he was mad and that. Wanted his own thingio – wanted a bit of a name and that. He's not a bad lad, to be fair. He'll be all right.

I'm sat there looking at the two tabs he's give us, thinking whether to take one or the both of them, and I leans back in the chair thinking about my brown adventures and the way we was both fucking *covered* in shite. And I starts thinking on that auld 'un before, the cleaning girl and that. And then I'm back to my aul' Rainhill hippo, aul' Hilda, my mud-loving aul' wool, and the way her big old tits was hanging down – like a kiddies balloon the day after the party, they was – and next thing I've gone on the nod. Not like myself, in fairness. I'm not usually one for too much sleep. But I'm spark out in the office there and the dream, man, telling you though, fucking unreal it were. Fucking *too* real, by the way. It's myself having a thingio with some big grock, having a bit of a word with him, and even though I don't know the lad that's in the dream, bringing it on with my good self, I half know that he can have a go and that I'm going to have to be on blob to do him in.

And that's where it went fucking horrible, by the way. Only asleep for about three or four minutes I were, but it was *deep* sleep. Dreaming sleep it were, and in this dream I'm just about pulling my fist back but I can't throw a punch. My arms are fucked – like lead they are. Can not make my fists do what my head's telling them. I'm just stood there like a knobhead, letting the cunt pick myself off. And then next thing, he's not picking us off, is he – he's got a big fucking sword. Coming at myself he is with a big samurai sword. I'm stood there, knowing that he's going to take my head off with it and next thing I've got one myself. But I can't lift it. Or I can't swing it and that – I've got a fucking samurai sword and I can not lift the fucking thing. And now the cunt is right over myself, lifting up his sword to do me right in and I can see the cunt, laughing in my face. It's Paul the fucking Hom. He's going: 'Need a tablet do you, lad? Need a tablet to help you get it up?'

I wakes up in a sweat, little bit thingio half, like, 'Where the fuck am I?' and that. Then I sees the two tablets and I thinks fuck that for a lark and I necks the pair a them.

Tokens

Paul

Well, he's made a holy show of me there – thinks he has at least, anyway. Truth be known, I would've been worse if it'd been in front of the workies. That would've been a bad one, la. But he's just a bully. I really, really am not going to lose sleep over the big bald grock. I just need to get out of here for a minute, get out of his way, get a breath of fresh air. I'll do my usual – leave a little token of my affection for young Gavin. And I'll go to the place and watch the lad for a bit. Breath of fresh air, he is.

Statutory Rape

Moby

Tell you what, though, it don't thingio you, that Viagra – don't make you rock hard just like that. I've heard all sorts from the lads about fellas who've had hard-ons for days and that, had to walk around bent double, can not get their kecks back on and what have you. Weren't like that for myself, in fairness. I mean, it *were*. Oh yes – Mr Moby did get one steaming fucking rock on when the girls started coming in and that. Some tasty fucking Judies in this establishment now though, la. Telling you – you'd beast on some of these little darlings. That was the thingio that got myself at the end of the day. It weren't the pills and that – weren't *just* the pills, end of the day. It was that little Lucy one getting her kit off. She's one of the few we kept on from Mikey's time and that. One of that Jade's girls, little Lucy – half begged us to keep her on and that and, in all fairness, I did tell the girl how it was going to be. Not going to be like it were, you know, kidder, I says to her. And look at what she's turned around and done, by the way. No way she can stay on now, in all fairness. Girl's going to feel a bit thingio herself at the end of the day. She knew the rules.

Brought it on herself, mind you. What's happened now with the young lad and that – it's all down to her at the end of the day. Is right. Knew I was watching, by the way. Oh yes – she knew that Mr Moby was stood there by the door getting a eyeful of her. You don't fucking come when you're taking your kecks off if you don't know you're half putting a show on for somebody. She fucking knew all right. Half done a little move, she did. Half done her stage routine and that – all snakes and wiggles and that, half touching herself as she got her jeans down (jeans that, by the way, that, *by the way*, are fucking skintight and sprayed on to her boss little arse and boss legs). Could swear that she done a moan and half touched herself, could a sworn she was strumming herself. That's when I come in.

Could not just stand there any more, in fairness. That Lucy one – I don't normally go for Judies like that, to be fair. End of the day that's why I've kept her on, in fairness. Not now and that. Girl *is* going to have to go, end of the day. Shame, in all fairness. Would not have minded going there again. Mr Moby would not half have minded doing the thing proper with the girl – and she would've fucking wanted that and all, too.

Looks like fucking Kylie, she does – *dead* small, *dead* fucking pretty, la, fucking beast on her, you would. But she's all there and that. She's a little doll but she's sexy, knowmean. Got great legs she has, lovely little arse and her tits, la – fucking telling you, her tits would drive you fucking mad. Fucking superb, she is. Knows it and all, too. Want to see the way she is when she walks past them workies. Telling you.

So I goes in and I goes: 'Don't stop on my account, darling,' and she half pretends like she never knew I was there and that. Acts like as though she's surprised and not all that made up to see yours truly neither, to be fair. Half tries to make out like she's covering herself and that, puts her arm across her tits and what have you. That don't wash, by the way. Does not wash for a minute with my good self, all that Modesty Blaise carry-on, covering herself up and that. I just looks down at my trackies. In fairness, my knob is like a fucking steel rod. Can hardly feel the lad, it's so stiff. It's stood right out, making my trackies stick out like I don't know what. I'm stood there, looking at it and she's stood there looking and you can see she's fucking loving it now. Can not wait to see the full root now, she can't. So I reaches inside down the waistband and pulls it out, and pulls my kecks down with the other hand. *Massive* it is. I don't mind saying so – my cock is fucking massive. Can see the girl is beasting on it and all, too. Can not take her eyes off've it, she can't.

I goes over to her, pulls her up to myself. She's fucking *tiny*. Can cup her arse with one of my hands. I'm feeling her little arse and the feel of it, the firmness of it just makes myself more thingio, more into her. She's half laughing but sounding that bit worried and that now, and she's going: 'Come on, Mr Brennan. That's as far as it goes . . .'

And I know exactly where she's going with that. Fucking *better*, by the way – I love all that. Half wants a bit of encouragement, she does. Wants myself to make her and that. I pushes her down on to the make-up table, and this one is good. Fucking shaking, she is, looking round at myself over her shoulder with big mad eyes, half would believe she was thingio and that, would think she really were fucking terrified of my good self.

I goes around her cunt with a couple of fingers, then I goes inside and that to juice her and I half stops and has a fiddle and that, gives her clit a bit of a working, gives her the time of day, to be fair. And then I pushes her right down with my forearm pinning her down how she likes it and I positions myself. In fairness, I don't exactly glide into her in spite of how hard I am at the end of the day. This little Lucy one is fucking *small*.

And that's where it all comes on top.

More Peeping

Paul

Could not believe what I was seeing, truth be told. Where I watch him from, right up in the roof, I could see into any of the changies if I wanted. There's one central beam running the whole length of the roof that's just about wide enough to crawl along, and if I wanted I could get a view through the mesh into any room on the top floor. Obviously I *don't* want. I don't exactly relish being up here with no end of dead pigeons and stink and what have you, but the less moving around you have to do, the better.

So I was all right up there, quite happy watching little Gavin stood there in that room right underneath me – the one the workies have taken over for theirselves. They use it to brew up, read the racing papers, have a ciggie, eat their butties – whatever. And my Gavin uses the room to have a wank. Yes, he does. More or less every day, more or less same time, young Gavin comes up here to pull himself off. It's brightened my day up, truth be told – although I was really really shocked when I first twigged it. I was more angry than into it, at first. I was. I didn't want to think of him doing that. Or, I didn't like the thought of him just doing it so cheap, so *routine* – just bashing one out like that. There should've been someone there with him. And I found out just now that there was.

What happened, happened quickly. Gavin's looking at himself in the mirror, like he always does. He's got his cock out, his gorgeous red-hard cock, and he's smiling at himself in the mirror while he strokes himself slowly. He's a showman, he is. You'd think he was putting a show on the way he leans back so that all the muscles in his stomach and his sides stand out, hard and toned and young and white. He's hard in the very, very best way. His body is hard and ripped and beautiful. My cock is hard looking at his marked-up, fighter's body, leaning back slightly with his cock in his hand. And he's watching himself in the mirror, smiling.

That's what I thought anyway – watching himself in the mirror. Because when it all kicked off, by the time I got down there Gavin's wank room was empty. All the madness was going off in the girls' changies next door. I seen it all – all of it. I seen Moby pulvering him and little Lucy hanging off him, clawing at his back. Moby, with his trackie bottoms around his knees, was battering my Gavin. The b*****d had him by the throat, driving his big fist into the side of his head again and again. I seen all this through the mirror.

Resolve

Jade

I'm so glad I was in. This time on a Friday I'm, like, *so* used to being at the club that I've just had to get out, these last few weeks. I just have to *do* something with myself? Fridays – I just lived for them. Here comes the weekend and all that – I *loved* it. Fuck, I still do, too. Sometimes, like, I've just gone up there. Sad, I know – that *so* is not me, yeah? I've just been like standing there? Watching the girls and the workmen come and go? Watching, watching, watching – that's what I do at this point in my life. I've seen that Paul coming and going. Couldn't be more furtive if you gave him those devil's-eye lenses and, like, made him look from side to side, that man. He comes out of Ultimo, walks up and down and around the corner until he finds like this battered old Peugeot 205, checks around himself and quickly slips a rose or a carnation under the windscreen wiper. He's a very odd man.

But today – today I'm struck low with the weight of futility and I *don't* go on up there to hang around and get myself down. I wait in my place for the day to be over? Tomorrow will be a better day? Whatever I try to think, I think of my Daddo. On another day, that can make me brim-full of cheer. His happy, hard, working-man's face peeping round the door. He'd always be happy, Daddo – always, *always* came home for his tea. He was never one of the men who stopped off for a pint. I wish he had. I wish he'd lived for *him*. It was like, the drunks, the gamblers, the wife-beaters – they weren't the ones who died. My Daddo did all the shifts that Sellafield would let him do. He did all the overtime that came his way, so that his little Jade could have it all. Would he still love me now? Would he understand? He wouldn't have to. Because what I do know is that I wouldn't be *me* if he was with me now. If Daddo hadn't gone, I'd be, like, a *different* me. I might be a me for him, perhaps. And that's what keeps me low today, this feeling that we *do* live and die for our men, no matter what. I'm thinking that, for all my freedom, for all my lust and spume for life, I *have* no life – because it only started once he'd gone.

So it *is* quite a miracle that I'm in when Lucy calls around. She's distraught, and it kills me to make her, but she tells me everything. Mikey's Mirrors. We *so* should have smashed those mirrors in joy and anger the moment he died. But we didn't, we plain never got round to it, they stayed and it's caused all this. And now, more than ever, I know I have to act. Even if I can't do it for myself, I can do it for others, yeah? I have to be hard. I have to be determined and I have to feel nothing. I have to care less. I have to act like a man.

Names

Ged

Big fucking huge fat lad picks us up. Not just a fatty, this lad, by the way – this one is fucking *yowge*, la. Fucking immense, he is – size of a industrial bin. Nice enough lad and that, introduces hisself as W9 and half gives myself a grin and that, half like he's expecting myself to know him or something. Never heard of the cunt. W9? Means fuck all to Gerrard Michael Leo Brennan, that don't. Nice enough lad, by the way.

He takes us down to Soho to that New World, one of Franner's aul' favourites. When he first got going down here and that, that was one of the places he always used to take the lads, just to show us how he was looked after by the fellas that had the gaff. There, and that Phoenix in Stratford. *Always* in that fucking Phoenix, by the way, Franner – him and Kathy Lloyd and Gail McKenna and thingio, all the boxers and that. Colin McMillan. Sweet C. Fucking reaming it he were back then, Franner. Fucking fat cunt he were – just like this fucking cunt here.

'Here y'are, lad.'

I gives him a tenner and that. Gives him a cockle, should I say. Lad don't look that made up with it in all fairness. Probably gets given all sorts down here. Should've give the cunt fuck all – do the lad a favour and that. He'll only spend it on sweets by the looks of him.

'Take care now, kidder. Go easy.'

Phoney cunt, me, sometimes. I pats the roof of his limo a couple of times and that's it. W9 is gone. Vamoosed. Not that you could really imagine the lad vamoosing anywhere, to be fair. One fat fucking lad, him, by the way. Maybe he was just that bit chocker 'cos I never knew his name or something.

TCP

Paul

Bad day, by the way. We all have bad ones, but this is turning into a *bad* day. The one good thing to come out of it was being able to console little Gavin. Lucy and me got him cleaned up. He didn't want no fuss, but I ran into town for a first-aid kit and I don't mind saying so, I got a bit of a tingle when I was dabbing the TCP on his cheekbones. He's got cheekbones like I don't know what, Gavin has. They're *brutal* cheekbones. Telling you la, it's not TCP he's wanting – it's TLC from PTH.

He's telling me his dad's this and that and what he's going to do to Moby when he sees what he's done to him. I'm trying to listen and I tell him that maybe he wants to think twice about any of that carry-on, any silly tit-for-tats and what have you. But really I'm just amazed by the shape of his head. His whole head is lain in my lap and it is the most beautiful, classical sort of head I've held for a long time. I'm dabbing the TCP on his cheekbones and he's trying not to wince, but I can feel the little tremors going through him and it gets me right in the solar plexus. I'm really, really stuck on this little man. And then he says it. Says no way is he coming back here to work for that effin bee. If he could've seen my face. Telling you, that Moby – he's a monster. He's screwing everything up. He's got to go.

Luck

Moby

Some lads are just born lucky. It's one of them, isn't it – either you've got it or you haven't. Well Mr Moby has got it in spades, la. It never rains but it shines on the big shiny dome of auld Moby Brennan. Oh yes. She's only gone and phoned myself, hasn't she – only picked up the mobie and asked my good self around to her gaff for a scran. Oh aye. Come around for a scran, by the way. That'll be the last thing she's eating. And my good self, by the way. I don't mind saying so – I've wanked myself daft over our Margi over the years. I have. That was one Judy I *always* fucking wanted to get a grip of. Always did know the score, by the way, Margi. I'm not fucking stupid. She's never wanted to know myself before. Never hardly give us the time of day when she was with aul' golden bollocks. But she hasn't wasted no time, has she? At the end of the day, word has gone around that Mr Moby is now a player, and aul' Marguerrite Lascalles is a girl that wants a bit of that. And that's exactly what she'll be getting, by the way – a very large portion and all, too. But not at her gaff, she won't be. I'm not a fella that likes to be told when and where and what have you. Did not want the girl calling the shots at the end of the day – can set a big thingio if you're letting her take charge right from the off. She's coming round the club to pick my good self up and we'll go from there. Oh yes.

On Reliability

Paul

And if the prospect of little Gavin leaving me isn't too much for one bad day, get this. My lad in Speke has turned gangster on me and all, too. Don't get me wrong – he's a nice lad, Nick is. Bit *too* nice. But he's got to understand what he's got himself into, here. I made it really really plain to the boy when I first took him on. I said to him, I did: 'I need to know I can rely on you, Nick.'

He can't turn round and say I didn't tell him that. I *needed* to know he was reliable. All's he was seeing was the dollar signs, mind you. Had a big mad student loan and an overdraft and no end of rent arrears – he would've said anything to get the gig. But I couldn't've been plainer with him. He was told.

'Five thousand tablets a week, every week.'

He told me that wouldn't be a problem. It hasn't

been a problem. But now he's saying he's got his finals coming up and he needs time out to study. He's having a laugh and a joke with me. Telling you, man – he wants to have a word with our friends in Soho Street if he thinks he's drying up on us. No chance, by the way.

Nerves

Moby

I don't mind saying so – I'm half shitting myself about this one. I am, by the way. Fucking Margi Lascalles – that is a fucking Big Shag by anyone's fucking standards. Forget that she was with our Ratts and that – fucking wrong 'un him when all's said and done. Do not even have a *mini* thingio about doing the dirty on that cunt. No fucking way. But she is fucking quality at the end of day, Margi, and I don't want to do nothing to put the girl off. I half like her, I do. That's the God's honest truth. End of the day, I like the girl. I want to impress her.

And then it comes to us. Only staring myself in the face, mind you. One thing that all Judies like is a boss bronzie. Oh yes. And what's just been installed in Mr Moby's own fucking gaff? Only four fucking top-of-the-range ultra-power all-over sunshowers, is what. Get paid, lad – get fucking paid! Gaff's fucking empty, to be fair. Can help myself. Give myself a proper fucking go-around. Don't give a fuck what the lads say about it, in all fairness. Do not give a fuck about none of that. Brown dome, brown fucking arse? Bring it on! Fucking let's have it! Oh yes.

The Use of Spies 3

Cormack

Knowledge of the spirit world is to be obtained by divination; information in natural science may be sought by inductive reasoning; the laws of the universe can be verified by mathematical calculation, but the dispositions of an enemy are ascertainable through spies and spies alone.

We can have our eyes open all the time and still not see. Then a stroke of luck – no, luck has an inappropriate ring of joy about it. Fate then, happenstance, pure chance brings it about that we should be in a particular place at a particular time. This evening, it is the rain that brings us indoors earlier than scheduled. We had mixed feelings about Jade's call. Pleased, because we shall see her. We were not expecting to see the girl so soon. But we're anxious also, for this was not the voice of the Jade Walker we know so well. She was agitated, irrational, undone. We were slightly hurt, also, that she preferred not to meet at the Colonnades. She made little sense. The girl was, if not distraught, then emotional, certainly. She was distracted.

But we've managed to get a cancellation at Hope Street. She's happy with that. One thing about young Jade Walker – for all her politics, she *loves* a fancy restaurant. More than anything, we'd have to say. We've never known her in love, but we've seen her light up over John Dory fillets swilled down with a crisp Pouilly Fumé.

Our plan was to perambulate the Canning Village

area. Until The Loin kicks in, this is still the best established and the safest of the city's red-light areas. We'd have to admit to a gnawing in the groin as we got closer to Percy Street, but this was no warm sensation, nothing so basic as lust. We'd have to confess, too, that the sorts of girls who work these streets are a fascination to us. Where most would find their brown teeth and their blank eyes repulsive, we find ourselves drawn in. It is nothing else – it *is* a fascination. But we have not been in the area at night for a long time. Tonight, the snagging in the pits of our soul is a product of, if not out and out terror, then something akin. We are far from anything familiar. We are tense and apprehensive as we turn from Percy Street into Huskisson. We watch the shadows dart and play, and we're relieved when the rain comes down so suddenly, and with such extremity.

We allow Sally to take our coat and we await instruction – upstairs, we hope. We don't want downstairs. Sally's a good friend of Jade's – an old course-mate. She'll find us somewhere nice. And while she's gone, in the minute it takes for her to find the boy who *should* be looking after coats and umbrellas, we hear him. We hear the unnaturally loud voice of that particular Bishop. His laughter, his unsuitably boorish joke-telling comes rolling down the staircase. It can be nobody else. It's him. We are alone and we glance at the reservations book. He's in a private room, the guest of an individual whose name is not familiar. We check around briefly and make a quick note of the diary entry. *P. Rattle/L.B.* is one entry. There's a note which says: *C.C. – no nuts.* And scrawled in pencil next that is *M.K. – later.*

Nuisance Calls

Margueritte

Talk about timing! I'm right outside Ultimo when he calls again. That must be half a dozen times this past week or so. I'm not in the mood. I *will* call him back some time, but for now I have bigger fish to fry. Jesus!

Heat

Moby

To be fair, I'm not one of your body beautiful teds. Have never gone in for all of that in all fairness. I do go the gym and that, half to have a laugh and joke with the lads and that. But at the end of the day, I've got all the gear on site, it's mine, end of. I'm using it. I don't mind saying so.

Tell you what though, la, it is fucking *hot*. I haven't worked out how long you're meant to give it, but way I sees it, aul' Moby can take a bit more punishment than most lads. It's one of them. You sticks the tokens in outside, you gets your kit off and you come on in. Shut the door, stick the goggles on and stand there like a fucking soft cunt. Would not be doing this normally, mind you. And at the end of the day, the place is fucking empty. No cunt's going to know, are they?

The first token drops down. That's two minutes. This is the fucking state of the fucking art by the way, as far as bronzie machines goes. This one does you like toast. I've put five tokens in — ten minutes, in all fairness. That's going to tan my arse nicely, that is. If that Margueritte one isn't biting my shiny brown arse in three hours' time I'm going to want to know the reason why.

Two tokens down and I'm wishing I'd just gone for the six fucking minutes, la. Telling you – it's fucking roasting. The sweat is fucking sliding off've myself and all's I can see is the tubes. Looking at them through these goggles, they look mad – all purple and weird. I gets a bit of a shock when the third token drops down. That's well past the halfway mark now. I'm half starting to feel a bit thingio now, that little bit chocker with myself that I was ready to give in so easy and I never put more tokens in.

It *is* fucking boiling, mind you. And I gets a sudden thingio and all, too – I can't work out where the door is, now. The door on this side, inside of the fucking tanning cabinet that is, is covered with tubes. That's all's you can see. It's just purple tubes. In all fairness, I did fucking panic there – where's the fucking door and that. Soon as the fucking money's gone, the tubes are off though, aren't they?

The fucking sweat is now pouring off've my own good self. Tell you what – fuck all that 'I can stay under all fucking day' thingio. Fuck that, by the way. I for one am fucking gasping here. Can hear my fucking heart thumping and that. Oh yes. It's one of them. You're that done in from the heat of the tubes – which are *right there*, by the way. They're as good as touching you. They are when you're a big lad like myself, in all fairness. Your arse is touching the back tubes and your grid's about a inch away from the front ones. Fuck knows where the fucking door is. I'm that done in from the heat, that horrible, boiling fucking heat that I'm ready to pass out. Can't hardly breathe, to be fair. And it fucking stinks and all too, by the way.

Should be time up any second now. That last token dropped a while ago. Always does seem that bit longer whenever you're waiting for something. That's what my aul' lady at Barnston used to say, aul' Mrs bang-up-for-it Moir.

'A watched pot never boils' she'd go. And then she'd give us that look that was going – come'ead. Come and unbutton this thingio and get your dirty fingers under my girdle and fucking fill your boots, lad. Feel my big tits as much as you want. Tell you what, though, you don't want to be getting a hard-on in here. That'd be game over on the Margi front, that would.

Token drops. Another one. Tell you what, though – it's that fucking hot in here I'm going mad. Half would've sworn that that last one was the last one and that. I don't mind saying so – I am fucking *melting* here. Can't hardly breathe at all. I starts checking around for the door now. As soon as them fucking tubes goes out, I am fucking out of here. I mean it. Fuck that – I ain't wasting one more second than I have to. Can not breathe at all, I can't. My eyeballs, la – telling you. And my fucking heartbeat. Can hear it loud and clear, in all thingio – fucking *racing* I am. Starting to panic that little bit, in all fairness. Need to get out of here.

Another token drops. And that's when the fucking penny drops with auld softarse here and all, too. Two pennies drop, in all fairness. That some cunt has boxed us in. Boxed us right in, by the way, and fed the fucking meter. And the other thingio that comes home to roost is that I ain't getting out. Can't hardly lift my arms at the end of the day anyway. Could not get the strength to have a wank in fairness, let alone smash the fucking cabin open from in here. Would probably get electrocuted from off've the wires at the end of the day. That's if I don't bleed to death from off've the smashed tubes. I ain't getting out. My fucking head is exploding and I can't fucking breathe and I'm going to fucking die in a fucking tanning cabin. Fucking bad one, la.

Doris Day

Paul

That's that, then. That's him dealt with. Didn't like having to do it, but *che sara*. What will be will be.

Eyes

Ged

Tell you though, that was just exactly what the doctor ordered, that was. Me and Franner had a good aul' rabbit about the auld days. Still is fucking weird to think of fucking Go-Inhead as a fucking Name, but that's what it is at the end of the day. He's a big, big fella – in more ways than one.

Half in fucking love with myself he is, though. Them fucking eyes of his, la – pure do my head in, they do. They always was fucking weird eyes, to be fair. Like fucking Scooby Doo eyes, in fairness. He never could keep his eyes still, Franner. Even if he was telling the truth he just always half looked shady knowmean, looked like as though he was guilty-as. His minces still do that, by the way – they slip about and that. No –

they *roll* about, they *slide* around in that big fucking gigantic head of his. He's sat there watching us all night, watching us eat and that, watching us *dead* thingio – and I know where he's going with it. I know he wants to get into that one – pat ourselves on the back, tell each other how good we've done for two lads from the barrio and that. I don't mind doing a bit of that carry-on if that's what the lad wants, but I feel a fucking cunt in all fairness. Feel like a bad phoney.

But then, just as I'm thinking fuck it la, it's going to be one of them – and I'm all right about it, by the way, I'm quite thingio about just having one of them with the lad – the cunt just comes out with it. That's what's so hard to get used to about the lad. I'm half still thinking about him as Fat Francis, aul' Go-Inhead the run-around. That's all's he were, by the way – and he was fucking lucky even to be a run-around. Lot of the lads wouldn't've give him the time of day, to be fair. But it is fucking hard to forget all of that. End of the day, the lad's not going to be one of the top fella's down here if he's a fucking knobhead though, is he? And that's what gets you about fucking Franner. He *is* a shrewd fucking lad. He just watches us, watches myself jabbing at my scran and that, spearing bits of duck and what have you and he just comes out with it.

'So, what is it then, Ged? What's troubling you, my friend?'

Says some fucking weird things he does. 'My friend', by the way – would think the cunt never knew us! Would think he'd never hardly met myself. But he's right, isn't he? He's right on it. And I tells him. I opens up and I tells him all of what's gone on this year. And fair play to the lad he just listens and chews and that –

nods every now and then, to be fair, gives myself that little bit of encouragement when he thinks I'm getting that little bit thingio about opening up to the cunt. He just listens. It would've been all right just to have sat there and told him everything. I didn't expect no big mad answers. There isn't any. But Franner's take on it all – just what yours truly needed, at the end of the day. And he's right and all, too. The fat cunt's only right what he's saying.

Medi-Tan 3

Margueritte

I have little time for cliché, but I didn't know whether to laugh or cry. Laugh at the sight of him – the great man-mountain Anthony Moby Brennan reduced to a red, skinned, scalded, whimpering cat. When I let him out he was in tears, the stupid bastard. Not a pretty sight – the tears *or* the seeping, flayed skin. As burns victims go, he's not too bad. He'll survive.

But I could have joined him in fits of tears on the floor. Firstly, because this sets my plan back. How long he's out of action has a direct bearing on how long it's going to take for me to get him on side. Looking at him, it could be a week, could be longer. I might have been better ignoring the screams, turning around and walking back out of there. That's my second regret. In many ways, a dead Moby might have been easier to control.

I have to make some tough decisions, and quickly. He's splayed out on the floor, exhausted, naked, barely *compus mentis*. I could finish him off. And that's exactly what I do, in a manner of speaking. I lie down right next to him and I speak to him in the crooning, soothing mamma's voice that Ratter loved so well. It works immediately. This boy's mind and body may be out for the count, but his dick has a mind of its own. I'm talking down to him, reassuring him all the time.

'The doctors are coming, honey. You're fine. Margi's here. Margi wanted your big cock inside her tonight, baby, but that's going to have to wait. Don't you worry, honey. We're going to have you back, big and stiff and strong in no time at all. You're going to be gorgeous. I'll show you, baby. I'll show you right now. Margi's going to show you, honey. Can you feel that? Feel my fingernails scratching your balls, Moby. I'm holding your big balls and I'm squeezing them, baby.'

I lean right into his ear and whisper it.

'Margi's going to make Moby come. Moby's going to come all over Margi, like a good, good boy. Come on, honey. Come on . . .'

It didn't take much more than that. I held his cock, stroked it two, three, four times and the great bear was nearly choking. His brain was fried, but his dick – I have to say his dick was fine. There was no way in the world I was letting the bastard come anywhere near me, incidentally – I was wearing Gucci – but he wasn't to know that. By the time the paramedics carried him away, Moby Brennan was in love.

Good

Cormack

Oh Jade, sweet Jade. The wily pleasures of her tongue and her caress – we should not allow it. It can't be right. We know we shouldn't let this . . . we know you only indulge us. And yet – and yet is it so wrong? It is. It is so wrong. For us to allow, to let, to lie back, gratified, as one so young and so *good* darts and delves to our groaning, collapsing pleasure – that should not be. That is wrong. But we allow it. And we allow ourselves to believe that, in some way, she is not the subject. That's what we want to believe. That one such as Jade would not in any case subject herself. If we are in some way the subject, then this is good. This *is* good.

An Obsession

Paul

All's I was going to do was take him some grapes and flowers, see how the poor lad's getting along. Anyone'd think it was *me* that'd done him in, the way his mam treated us. I wasn't going to push it, anyway. I know when I'm not welcome. But that changes things between young Gavin and I. Seriously, it really really does change things.

Harold Shand

Ged

W9 drops us off at Euston and Franner walks us to the

platform. He's had a good time, Franner has. I don't mind the lad playing the kiddie with us, to be fair. He's half doing it now, putting his hand on my shoulder as we walk, half trying to make it look like as though I'm one of his men. Maybe that's the way he sees things now, by the way. In all fairness, the lad has sorted out one or two things for myself. Was him took care of the John-Paul thing at the end of the day, so he's got a point, to be fair. Maybe in some way he thinks I'm under him and that. Don't think so myself, mind you. Do not fucking think so at all.

I gets on the train and talks to him from out of the window. He's stood there on the platform, looking up. Don't half feel close to the lad, in fairness. I haven't really got that many close mates at the end of the day. Was close to Coley and that, but when the shite hit the fan, where was he? Franner though, he's a good lad. Fucking solid, he is. Guard blows the whistle and I'm half sorry to be headed back. He turns to go and I remembers something.

'Your lad there. Why the fuck's the cunt called W9?'

Franner starts laughing.

'Why d'you think, you cunt?'

He's doing his half Cockernee, half Scouse thing. Fucking Harold Shand, he is. Laughing and talking at the same time. I shrugs at him. The train starts to move off. He shouts after us.

'Because he drinks so fucking much!'

I goes to find my seat, plonks myself down and gets a pen out. I'm going to do what he said – make a list and that. Work out what needs to be done and what's just shite.

Out-of-Body Experiences

Jade

A lot of the girls have, like, got this big stance? On received notions of aesthetic beauty? It's the old Dworkin one, isn't it – why should we, like, conform to orthodox perceptions of desirability? Good point. Do whatever makes you happy, yeah? But it begs the question why she or anyone would want us to conform to a *different* stereotype – like, the overweight, comfortable, Mother Earth lesbian. This is the argument Shelagh and I had this morning. It wasn't an argument so much as a meandering difference of opinion.

I'd made her come – I'd done that with my fingers, done it because I wanted to and because she wanted me to. She lost control. I've never quite seen her so overcome – she was gone, you know, she was at another place. Even with her, like, body form, the power of her orgasm almost took her off the bed. There was only her feet and her head touching the mattress – everything else was arched, quivering, ready to blow.

It was great for me to take her out of herself like that, but the ecstasy was as short as ecstasy always is. She became silent and brooding, and I knew what that was all about. She's always the same – she feels a deep and immovable shame. She feels it's wrong? For an old lump like herself to take any kind of gratification from a child such as I, she feels it's wrong? She beats herself up over it. She knows that her thick waist and her grey and sunken breasts spark no desire, anywhere. She believes in the natural order of things. She believes that she does not *deserve* physical gratification, yeah, that she has no place next to me? I don't see it like that – and I bend her to my way. Every time, she succumbs. Each time, she is powerless. She will acquiesce to my touch, to my lips. She will let it be. She acquiesces to the inevitable – the fearful and shuddering thrill she knows my touch will bring. And afterwards, she will want to know why. Why do I do this for her? My answers seldom vary. I do it because it gives her such pleasure. Because it isn't hard to do.

I don't want to go over and over the sexual politics of this with her. I'm a firm and lissom girl and she is old and loose, yeah, flabby and hirsute. She has a stern and masculine face, yet she looks kind? She has love to give? I do, too. I sometimes bring her to climax. If that disturbs her, if she wants that to stop, she need only say. For now, yeah, there is so much more that needs to be done. We have work to do.

Shelagh told me all about the unholy trinity in Hope Street last night. I couldn't even get a minute with Sally – girl was run off her feet. But we'll catch up today. She'll tell me what she knows.

Yet More Peeping

Paul

Well, well, well! Little Lucy as I live and breathe! Don't see *her* getting the once over from that aul' cow, by the way. Oh no – it's straight in for little Lucy Locket! Little slag! That's been going on in *my* gaff right under my fucking eyes! They've got me really really angry, now!

Lists 2

Ged

I'll admit it. I'm not a fucking scholar. I've never said I were, to be fair. I've spent the whole fucking train trip with a fucking pen in one hand and this fucking napkin sat on the table, waiting for the list to write itself. I've had four cups of coffee – the tea's fucking horrible on these trains, pure fucking swill it is – and two KitKat Chunkies and the list has gone no-fucking-where. We're at Runcorn, and this is it:

1) *Sack S. Vill caper. (speke to M)*
2) *M*
3) *Sort Stephen*

There should've been more. There should have well been more. It was fucking flowing when I got back to my hotel room last night, but now it's thingio. I can't fucking remember the half of it, know where I'm going.

But those ones are the important ones, knowmean. That'll do to be going on with at the end of the day. I've got the big ones down, and Franner's got it spot on. Lad's only fucking right, by the way. This whole fucking property caper – not for Gerrard Brennan. Is right, by the way. Just is not for myself, all of that.

What I'll do soon-as is, I'll hand over to Margo. Fuck k.d. lang and her crew, they don't have to know nothing. I'm not taking out a advert in the *Echo*, am I? Ged Brennan has left the building and that. I don't mind staying on as a adviser and what have you, move upstairs and that, Director of Football, if you will – but I've only been fucking kidding myself. Franner's got it in one. It ain't me. I'm a man of the streets, not a fucking property developer. I'll find some other caper, but the sooner I lash that South Village, the better I'll feel. Been bringing me right down, all of that. It has – pure and simple.

Margo'll be made up, by the way. Made up, she'll be. And that, just thinking on it now, gives myself a extra little thingio. She's Thing Two on my list, Margo. Don't know what to do about the girl. Can not get her off've my mind. Going to sack it, by the way – not even going to give it a second thought. By handing her what's hers and that, give her the South Village back, I'll probably be coming as close as I'm ever going to get. Shame, at the end of the day. I do like the girl. Think a fucking lot of her, I do, by the way. End of the day, in all fairness, I myself have got fuck all to offer a girl like that. Got my own to look after and all, too. Item Three. Our Stephen. That, I can sort.

Language 1

Paul

All's I wanted to do was talk to the lad, make sure he's OK and that. As his employer – well, sort of, aren't I – I'm responsible for the well-being of everyone on site. All's I wanted to do was let him know that we *are* there for him. I didn't exactly expect him to greet me with open arms, in all fairness – but I really really did not expect that foul-mouthed abuse, neither.

This changes things. I keep my distance and, once I'm certain he's started to simmer down a bit, I follow him. I'll follow him for as long as it takes.

Plot

Jade

Shelagh is so not going to like this. It's like, fuck knows how we stave this one off. That's Shelagh's greatest strength, yeah? I know that she will not panic? But this is getting tasty. Sally's news is that, like, there *were* three guys? Running up a horrific tab on a company account? And a fourth guest joined them for coffee. The company was Little Brother. They're one of the biggest suppliers of CCTV and surveillance equipment in the country. Phil Rattle was the guy doing his pitch and paying the bill. The Laughing Bishop was one of his guests. The Chief Constable was another. And the latecomer was Marc Kelman from City Focus.

Paul

I check the clock on my new mobie. I watch the digit change over from a 2 to a 3. It looks beautiful, all in a line like that, 3.33. Probably my favourite time of day, 3.33 – morning or night, I don't care. That and 11.11 – that's my favourite, too. And I really really do like 5.55. Those are good times of the day.

Little Lucy Locket lives in Cheviot Road. There's only really one way in, so I can sit off here all day if needs be. I've been and bought a new phone. That Carphone Warehouse is just there. The staff in there were really, really lovely – did not make me rush into nothing. They treated me nice. Treated me like a real human being. I bought this boss little Nokia 8310 that's got all the new games on it – *gorgeous* it is, sort of matt black and chrome. Perfect. I'm quite happy to be sat

here, playing Snake IV and waiting for him to come out
of there. He can take his time for all's I care.

Souls

Cormack

Not good. Not good at all. Marc has been transparent
about his need, indeed his *desire* to solicit rival visions
for the city centre. He has been less forthcoming about
the nature of some of those bids. In a nutshell, Marc
Kelman has had dinner with a major supplier of closed-
circuit cameras, along with the Chief Constable – not
exactly renowned for his support of any manner of
decriminalisation of *anything*. Far from it – the Chief
Constable would very much like to criminalise as many
things as possible. The presence of the Champagne
Clergy is neither here nor there. He'd join Satan for
supper so long as it was at Heathcotes.

To be scrupulously fair, Kelman did not have dinner.
He joined them a lot later and, according to Jade's
friend, left before anybody else. He was, no doubt,
being politic. Nonetheless, I'm far from elated at this
development. I tear away those few stubborn weeds that
have taken hold with the recent rain, and place new
flowers in her vase.

Jade

I wasn't sure at first. Like, I really did not fancy it?
Coming up to a graveyard on a damp afternoon? That's
what this is – it's a graveyard. It's not really a cemetery
at all. And it's *her* graveyard. This is Shelagh's retreat, in

every sense her *resort*. I've sensed that sadness about her, underneath all the drive and the vision – and now I know it. I know it all. It scares me slightly, too – because I see also now why she took such an interest in me.

But I'm pleased that we came. Like, Shelagh's shared this with me and I'm glad she's done that. It's so peaceful up here. It makes you think all sorts of things. I think that, like, just by coming here, I know her so much better now.

She seemed so *guilty*, this morning. No, *not* guilty, actually – she seemed *tired*. She was defeated. Her suggestion to come up here came right after our disagreement. She'd been beating herself up over the sex, I know she had. She'd gone quiet, which is *so* not Shelagh. Even when she's down, there's always that cracked Stranraer accent trying to make sense of *why* she's down. But not this morning? She just looked at me for an eternity, those deep and mournful eyes burning into my soul. Then she looked down and away, looked out of that big tall window. She stared out to sea for ever. Then she said: 'Jade, darling. Most people, at some point, need to take a step backwards before they can move on forwards. People like ourselves, though – we might just need to keep going before we can confront the past. Is that right, darling?'

I think I know what she meant by that. I think I do. Like, standing here now and knowing what she's told me about her sister, I see how her personal mission has grown and grown and, like, *blended* into this huge and spectacular vision for the city, for good. And she's right. I think I'm the same.

Blue

Paul

All's I wanted was a little chat, but he's made that very, very difficult, now. It's hard enough to chat when only one of you wants to talk. It's harder still when you've got a plazzy bag over your head, in all fairness to the boy.

He's give me no choice. He would not listen to reason, so I've had to calm him down. I didn't want to mark him up again, so I just give him the one slap. Just a backhander to shut him up. I pulled him into the passenger seat and that's when I seen the plazzy bag on the floor. Lovely bags they give you at that Carphone Warehouse. They're real quality – thick blue plastic with a nice drawstring, like a duffel bag. I bit off the corner so's the boy could breathe and that – and then I bagged him. Weren't that hard. He's not as tough as he thinks, little Gav. I got the bag right over his swede in one. Got to say that he looked really, really funny. Looked like he had this blue robber's mask on. Looked like a blue Jim Carrey, he did. Half *The Mask*, half *Scream* he was – but blue. Sort of a dark petrol blue, really. And he *was* screaming and all, bless. I didn't want to attract attention to us, so I've bunged him in the boot. Just to slow him down, know what I mean. I need to slow the kid right down then we can both start again. I've got no real idea where I'm driving him to. I'll head for the river, see if the change of scenery makes him feel like talking.

Mine

Marguritte

Can't say that I'm one for surprises, but this was very pleasant – two of my favourite femmes, both at once. Very gratifying. Their news was not quite so gratifying. The councillor's surmise is that, far from legislating for a new and bold city pulse – a leisure quarter like no other in this country – those with the gift might yet opt to play safe. They might simply duck the controversy, head off the storms of protest and save themselves millions by merely making the city centre *safer*. They're looking at installing webcams and CCTV *everywhere*.

I'm all for that. If you've got nothing to hide, you won't mind it being filmed, hah! A safe city centre is a vibrant city centre – that only makes sense. See, what the good Shelagh Cormack forgets is that I don't give a fuck about her Loin. It's got nothing to do with me, all that. She excluded me. It's not mine. The reason, the *only* reason I'm pulling for her now is because I have no alternative. If I thought for one minute that the men, the *men* who oppose this would conspire with me, I'd stab her through the heart today. But they won't. Not one of those bastards is about to hear my voice. So it's Shelagh and Jade and *moi*. I tell them my plan.

Andy Williams 1

Moby

I'm sat here in the window table at Dool's and I feel like every cunt's staring at myself. Dava and their Brian have been good as gold. Haven't even give us a second look, them two, as though it's the most normal thing in the world for the fucking Elephant Man to walk in and have a brekkie. Mind you, kip on some of the Billy Bunters in this gaff, maybe I'm one of the better-looking ones, even like this.

Our Gerrard, as per fucking usual, is late. Fuck knows what he wants, by the way. It's not like as though we're planning fuck all. I only hope he's called myself out for something fucking important for once. I feel like as though my skin's *trickling* non-stop. It's still seeping from the burns, I look like a Cherokee with acne, and bed is the only place I want to be. If he's getting on my case again for them Andy Williams tickets, I swear I will knock the cunt out. If he's asked us once he's asked us a thousand fucking times. Same fucking rap, by the way.

'It's not for myself, kidder, it's her – fucking loves the cunt, she does.'

I know for a fact that their Debs does *not* love the cunt. She fucking *hates* Andy Williams. There's only our Gerrard under the age of fucking seventy that likes Andy Williams. But I'll sort the briefs for him. Not a problem at the end of the day, but not worth getting us all the way over here for, neither. If that's all's it is, I for one am going to be fucking cross.

Me and Dool and their Brian are talking about the olden days, how girls used to try and put you down even if they fancied you. That's got me thinking to aul' Margi again. Telling you, kidder, that is one Big Shag, fucking Margi is. Superb, she is – talking quality there. I used to go up to her when we was kiddies, ciggy in my mouth, thinking I was hard, thinking that that was the sort of thingio she'd go for. I'd go up to her, this tall, gorgeous, fucking sexy brown girl and I'd try and look cool and I'd go: 'Got a match?'

The look she'd give us was nothing but contempt. Looked at you like you was a worm, she did – told you you was fuck all just through the way she looked at you. And she'd look at you like that for a minute, then she'd go: 'Your face, my arse.'

That was about as thingio as she'd get, back then. She weren't one of them that you'd hear effing and blinding. You wouldn't hear no language out of Margi – she was different class. But you'd keep on going up to her and asking her if she had a match, just to hear her say that.

Three seagulls are having a little go-around outside the window. Fight started over a little pile of sick, by the way – little pile of spewed-up chips and that and the seagulls are on one, killing one another over it. It's two on to one, to be fair. Never knew they had fucking seagulls in fucking Birkenhead. No reason why not, to be fair. It's by the sea, isn't it, at the end of the day. These ones, though – two of them must be fucking doorman seagulls, throwing this bit of a aletank seagull out the club. Bullies, they are. Telling you, la, they're fucking bullies. One of them's gripping the lad's wing in its beak, half holding him down and that, and the other one's running in from behind giving it to him with sly little pecks and that, gouging his arse and what have you. Fucking savage, they are. Half feel like going on out there and giving the lad a hand. Fighting over a pile of spewed chips, if you will. Lot of takeaway places on this drag, there is. Dool brings my brekkie and that's that – happy days.

Issues

Ged

One thing that's cast-iron guaranteed to do my swede in is fucking Lurch-ups. Fucking Lenny Lurch-ups – telling you, man, they don't know how close they're coming to bollocks when they do that. Pure fucking does my head in, that does – always the same MO and all, too. You're wanting to get out into the main road and there'll be no cunt coming, or they're a hundred fucking yards away or something. Either way, there's no danger. There is no fucking danger, by the way – that's the God's honest truth, that is. *No. Danger.* You're pulling out onto a empty road. There's a car fifty yards behind you, thirty yards, whatever, but the cunt is fucking *guaranteed* to all of a sudden speed up as soon as he sees you've pulled out. It's a fucking nap, by the way – cunt's going to speed up. So what happens is, instead of pulling out and that in good thingio, all of a sudden you've got this beaut in your mirror that's come lurching right up behind you just so's he can make a big fucking song and dance of how he's got to slam on, so's he don't go ramming into the back of you. That's what it is, by the way. Cunt's teaching you a lesson. He's going:

'I-have-had-to-brake-sharply-and-suddenly-as-a-result-of-your-rash-decision-to-pull-out-into-the-main-flow-of-traffic.'

That's exactly what he's doing, by the way – fucking gobshite. Had that twice already this morning, two fucking Lenny Lurch-ups and it's not even ten bells. I'm not happy.

I'm not happy, but that don't make me start acting

like a cunt myself, though. Just because certain people are acting like pricks don't mean we all have to be arseholes at the end of the day. For e.g., I for one don't personally believe this *Big Issue* is a good thing. For myself, it looks like a excuse for no end of smackheads to get a few bob together and carry on buying gear. End of the day, no cunt *has* to be homeless. I don't buy this homeless thing at all. Homelessness is a option, end of. Cunts have *chose* to live in a doorway, end of the day. That don't mean you have to blank them, though. That's what our Cheyenne's told us, by the way. Don't just walk past the cunts like as though you haven't seen them. Say: 'No thanks and that, lad.'

That's what I done. Even though I'm late for our Anthony and them Lurch-ups have fucking done my head in, I'm not going to blank the *Big Issue* lad. I looks him right in the eye and I goes: 'You're all right, lad – we get that delivered.'

And you can see he's made up. Big grin on the lad – want to see it, man. Costs fuck all at the end of the day.

Jade

I'm so *not* a politician but I do like Margueritte's strategy. If nothing else it'll achieve two things. It'll buy us all some time – which we badly need. And, like, it'll bring the real issues here right to the surface?

What she's going to try and do, yeah, is to persuade Moby to go even sleazier with Ultimo. She wants him to run it as an escort service, and absolutely plaster the city centre with fly-posters. I know for an absolute fact that a lot of the girls will go for it. They'll buy it. Whether they're students, single mums or good-life girls, the reason they're there is to make money. So they're not daft? They know they can make three or four times as much if they're getting to the bottom line? That, incidentally, is what it's all about, yeah? For the girls, money. For the Billies, flesh. And, like, escort agencies, if carefully and correctly run, are not illegal, yeah – but they're *fucking* controversial! Margueritte's talking about *covering* town with purple posters, hitting all the phone boxes, leafletting the football grounds. It'll be interesting to see, too, whether the local cable station will take an advert.

What it all adds up to is Armageddon. Liverpool, within the strict confines of the law, will very quickly be transformed into Sin City, Vice Central, Sleazeville UK. Oh, and she tells us there'll be a working party from Brussels in town to finalise their verdict on further funding for the city! *That* was the moment I knew Shelagh was buying it. The look she gave Margueritte – it was, like, *total* respect, yeah? I mean, her plan's, like, very, *very* crude – it should work a treat.

Out

Ged

I should get out and about more, me. It's a boss feeling sometimes, just being *out* and that. Fuck knows how Moby's going to react to all of this. All's it is, is – I'm fucking this South Village thing off soon as I've worked all the angles out, all the compo and that, any hidden penalty clauses and what have you. But I'm fucking it off, man – that is a fact, by the way.

Need to get a feel of how the boy Moby's seeing things now, at the end of the day. If the lad's happy with his new-found life as a club grock, then maybe we just lets that be as it is. Maybe I goes on my own and that. First time for everything, in fairness. This is one of them, isn't it – just have to sit back and listen for once. See how the lad sees things himself.

New Deal

Cormack
Having thought it through, we think it's a good option. In many ways, those who oppose us do not care one iota whether the city shows badly in front of Brussels. Yet they do – of course they do. And in particular, Marc Kelman cares. Agencies like City Focus depend in large measure upon support – directly or indirectly – from European funding. Looked at another way, the City Focuses of this world need to look good in front of Brussels. Their profile, their future efficacy gets such a fillip from a good European rating.

What we're threatening them with here is humiliation. It *is* crude but it's all we've got – and it could be devastating. We can *really* embarrass them, here. In front of next month's delegation from Brussels, we can make them and the city look extremely amateurish. If we follow Margueritte's redprint, we can paint a picture of a city council that's lost control of its heartland – and that's the big one for our lot. Everything they've been working for is geared towards painting Liverpool in a new light. The words *strike* or *Militant* or *black economy* have been scorched from the council ledger. This is New Liverpool. We, no – *they* do not want to be made to look foolish.

Moreover, this can serve as a taste of how things will be. It's very much a worst case scenario, but once our noble fathers have seen the other side of the coin – a completely deregulated sex industry, a city fighting a losing battle against vice – they'll be back at the table in a jiffy. It's a good ruse. She has such a brilliant mind, Margueritte – such a brilliant girl.

Eyes 2

Ged

Fucking state of our Anthony, by the way. Looks like fucking Merrick, he does. Telling you, man, I've seen some better sunbed cases, Judies in that Living Room and what have you, but our Anthony's in a class of his own with that tan of his, la. Fucking different class he is. Mad red grid on the lad, skin all flayed and that, starting to peel and hang off've him and what have you – but the best of all's his eyes, man! Tell you la, too much, that – all his eyebrows has singed off and that, and his eyelashes have gone and he just looks dead . . . *surprised*. All's he is, is *eyeballs*! Lad has got a total look of surprise about him, fucking full on. Fucking better, he is – looks a total fucking divvy. I can't help myself, to be fair – know I should lay off at the end of the day, but it's fucking there, isn't it? He's done the same to myself often enough, hasn't he? Pure can't stop myself, by the way.

'Boo!'

I just keeps going like that. It's his face. Fucking in shock, that face. Tell you la, it's like as though lads keep popping out at him and going: 'Boo!'

He's not having it, Moby. Sat there with his kite down, munching his butty. He's made a butty with a egg, black pudding, tomatoes and bacon – fucking doesn't half look nice but I can't copy the cunt now, in fairness. He goes: 'Listen, kidder. I *have* got things to do, you know.'

Mad deep voice on the cunt, by the way. I wouldn't've stood for that if it was any other cunt – pulling us up like that, half trying to tell us he's doing us a favour. He can fuck off. But we've got to discuss this thing between us and that, so I've let it go.

Shellshock

Moby

Tell you what – that shut the cunt up! I never meant it, neither – never meant to thingio him and that. Never knew he'd thought that way about her. I was half – I weren't going to tell him nothing about Margo getting into us and that. Know what he's like, our Gerrard. He'd be half: 'Here y'are, bollocks – our Ratter's not dead a year and you're getting a grip of his missus.'

Bit of a choirboy on the sly, Ged is. Won't let you do nothing. So I weren't going to say nothing about her, only it just come out. We was just talking about the club and that, all this *Red Zone* that's in the *Echo*, how they're going to be bringing in legalised brasses and legal drug dens and what have you. All for it myself – I don't see what he's getting so aeriated about. But that's how it come out. I'd been telling him how Margo's come to talk to myself about all of that malarkey – telling you, la, she is *bang* in favour. She's wanting the whole fucking tea party, aul' Margueritta is!

From the look on his grid, Ged knew nothing about Margo being into all of that. Or, more like it, he didn't *want* to think of her being like that. She's half his business partner and that now, Margo, so he's going to be wanting her to be pure-as, innit? So I probably done the wrong thing in telling the lad she give us a wank and all, too.

Not business

Ged

It's the spew that brings myself round. I've half been in a daze after all's Moby's told us there. Can't blame the lad, by the way. Do not blame our Anthony one little bit. She's a fucking good-looking girl at the end of the day, and if it's there it's there – is right. Get fucking paid.

It's fucking her that's got me thingio at the end of the day. I'm not jealous and that – I myself am not a lad that gets jealous. It's not that, it's more a thing of I'm just that bit surprised by her. It's not even surprise, by the way. I'm disillusioned with what she's done. Not with Moby and that, that's up to her if she wants to be rolling around giving out wanks to fellas with third-degree burns. That don't bother me, that don't. Could not care less about all of that – girl can wank off any cunt she wants, far as I myself am concerned. It's got fuck all to do with me. It does just leave me that little bit thingio at the end of the day, though – little bit disappointed in the girl, know where I'm going.

That's all's it is, by the way – I'm badly disillusioned. That's opened my eyes, that has. All of what our Anthony has told us back there, that has done myself no fucking harm at all, by the way. I've come on out of Dool's and stepped in a pile of spew and that's what's snapped me out of it. It's brought myself right back down to earth. It's half 'who the fuck are *you* kidding, la?'

For myself and that, there's something that's *pathetic* about the sight of spew. Not the mess itself, by the way, more the actual thingio of someone throwing up – it's *personal* and that, isn't it? It's what's inside of you, coming up for all hands to see.

That, and small tins of tomatoes. End of the day, a *big* tin of tomatoes only costs about nine fucking pee. But sometimes you'll be stood in the queue at Tesco's and there'll be a aul' fella in front of you with one little basket and it's a nap that it'll only have sad, small, cheapo things in – a small tin of tomatoes and that. Does my head in, that does. That and fellas throwing up. End of the day, that's their own personal thingio and no cunt should be stood around seeing it.

Distress

Paul

It don't come easy to me, things like this. I'm driving around with this one in the boot, and that's all's I *am* doing. I'm driving around in the lad's VW – just driving and driving. I don't know where I'm going. And this clutch is playing up something terrible. Can *not* get used to it, but at the end of the day that's *his* problem. Was.

There's tears in my eyes and all's I can do is just drive. I
don't do this sort of thing well at all. I should just get on
with it and get back to the lock-up. I haven't even
thought what I'm going to do about *him*. And Brian'll be
starting to wonder where his tea's got to and all, too.

Andy Williams 2

Ged

Don't really like to pick up the phone while I'm
driving, but it's Moby. He's that little bit thingio with
myself, after all of what's been said in Dool's. He don't
have to be thingio with my good self. I'm his fucking
family and that, I'm half his fucking brother end of the
day – he don't need to be thingoing what he does with
yours truly. Do what the fuck he wants when he's out
of school.

He's got good news – he can sort Andy Williams for
me and Debs. She'll be made up. We've seen Andy
before and one thing you can say for certain about that
bastard is he's one fucking boss showman. Oh yes – he
knows how to put a fucking show on, by the way. Full
backing band, singers, dancers, the works – and he must
change his costume about four fucking times a show.
Fucking sound, he is. This one time we seen him, he
half forgot the words to 'It's So Easy' but was the cunt
flummoxed? Was he fuck. Just done a little dance,
didn't he? I was with the ginger-haired lad and the
German fella and they was in bulk, to be fair. Andy just
stood there in his mad red suit, *crazy* white teeth and
that, doing a little dance until the words come back to
him. I thought it was sound. It's in a big tent down by

the dock, this one. That Heathcote's are doing the catering and that. She'll be made up. That's cheered us up, that has. Do not know what the fuck to do about aul' Margo, though. Half got myself in bits, that has.

Happiness

Margueritte

He's been calling me for weeks now and I really have not been in the mood, but today I feel good. I see it's him – again – but this time I take the call. And I surprise myself with how pleased I am to hear his voice. Thom.

Business

Ged

I had been hoping to get this whole thing with our Stephen took care of low key. Before all of that thingio about Margueritte, I was going to ask Moby about the lad he's always going on about. Lad lives round by theirs, meant to be a little bit handy and that. I'd been meaning to say to our Anthony, here y'are, give the lad a score and let him take care of these beauts that's bothering our Stephen, but obviously things got that bit ahead of theirselves.

Happened right in front of myself, by the way. I can't just let it go, in fairness, not now's I know who's involved and that. It's broke my heart, it did – but what else can you do?

What's happened is, I've been driving back to ours in

a much better mood. I'm over the thing with her, over the disappointment and that. I'm more thinking: 'Here y'are, Ged lad – get your head together. You've got it made and that.'

I've got my *In The Lounge* CD on, I'm starting to feel like as though I'm sorting my head out and I'm going to give her a treat by getting back handy and taking her out for a nice scran. Them two can stay in and watch *The Weakest Fucking Link*, but it ain't going to be softarse here tonight, man. Oh no.

I've overtook a bus and I've half left it right behind when I realises that that's our Stephen's school bus. I'm took over by a bit of a glad feeling and I slows down and watches the bus in my mirror. I'm thinking I'll pull over at the petrol station, let the bus go past and I'll pick Stevie up as he's walking down. It don't quite get to that.

It's one thing knowing your boy is going through a bit of a hard time and that – but it's a total different ball game when you sees it happen right in front of you. That's what's gone on. Our Stephen comes flying off've the bus and his bag comes after him. His stuff is strewn all over the road. That's another tragic sight, by the way – someone's personal things strewn about in a place they shouldn't be. It broke my heart to see him like that. To be fair and all, too – if I'm honest with myself and that – I was half ashamed of him. I was – I'll admit it. I wanted to see him get up and fuck those little gobshites that done it to him.

But he never. He's not like that. It did – it had myself in fucking bits to have to sit back and watch what went on. They've gotten off've the bus behind him and one little cunt's booted him up the arse. They're from a different school and that – different uniform. Little dickheads they are, not hard at all. One of them's got a nasty face – bad teeth and that, screwed-up. He's half got wrinkles round his eyes – at his age. He's got wrinkles from pulling all them hard-case faces, but he's a little gobshite. If I'd've had the chance to get the lad from by Moby's over, he'd've battered all three of the little cunts. The other two twats are laughing and one of them kicks his papers away as he's trying to get them together.

That nearly kills me, by the way. To see him getting that, from the three of them – it's fucking horrible. But I know I've got to just sit and watch and bide my time. If this was our Anthony, he'd be over there banging heads together by now. That might make *him* feel better, but it wouldn't be the way to deal with these little cunts. It's not how I'm going to do it neither, to be fair. I've got to let the hurt and the anger fill myself up, and use it as a sort of energy, if you will.

After a while they've let our Stephen go. It's fucking pathetic, it is – fucking horrible, by the way. His blazer's all fucked and his books and homework are covered in shite from the road and the grass verge. The lad's no harm to anyone – that's his fucking trouble. I wait for the little twats to split up, then I follows the main dog, the ringleader. Wrinkles. Follows him all the way to his front door, I do – and then I sits and waits and keeps the whole thing alive in my mind.

In our sort of circles, there was always half this thing about 'we know where you live' and that. It was meant to be a big deal for some cunt to turn up on your doorstep and have a word. The fact that they knew that much about you was meant to be that bit sinister, and the fact that they didn't give a fuck, they'd come and do you in right on your doorstep, right in front of your family if needs be. Never bothered myself, in all fairness. It's come on top like that once or twice for my good self, but I've never lost a wink's sleep over none of that. Let them come and that – bring it on.

But I'm not a fella that's ever liked turning up on doorsteps, myself. Pure do not believe in it at the end of the day – it's a cunt's trick that, bringing women and kiddies into it and what have you. It's not on. But this is different. I'm not about to go banging the door down and going: 'Outside now, you prick, if you don't want your kids to see you get burst!'

I won't do nothing like that. I waits nice and calm for the man of the house to pull in, and I waits for him to get out and approach the front door before I makes my move. In all fairness, I do have a bad feeling about the cunt. He looks like a bit of a thingio – looks that bit pleased with his self, know where I'm going. Got a bit of a tan, bit too much of a spring in his step, and *bad* clobber. Can see from here that it's all the right names, but he's bought the gear they've made for a laugh. He's got a *dead* tight Prada leather – not advisable on a frame like his, by the way. Even though you can see he does the weights – looks like a typical home-gym beaut – he's also got one vintage fucking ale gut and all, too. He's the sort of cunt that's got a bit of a business – pine doors or double glazing or what have you – and puts on a phoney posh voice and is banging his secretary. He's a gobshite. Every single thing that I need to know about the cunt is wrote all over him. I know how he's going to try and deal with this and he won't be making life easy for hisself. I goes over.

'Have a word with you, lad?'

I don't see no need for airs and graces. His lad has just made a holy show of my lad, numbers on his side and all, too. His dad needs to know that his lad's a bully. His lad's a wretch and his aul' fella is going to have to do something about it. He's going to do the right thing and he's going to do it right now and all, too. If he don't, then he gets it hisself. Either his lad gets it or he gets it right in front of his lad – I'm not choosy, to be fair. He half gives me a 'who the fuck are you – do you know who I am?' sort of look. He ignores us and carries on walking to his front door. I quickens my step and blocks the cunt.

'You and me need a little word, kidder.'

Kidder. Hardly ever say that nowadays, in fairness. The fella isn't sure whether I'm a nutter or what. His eyes are more puzzled than anything – he's not shitting hisself. Not yet, by the way.

'What's the problem?'

'Your lad is the problem.'

He looks relieved for a second.

'What's he done now?'

'Oh, it's a regular thingio, is it? You half think it's funny and that, do you?'

That gets him that little bit mad. He steps backwards.

'Listen, mate – I don't know who you are . . .'

He goes to push us. He's Scouser Tommy, now. His I-am-a-respectable-businessman rap has been sacked. He's a hard case now, by the way.

'. . . but you can fuck off off've my property.'

That's all's I needed. I gets him in a headlock, and walks him to the front door. I rings on the doorbell. He's trying to say something, but in fairness I am holding him tighter than what I really need to. His lad comes to the door. Was worth it just to see the look on his face when he opens up to find his dad being served up to him.

'I'm glad it's you, you little dog. Let's go in, shall we?'

The lad is a proper fucking shithouse, by the way. It's waterworks right from the off. He starts crying and his ma comes in and next thing there's palaver all over the show. I slaps the old man to shut him up. I tries telling them why this is happening to them.

'Your lad here – ask him to tell you what he's just done. Ask him what he done when he got off've the school bus today.'

The lad goes running to his ma and the pair a them are in bits, to be fair. The aul' man is cowering on a chair and I'm just thinking: 'This ain't going to plan. These think I'm after robbing them out.'

I goes towards the lady, but she starts backing off.

'That's it. I'm calling the police,' she goes, but she don't move from the spot. She just stands there, shaking. I do, I feel bad bringing her into all of this, but they've give me no choice. I tries to sound reasonable.

'Call the law. Get them down. They can do whatever the law says and that. The law is the thing that's wrote down and tells us what we can do, yeah?'

I goes back and leans close in to the lad's father. Shithouse, he is. He's shaking like a fucking gobshite. Fucking pathetic. I lowers my voice that little bit so's only me and him can hear.

'But there isn't a law that can stop me doing whatever the fuck I want to you in the next five minutes. Oh aye – they can lock me up after I've done it. They can chop my hands off. But that don't help you one little bit, matey – because none of it, no law, no threats, no promises can stop me from hurting you bad, right now. Do you know where I'm going?'

He's closed his eyes now and he's crying. I looks over at the young lad from Stephen's bus. He's in shock, to be fair – white as a fucking sheet, he is. I tries to sound gentle – let them know they're dealing with a reasonable fella and that.

'Only *youse* can help yourselves.'

I changes my voice again to sound half sort of still reasonable and that, but like as though I'm not messing around, neither.

'Make the lad tell youse what he done and make him pay for it. Simple as that.'

It's the woman that asks him. He breaks down crying again and you can't get no sense from the little cunt and at this point I thinks to myself that there's not much more can be achieved here. I goes over to the kid. I don't feel *nothing* for the little wretch.

'The lad you've been making a cunt of – his name's Stevie Brennan. Yeah?'

He can not look at myself. I goes and puts my mouth very close to him. I says it quietly.

'You, or any of your raggy-arse crew lay a finger on Stevie again and it's you that's going to answer the question – not your aul' fella. You understand that?'

He nods and buries his head in his mother's lap. His dad can't look me in the eye. His mother can. There's fear there and relief and all, too. Oh yes. But there's something else there. There's contempt. She despises my good self.

Choice

Paul

Eleven eleven. I've waited until the time was right and then I've just done it. I've just let his tinny Polo slip down the jetty and into the dock. I really really hated that. It didn't have to be that way, but now it's done. He gave me no choice.

What I'm thinking now is that I should just get some miles behind myself. I could jog as far as Brunswick station and hop on the first one that comes – Walton or Rice Lane, makes no difference to myself. Could even hop off at Kirkdale. But then I'm thinking that maybe that's asking for it – CCTV and all that. It's everywhere now. I can zip myself up and face away from the cameras, but why risk it? So what I do instead is I jog all the way along the front, right past all the car showrooms and past Harry Ramsden's and then I head up Parly, just to get myself away from that whole waterfront vibe. I could be anybody, now. There's nothing to link me with Garston Docks.

I sees a taxi with its light on, and suddenly I'm fine. I feel like as though a crashing headache is starting to clear at long last. I feel happier. I decide that what I'm going to have to do is go back to the lock-up and terrorise the little B so badly that'll he'll be grateful just to walk free. He won't snitch when I'm done with him. No way in the world will he even think about snitching.

And then I can think about my club again. I've

always wanted my own club. After the way I've dealt with their problems this evening – swiftly and efficiently – the message has gone on out to Liverpool's players. Here comes Paulie.

Help

Ged

Telling you, man, you could get depressed reading this shite. This city's going to the dogs. It's not just here, to be fair, it's every-fucking-where. Look at what's gone on with our Stephen. People are turning into dogs. There just isn't no right and wrong no more – it's all wrong 'uns. Look at this, for e.g.

> 'BODY IN THE DOCK' identified. The body of a driver whose VW Polo was found in Garston Docks earlier this morning has been identified. Police say Nicholas Short, 21, of Derby, was a final-year pharmaceutical student at Liverpool University. They are treating his death as suspicious.

That's a disgrace. Don't care what the lad done or who he's upset, rubbing out a doctor or a fella that's going to help save lives – that's disgraceful, that is. Young student and all, too – got his whole life ahead of him and that. His poor mam. Sends her lad off to Liverpool, wipes his mouth with her hanky and goes: 'Watch out for yourself, son. They're a bit thingio up there, them Scousers.'

And she's been right, at the end of the day. And just as I'm thinking that, who fucking phones up? Who, of all people, picks up his mobie and gives aul' Ged Brennan a tinkle? Only Ray Cole, by the way. Oh yes.

Ch-ch-ch-ch-changes

Jade

As soon as Shelagh told me all that about her sister, yeah, so many things just slotted into place. It was just, like – *sense*, at last. I booked the train ticket there and then.

Margueritte

'You don't seriously believe that this Red Triangle madness can actually *happen*, Margo?'

He's one person I never minded calling me that, Thom. He always made it sound rather sophisticated. I liked the way he said it, whereas somebody like Ged only debased what there was of my exotic lineage with his shortening and coarsening of every single word he was given. And sitting there, at that moment, I felt the scales drop from my eyes. I, who have spent my adult life *seeing* things, realised something about myself. It was a big, crushing realisation, too – almost as though I were looking down on myself, watching another person. There were several aspects to this out-of-body experience, but a big part of it was an understanding that Thom is a *good* guy. He's a good and honest man who is absolutely devoted to me. Instead of that being a reason to despise him and abuse him, it made me feel warm.

'You don't seriously believe that this Red Triangle madness can actually *happen*, Margo?'

No. I don't.

The Art of War 3 – Variation of Tactics

Paul

If you are powerless to inflict a real defeat, refrain from attacking. But if in a desperate position, you must fight.

I've let Gavin out of the lock-up and he's been as good as gold. He knows the score, now. That whole thing, the thing with little Gavin has given me a mild diversion. That's all's it was. I'm back in control now. I feel . . . I feel *invincible*. Really, really strong. I've done extra weights, hammered myself, I have – but I do feel fantastic. The refurbishment's as good as done, the girls are all auditioned and primed, it's all systems go for Friday. It's only 10.57 but I don't care. I'm going in. I'm going in to run my club.

Butterflies

Jade

I've had butterflies since the Glasgow train pulled in at Carlisle. But now the local chuff-chuff's slowing into town, I'm almost faint with excitement, worry, giddiness. I so should have done this a *long* time ago.

On Cut-Ins and Other Driving Menaces

Ged

Fucking Cut-ins, la – they do my head right in! Bad

enough that the cunts do it in the first place, but they fucking *know* they've done it and all, too. They come steaming down the outside lane of the motorway, decide they've had enough of the high life and that, cut *right* in front you – you, who by the way, is doing a nice seventy-five all the way – and then what? They fucking slam on, don't they! They cuts in at about ninety-five miles an hour, *squeeze* their fucking shitty Megane into a gap that weren't even there, by the way – and then they fucking slam on! Cunts *know* they're doing it and all, too. They fucking do – they slam on and nearly put you through your own windscreen and then they make a big fucking show of having a oh-so-casual conflab with their bird or whichever other cunt happens to be sat in the seat next to them. They're going:

'I've just nearly killed you, lad, but I'm now going to act as though fuck all has happened by having a very casual chat with my bird. I'm going to turn and face her a lot and nod my head and that, so's you can see that I'm half engrossed in what she's saying to myself. That's so's you also know why I never seen you when I cut right in front of you and slammed my fucking brakes on! I'm a TWAT – that's why!'

I shouldn't drive.

Me

Jade

For so long I've believed – I've *let* myself believe – that Mum disapproved of me. It was, like, when I came away to Liverpool so soon after Daddo died, I could *sense* her disappointment in me, yeah. That's what I really thought? That she wanted me to stay there by her side and help her through the next stages of her life? She didn't just want it, she *expected* it. She wanted to lean on her daughter, but her daughter had other plans.

If only she knew. If she only had an inkling of what it was to be *me* back then. Who could *I* turn to? The thing with Babs and Susan happened and they made me feel something else – but who can you talk to about that when you're seventeen in Whitehaven and you look like Patsy Kensit? There were two people I *so* was not going to confide in. Babs herself was one of them – rapacious bitch. And my mum. I just couldn't go there?

Maybe I went a bit remote. I don't know – I don't think I changed that much. I was always going away to uni – that was what Daddo always wanted for me. If anything, it was Mum who went distant. It was, like, I *felt* her helplessness? And I knew it for sure when I got to Liverpool and she didn't write once. I did. I wrote once. I wrote to tell of my sense of loss and despair. I wrote of my confusion. I wrote about the heavy, low, grey-white skies and my feelings of total confusion and *utter* insignificance. She didn't write back. She didn't need to. I could feel her reproof from many, many miles away.

'You left me,' she was saying. 'And you're weird.'

So it wasn't so difficult to make the choices I made after that.

And what have I found out today? That I was wrong, yeah – wrong in my motivation, at least. Because somehow, somewhere, I *needed* to know that isolation. Those early days in Liverpool, they, more than anything, are the moments that defined me. Those were the days I became me, yeah?

I don't know whether Mum knew that, *sensed* that, guessed that there were things I needed to work out for myself, on my own. She's not the sort of woman who'd tell you, to be honest. She's just not that sort of woman. With tears in her eyes today – and not absolutely tears of sadness, it's true to say – she's batted away my plight of neglect. She's not even pretending to sympathise. Her whole stance is 'stupid girl – don't talk such rubbish', and she's right. My complaint was the fancy of a bruised and self-pitying child.

Why didn't she write? She was terrified of what I'd think of her grammar, her spelling, her handwriting – I could, like, hug her to death, I love her so much! In front of me is one of those women, an *old-fashioned* woman, that, like, makes me ashamed not of the choices I make, but the choices I *have*. I'm going to be such a friend to her from now on.

I told her Shelagh's story. Shelagh came to Liverpool, like me, a student from an insular and unfashionable town. She came with her twin sister, Annie, to study politics and economics. They both loved the city, the nightlife, the sleazy and winking charm of clubland, but Annie loved it more, yeah – she loved it to death. She fell in love with bad men and bad drugs and she dropped out of classes and went on the game. Shelagh only told me that the other day? Her bright, cheeky, impulsive sister lived in Liverpool for less than a *year*? She lived and died in Liverpool 8. When she was telling me the story – well, she just *told* it, yeah? She seemed, like, *resigned* to it. But it killed me, that story – it fucking *haunted* me. It's one of the things that got me back on track again. It's like – who the *fuck* have I been kidding, yeah? I talked and talked and got it all out, and Mum just put her arm around me and didn't say a thing. Right answer.

I'm going back to Liverpool. She's got under my skin, now. But I feel I've grown up a lot – and quickly, finally. I'm going to be such a good friend to my mum.

Strawberry Field

Margueritte

'You don't seriously believe this Red Triangle madness can actually *happen*, Margo? In *this* city? In *this* day and age.'

I'd forgotten quite how much his overemphasis on certain words – every *other* fucking word, actually – irritated me. But it's small beer. Thom Harries is good-looking (if you like Will Carling), going places (if you're turned on by property lawyers) and *fucking* rich, now – he's not so thick as to let that go unmentioned. Oh yes, indeedy, Thom's dear old randy old daddy has done the decent thing and passed away to that saucy whorehouse in the sky, where busty wenches will spill sack down their fronts and ol' dirty dog Harries will lick it off, day after day, for ever and ever. Amen to that, though. In croaking, he's transformed his previously dull and doughy boy into quite a desirable and dough-laden little honey. And he's trying *so* hard, too. He's *begged* me to see sense over The Loin and come on over to the winning side. He really has, the little poppet – he's been extremely loose with some *extremely* sensitive information.

'I *assure* you, darling – Marc Kelman and Focus have no *intention* . . .'

Do wish he'd stop overemphasising *every* other *word* . . .

'. . . of backing this *madness*. Shelagh Cormack is out on a *limb* over this. She's *totally* isolated herself and she *will go down* with this. It's utter *insanity*. Mark my words, darling – we're handling *all* the land transactions and I can tell you what the finding of the Brussels delegation will *be*, yes? HMS *Cormack* is *sinking*, darling. Get off. Get off *fast*!'

I tell him that the initiative received majority backing from our esteemed and able city council, with or without Brussels.

'Conditions applying, Margo – conditions *applying*!'

'So? Conditions *do* apply . . .'

He sighs and goes through the entire routine – I can only help you so much, et cetera. You have to help yourself et cetera. Then he cracks.

'Look – City Focus are recommending a vastly toned-down version of The Loin. They've never been happy about the drugs – or the prostitution.'

He goes all self-righteous and frustrated on me – that 'why won't you see *sense*' attitude that I find so grating in men. It brings out the worst in me, that does – it makes me stubborn.

'Just look at the Dutch Experience Café, darling . . .'

Attempt at a Brown Café in Stockport, Cheshire. Brave and noble attempt to give people what they want – a smoke in peace. Local law didn't like it. Leant on them so much that they hardly had time to run the business, they were in court so much.

'You'll go the same way as *they* did, darling, I *promise* you. The Loin is seen in *exactly* the same way. People don't see it as *visionary* – they see it as *sleaze*! Brussels is putting its money into a *family*-oriented venture – we *know* this!'

Now he's going for gentle persuasion. He's softening his voice – although he still can't help licking his lips – and trying to come across reasonable, sensible and *right*. He's not good at this, to be honest. He stinks, poor boy – and I'm not about to make it easy for him.

'So, they get their own way at last, hey? Liverpool gets turned into a theme park?'

His shoulders slump.

'So, let me guess. Strawberry Field, a Beatle-themed pleasure park with fun for all the family, and only two minutes from Liverpool's teeming Albert Dock?'

He tries to make light of it. I remember that he has quite a big dick.

'That's not such a bad idea, actually – that's *good*!'

'Spare me. I'd rather have the Liverpool Kop Mania Total Football Experience Park!'

He seems to think this has marked a breakthrough.

'Hey, kiddo – you're the nuts! Want a job?'

He flashes his teeth at me. They're ridiculously white, square and bulky. He does have one hell of a lash on him, though. And he inherits the pile. He tries once more.

'Margo, honey – see sense. This will *not* get through at *any* level. *Certainly* not *locally* – I was in the Athenaeum last night. *So* many key figures feel they've been misled and coerced – they'll vote for the new template . . .'

'Which is?'

He's flustered. He wipes his beady brow. I have to admit – I'm enjoying the show. This is fun.

'Which is a twenty-four-hour leisure quarter – bars,

cafés, restaurants, clubs, galleries, theatres, hotels and so on – perfectly lit, safe, open and transparent. And *yes*, it *is* aimed at the family actually, as *well* as the individual. Its philosophy happens to be the opposite of The Loin's. The Square . . .'

'The *Square*? Fuck off, Thom!'

He's all perplexed and ruffled. I knew he would be. He's blinking at me, unsure what to say. I say it for him.

'The *Square*, Thom? Are you serious?'

He juts his jaw out, trying to look robust.

'Absolutely!'

'Hah! Well, that says it all, doesn't it! The Square!'

'The Square is bright and safe and . . .'

'Boring . . .'

'The Loin is all about the dark side – it's hidden, it's shady, it's lawless . . .'

'No, Thom – it's exciting. It's *real*!'

I'm really enjoying this – there must be something wrong with me. I'm loving it. I don't mean a single word I'm saying. Thom's getting his mad up now.

'It's impossible!'

'It's what people *want*!'

'It's *illegal*!'

'People will flock to it – from everywhere, dammit! Like Cream, Thom – there'll be coachloads! Build your hotels, because we're going to fucking well need them . . .'

He looks away, tense and frustrated. He never liked me swearing – doesn't like women using 'language' at all.

'You're intent on going *ahead* with this, then?'

Of course I'm not, fool. I've never been one for valiant losers. Thom knows that, or he ought to. He reaches for my hand. I let him. His face is a picture of crumpled, old-before-his-time sincerity. The guy loves me. The guy loves me. He fucking *adores* me. There's something to be said for that at the end of the day. He looks into my eyes. His are bland and unchallenging.

'We can do this *together*, darling. I can get you in with JDE – you'll be a shoo-in if you'll only declare yourself *now*. There's nobody *better* than you at this fucking stuff.'

I know. But I stay silent.

'You could take back the South Village, for starters. We can *absolutely* do that – there isn't a *doubt* about that.'

'Starters? What's the Main?'

He smiles. For all that his teeth are so chunky, he's got quite a nice smile, Thom. Dimply and safe and pleasant – he's a very pleasant boy.

'That's a *bit* more complex. That's what we've been looking into all this time – the underleases on Ultimo and that surrounding area. It's tricky. It's up to you, really . . .'

'How so?'

He gulps. He gulps a lot, Thom does – but this is a *real* gulp. This must be important. He goes for it.

'The leases, it would *seem*, are *per*fectly legally sound . . .'

I'm suddenly liking the sound of this.

'Go on . . .'

He gulps again, gulps hard, wipes his perspiring dome. His was already thinning when we were at college together. He's not totally unattractive, though. Women like him, by and large.

'Um, ah, well – it hasn't gone *unnoticed* that you, ah,

um, wield a certain amount of influence in those quarters. Am I, ah, right *enough* so far?'

Why beat around the bush, I think. He's doing more than enough of that for both of us.

'He's persuadable, yes. Anthony Brennan is eminently persuadable . . .'

For the first time Thom's chubby face breaks into smiles. In fact, no – it *collapses*. He is *so* relieved that his face simply crumples into a malleable lump of joy. He takes my hand again.

'We can do this, Margo.'

He pauses for such grave added sincerity that I have to stifle laughter.

'We can do this together, you and I.'

He doesn't need to sell it to me. I'm sold. Have been for a while, truth be known.

Self-respect and that

Ged

Pulling through town and that, heading through traffic along the Goree and past the dock and that, gets myself to thinking about John-Paul and all the bad that become of him. How that lad turned into such a wrong 'un is beyond myself, in all fairness – I for one will never know what went wrong there. But then, thinking of Ratter and all's that's gone on with him gets myself thinking about Ray Cole and all, too – and that's cheered myself up. It has, by the way – it's put a grin on my grid that aul' Coley's been in touch.

What it is, is – Coley's asked myself if there's anything I can do, anything that I myself can think of to prevent this demolition thingio going ahead. He's dead upfront and that – half tells myself it's a desperate measure and that, him contacting the likes of myself for help and that. But I'm not arsed – I do appreciate that, to be fair. Ray Cole coming on the line and going: 'Ged, this a weird one, lad, but I half need your help and that.'

I don't mind that. Do not mind that one little bit at the end of the day.

What's happened is that these contractors that's wanting to bulldoze this auld hotel have got wind that Coley's lot has been trying to rush through a protection order on the gaff. There's measures and that that Parliament can take to slap a Hands Off've It notice on aul' piles like that. It's not a listed building at the end of the day, but they're looking to *make* it listed. But the builders have got on to it, and the word is they're going to smash the place down before Coley's crew get a chance to do fuck all about it. Once the place is in rubble, there ain't that much for the heritage crew to protect at the end of the day, is there? They'd be crying over spilt milk and that.

To be completely fair, I'm not that certain what Coley's saying to myself here. Is he half sort of saying to myself: 'Here y'are Ged lad. You can get a bit of a mob together and that. We'll look the other way and that while youse do the business on the cunts.'

Or is it something else? Can't tell, by the way. I for one do not know where the cunt's going with all of this, but I do know one thing. My lad Stephen and my girl Cheyenne will be *made up* when I tells them that we're all going down there, going on site to protect some half-listed building. We'll be there and that, the three of us, shoulder to shoulder with them – solidarity and that. If Coley wants the likes of myself down there on the front line, it's as good as done at the end of the day. Lad don't even have to ask twice – I'm there for him. And to be perfectly fair, I'm made up that he's asked us. I am, by the way – I'm made up about that.

I pulls in to where I've said I'll meet Margo and checks myself out in the car mirror. Looking all right, mind you. Has to be said that yours truly is not looking that bad at all, in fairness.

Thoughts

Moby

Telling you, man, that Georgie Thompson – shouldn't be allowed that, kidder. Should not be on the telly in a blouse like that – not at this time of day. Fucking gorgeous, she is. Black silky blouse and that half-stern kite on her, *dead* fucking serious she is, but in a sexy way. Phone goes again but there's no chance of any cunt speaking to my good self until I've finished with little Georgie here.

'. . . mail us your thoughts on that subject or on anything else you wish to discuss.'

I'll give you my own thoughts on that subject for fuck all, girl. *You* look fucking *boss* in that black blouse – end of. That's my thoughts.

I dials 1571. Ged's called. So's Margo. So's fucking Paul. All wanting meetings and conversations and what have you. Fucking Paul the Hom, by the way – half getting on my case, he is, 'cos I'm not at the club.

'Anthony — Paulie . . .'

Cheek of the cunt! No 'All right, Moby lad, how's it going and that', by the way. Just straight in there with his fucking *Paulie* rap. State of his voice, by the way. It's one of them, isn't it — I-mean-business. I-have-no-time-to-fuck-around-with-how's-it-going-and-that. That's him, the soft cunt. It's all this I-am-a-fucking-businessman voice, telling myself what time it is and that, telling us he's been in the office all fucking day. Not on my say-so he hasn't, the cunt.

'I'm just wondering whether we're going to have the pleasure of your company today, because there's things we need to discuss . . .'

The cheeky fucking turd-burgling faggot, by the way! I'll show that cunt who calls the fucking meetings around here, and it ain't fucking him! Fucking Paulie, my arse!

Atonement

Jade

I settle down to a cup of jasmine tea in my own flat and *still* the thought of him makes me giggle. I must say, he's not looking too pretty now, the bastard! But, like, Moby Brennan was the last person I was expecting to see. I mean, like — when I jammed him inside that sunshower, yeah? I *meant* that. I didn't *care* what happened to the big monster. I *wanted* him to suffer. For all the girls I knew about and all of those whose lives he'd spoilt before, I *wanted* him to burn. He was evil, he was an ogre and I was so going to fucking burn him alive. That's how I felt. That is *so* fucking how I felt. I'd taken a man's stance — I wanted him dead.

But, like, I'm glad he's OK? I wasn't like *myself* when I shut him in like that? I mean, it's, like, *so* spooky to think that was only a few weeks ago. It's like I'm dreaming? Like I was a different me?

I don't think Moby'd recognise me anyway with my hair like this — only as someone he'd vaguely, like, *ogled* at some point in his dumb and wretched life. But the guy looked, like, *irate*. He cut, like, *right* across my path, face like murder. With his face all scabby and, like, with all his eyebrows bald and his eyelids burnt, he looked insane anyway — but he was *furious*. I couldn't stop giggling, though? Even when I think of him now?

Playing

Ged

Was just going to walk in there, by the way — just lay it out for the girl.

'Here y'are Margo, girl. I've been in that London and that and I've had that bit of time to think on things and where it's all taking us is that this whole caper ain't for my good self. Inner-city regeneration and that, property redevelopments and what have you — not for Gerrard Michael Leo Brennan, all of that. What I'm saying to you, girl, is it's all yours. This whole carry-on — it's for the likes of yourself, all of that. You've got the noodles. You've got the know-how. Fucking go for it, girl. Is right.'

Was going to say all of that to her, in fairness. Was on my way to see her and that, fucking giftwrap the whole fucking carry-on for her, give it her on a plate. But after she's called us up and that, way she was talking to myself on the mobie – I knew she was up to something. Was wrote all over her voice, in all fairness – girl was trying to play us. Did not have a clue beyond that what the fuck the girl was up to, but she was trying to play myself on. So I've bought it. I've gone: 'All right, girl. I'll see you.'

Margueritte

If he but knew it, he's just dropped a gem right into my lap. He's such a loyal old dog, Gerrard. In so many ways, he'd make for the perfect partner. His eyes just *glisten* with devotion. He *adores* me. I could get him to kill for me – but therein lies his weakness. He's *uncalculating*. He's slavishly loyal, and that's a weakness.

He's sat with me just now, so smitten that he'll do *anything* he can to help me, to impress me, to make me like him, love him, *value* him. I can see it in his eyes. I've asked him to help, so he's trying to help. He's said he can handle his big daft cousin, no problem. But he's as good as admitted that someone else is the *real* danger. In all his innocence and desire to please me, Ged has given me another name. And *that* has *really* got me excited . . .

Ged

Disappointing at the end of the day, is all. I thought a lot of the girl – would have done a lot for her. All's I've thought as I've sat there, listening to her rap and that, listening to her thinking she's playing me on with all her shite – I've just felt let down. I feel last, in all fairness. I feel shite that she thinks that little of myself. Girl must think I'm a fucking clown by the way. I've come from the same barrio as her, I've been through the same thingio. Fair dos, I haven't got a college diploma that says I Am Smart By The Way. But, know where I'm going, she didn't need to treat me like a knobhead.

And I could have had her for brekkie, by the way. Simple fact of it all is, I know her game – she thinks I'm soft. That's a win–win position for my good self, thank you very much. But know what la, I'm fucking sick of it all. I've been in this caper for less than a fucking year and that, and I'm *tired* of it.

Bottom line is she's trying to play me on over the South Village. Or, to be fair, she's talking as much about our Anthony's gaff, that Ultimo. Wish to fuck I'd never got involved with none of this lark, by the way, the Ultimo, the South fucking Village – none of it. But that's her game – for whatever her reasoning, she's wanting me to mark Moby's card over the way he's going with Ultimo. Fucking painful it is, by the way – this good-looking young girl that I think a lot of, sat there thinking she's working my good self over. Thinking she's playing me like a fucking Stratocaster. Girl can hardly keep that smug grin from off've her kite.

Her basic thingio is this – she's looking to start bollocks between myself and Moby over his club and what it might do to our fucking *investment*. Kid's got no shame, by the way – she's going on about how fucking *extreme* Moby's took the gaff, how it's half ruining the good name of the barrio and how he's bringing on no end of lairy reviews from fucking Plod and licensing and what have you. She's basically looking to use myself to get to Moby, get the fucking official line over to our Anthony. Why? Only she fucking knows – I don't give a fuck. I've only come in here now out of curiosity, knowmean – just to see how far this little viper'll go. Knowmean, is the girl that fucking stupid? Does she think that myself and our Anthony never fucking talk? Fucking risky business if that's how she wants to carry on, by the way.

Thinks she's being dead thingio about it and all, too – thinks she's working myself over good style and know what la, telling you – I don't give a fuck no more. I am *weary*. I'm sat here, listening to her telling me stories, watching while the girl smiles and lies into my face and I'm thinking that I just do not give enough of a fuck to even answer her. I'm thinking: 'You give our Anthony a wank, you did.'

What I'm going to do as of the moment I gets out of here is I *am* going to get on to our Anthony. I *am* going to pull him out of that gaff – and he'll have it, at the end of the day. End of the day and that, our Anthony has always done what I've told him. We'll get out, me and him, and we'll start again – do something proper. So I'm like that. It's one of them – I'm just fucking *done* with her and her games and I want out of there and I never want to see the girl again. She's telling Moby one thing, she's telling myself another thing and know what, I do not give a fuck. She means fuck all to myself, now – serious. I'd be lying if I said she hadn't got to us and that, but I'm over all of that, now. Lasted about thirty fucking seconds at the end of the day. That's the God's honest truth, by the way – I feel fuck all for the girl. I gets up to leave.

'You'll have to take care of Paul yourself and that. I hardly know the lad, in fairness.'

For about half a second she sparks up.

'Paul? Who's Paul?'

The look I gives her there and then is about the only bit of enjoyment I gets from that whole fucking encounter. I just looks at her dead serious, not even a glimmer of any thingio, no emotion or nothing. With that look I've let the girl know. She's not soft – she'll fucking know now – know that I was on to her the whole time. It was myself playing her, end of the day. I waits a minute, then I goes: 'He's half Moby's partner, know where I'm going. He's *not*, like, but he is – do you know what I mean?'

I gives it another big mad pause while she wets herself trying not be too fucking eager.

'No. Tell me.'

'Nothing *to* tell at the end of the day, queen. He's a ambitious enough lad, not a dickhead, knowmean – he's after running his own gaff, end of story. I'm just telling you girl – he's *in* there . . .'

Want to see her fucking *wince* when I calls her *girl*, by the way. But fuck her. She's fuck all.

'. . . I can say something to Moby – but him? I don't know him . . .'

Margueritte

. . . and neither do I – but I fucking well will do, and soon. If this Paul is playable, he's going to be saving me one fuck of a lot of bother with those Brennan dickheads. Thanks for that one, Ged. You've been a mine of information. Over and out.

226

On Snipes

Paul

The big bully – he never even give me chance to defend myself. End of the day that's all's he is – he's a bully. He's just stormed in here, face like a napalmed jellyfish, and kicked off for no reason. Well, he might've give a reason, in all fairness, but with all his screaming and shouting, all's I heard was language at the end of the day. Terrible, some of the things he's said back there. I won't be forgetting none of that in a hurry, by the way. He can repent at his leisure, because it's coming his way soon.

I've managed to staunch the blood, but he's definitely definitely broke my nose, here. Like, one thing I've half been proud of over the years is the fact that, knowmean, in all the time I've been doing this sh★★★e I've never got myself badly marked up. Like, when I'm out and that, no one can believe how old I am. Everyone says I look about late twenties and that, early thirties at a push. I've never had no stab wounds, scars, slash stripes, nothing. I've looked after myself, end of. I've managed to mainly steer myself clear of any serious thingio at the end of the day. Like, my nose – which I like to think of as being half sort of one of my good points at the end of the day, sort of, like, *regal* my snipe is, people have said – it's stood up to a lot of punishment without so much as a kink in it, my snipe has. He never even give us chance to stand up, by the way. It was just:

'What the f★★★ are you doing sat there in my f★★★★★★ chair, you f★★★★★★ dog, you!'

I goes to stand up and ask him what it's all about, and just as I've bent my knees to take my weight and put my palms on his desk to push myself up he's thrown his dirty fat bald head right into me. I'm in a basic crouching position, stuck in no-man's-land, neither stood up nor sat down, and he's smashed his fat head into my dial. Bang!

'F****** faggot! Get the f*** outa my f****** chair, you c***!'

Then he starts really really laying into me, fists and boots and what have you and I've just curled up in a ball and all's I can hear is this *insane* carry on about *me* phoning *him* and how I never, never have the *cheek* to phone *him* and then I've blacked out. When I've come round, he's half trying to be all right with myself, he's got a damp cloth and he's held it to my face to stop the blood. I've got up and shook him off and I've held the cloth to my nose until it's stopped bleeding so bad. Definitely broke, it is – he's bust it right across the bridge.

By the time I've cleaned myself up and that, he's gone. Typical bully and that – can't bear to stick around and face up to what he's done, can he? It's not so much what he's done, by the way, it's what he's said. I've never really liked him, to be fair, but I never thought he was one of them to come out with all that sort of carry-on. I'm not going to forget what he's said today. He can repent at his leisure.

Machievelli 4

After deliberating on all things I asked myself whether in this present day the times were propitious to honour a new prince, and whether the circumstances existed here which would make it possible for a prudent and capable man to introduce a new order, bringing honour to himself and prosperity to all citizens.

Margueritte

It's quite a little feat of time management just keeping on top of my various players, but it's *fucking* exciting, too. Under my previous plan, I'd need to play Cormack along, let her believe that when the Brussels delegation wakes up to Liverpool next Saturday, they'd find a city awash with sex options. There'd be posters, flyers, calling cards and ladies of ill repute strategically positioned in every hotel lobby and on every wall outside every bedroom window. And at that point we call each and every key figure – from local media to local government – and we inform them that this army, this *flotilla* of scarlet can be made to vanish and reappear at any time, at our behest. Now get around the fucking table with us! Shame we won't be seeing that one through, actually – would've been a lot of fun to orchestrate.

So that's where old muttonchops thinks we're at, and I for one have not told her differently. Her role in the grand scheme of things is rapidly running down, but I know better than to rattle her cage any sooner than I strictly need. The longer she remains in ignorance, the better for all concerned. Well, no, not strictly true, actually – the better for *moi* is what I wish to say.

But then, under that selfsame plan, I was counting on working the idiot Brennan boys to a frenzy of internecine paranoia. It was a challenge I was anticipating greatly, a real challenge to my techniques of persuasion, my skills of seduction, duplicity and political treason – and one I could not lose. But, equally, it was a game I could only win once. Whichever way I schemed it, I could take Moby and Ultimo, or Ged and the South Village. Thom wanted me to go after Moby. My heart was telling me to take back my South Village – mine, mine, *mine*! But for the fuck of it, I could not immediately see a way of closing the pair of them out.

That was PP – Pre-Paul. And now we can remove that great imponderable. It seems that I *shall* have my cake and eat the fucking fucker. I've made contact with young Paul and he does sound *terribly* keen. Onwards and upwards!

Cormack

At times such as this in the past, we've always taken solace in our philosophy of gentle existentialism. We live our life on the basis that our work is important while knowing, of course, that it is not. And from a position of fatalistic *che sara*, it is difficult to lose.

Nonetheless, this has always been a fight and, because it was always a scrap worth fighting, it is therefore a fight worth winning. We've spent the past few days cutting a way through the surmise and uncertainty, lining up those things we know for sure. We took two pieces of coloured card – one green, one red. Then, with a thick, fibre-tip pen, we marked the cards as follows. Green is for Go (and Good). Red is for Stop (and Bad).

GREEN CARD

Brussels v. supportive.
Key council figures in favour. (Poll major players again.)
Kelman needs Loin success for City Focus credibility.

Majority of opinion formers still support Loin. (Check Knighton for update.)

Govt has all but decriminalised certain drugs, wants to consider more. L'pool ahead of the game and could get Tracer status.

No council taxpayer's money needed.

We leave a space and then, in light pencil, we note:

Margueritte's escort agency leaflet blitz as tactical reminder. (Go ahead anyway to show gruesome alternative?)

Then, back to the bold fibre tip:

Margueritte

She's the real plus in all of this. We should have seen her strengths earlier, but having her on board at last is the thing. Better late than never, and what an ally! And then we circle this last.

Do this, then retire.

That was the wonderful and saturating realisation of yesterday evening – that come what may with The Loin, this marks the end of the line for this old warhorse. Inconceivable how liberating, that moment of truth. This *has* been the ultimate battle. The *ultimate* battle. So we need to ensure victory. The negatives don't look so daunting, written down and laid out like that.

60 Hope Street cabal – CCTV + police = The Enemy.
Kelman – can not rely.
Moby Brennan/Ultimo – loose cannon. (Sacrifice Ultimo/safeguard the Stables?)
Easy campaign for Moral Majority. (Bishop? Any threat?)

Laid out like that, we still look strong. Assuming Margueritte delivers on the Brennan front, the art now is in the final lobbying process. The Brussels contingent arrives next Friday. By the Monday, their decision will be made. We have it all to do. And yet we feel serene. We feel marvellous.

We Shall Not Be Moved

Ged

Tell you what though, lad, that was something else, that were! I weren't expecting nothing like that at all – fucking *better*, it were! Knowmean, not that I'm saying I've thingioed or nothing – I haven't changed sides or nothing like that. We was all down there shoulder to shoulder and that, me, our Cheyenne, our Stephen. She never come and that, but I weren't expecting her to, in fairness.

Telling you, la, the atmosphere was fucking better! All these batty auld dames doling out mugs of soup and that, big mad hotdogs and that, thanking ourselves for coming along and lending our support and what have you. And that's what it's all about at the end of the day

– that's what makes life nice and that. All's this was about was decent people that haven't got no axe to grind with no cunt, turning out in force for something that they believe in. I felt proud to be there myself, in all fairness. All that shite with Lady Margo and that – it's forgotten, to be fair. Things like this – they put all of that into perspective. Don't know where my head was going with her, mind you. I don't mind saying so – I did half lose sight of the ball with her. But, knowmean, this is what it's all about, me and the kiddies and that, doing something on the fucking level. Nice people, pulling together – end of. When they all started singing 'We Shall Not Be Moved' I was filling up, to be completely fair. And when the bizzies moved in and Ray Cole goes: 'If you're expecting your overtime chits signed by me, you can fuck off!'

Telling you – nice people. Everyone was in bulk, to be fair. Even though we was thingio with each other, we was on opposite sides of the fence and what have you, we was all still in bulk at Ray's shout, bizzies and all too, in fairness. Just, knowmean, a pleasure and a honour to be stood there side by side with them at the end of the day. And our two, they was fucking buzzing on it, by the way, fucking *loving* it, they were. I was made up myself that *they* was so made up – what it's all about at the end of the day, isn't it? My two fucking loved it out there. Little Shy went and run out in front of a copper that was trying to haul these two aul' ladies back. Fucking case, she is – flew in, kicking the bizzy in the shins and calling him all kinds of bastard. Couldn't do nothing at the end of the day though, could he? Girl's only fourteen and that. Chip off've the aul' block, isn't she?

Know your rights and that, say fuck all – is right.

I don't know what Coley was expecting from my good self at the end of the day, but the way it all panned out and that, there wouldn't've been nothing I *could've* done unless I had access to heavy militia – which I don't, by the way. Know where I'm going, I was there to help the little people out, help the *nice* people preserve something that they all care about, this aul' wreck of a hotel that was getting demolished. But, tell you what though, the way it went up, la – fucking better! Plod starts coming on that bit heavier, know-mean, half starting to panic and that, starting to get that bit impatient with protesters that wouldn't fuck off out the way. Like, I myself was on the side of the good guys and that – but it *were* fucking boss when they jellied the gaff! Fuck off! Come crashing down like a bag a shite, it did – one minute it's there, next thing it's fucking dust, la! Superb, it were. I mean, like, know where I'm going, I kept my face straight and half looked like I wanted to run over there and chin one of the coppers. Then little Cheyenne starts crying and that, doesn't she, so that's that – game over. I tells our Stephen not to glare at policemen – they're only doing their job at the end of the day, aren't they – and we fucks off handy.

New Order

Jade

I wake up and while I'm blinded by the first hot clear sun of summer, another blind spot is lifted with equally dazzling clarity. I just *see* it, yeah, see it for the first time. The Loin. The Loin is not going to happen. Just who the fuck have we been trying to kid? It's all well and good prattling on about Queer Theory and trying to subvert from within – but I have a different take on it, now. I think that can only work when men are on the receiving end. As good and as righteous as mine and Shelagh's putsch has been, we're ultimately only seducing each other. We're preaching to the converted. It's the chief constables and the council leaders and, fuck, the Marc Kelmans I should've been working on. Shelagh must know it. The whole project is doomed.

And in recognising that, I don't feel down, or used, or beaten in any way at all. I feel invigorated. I know only now how much I want this whole thing to happen. I *want* The Loin, want it for Liverpool, want it in the way that Shelagh Cormack wants it. I'll do anything to see it happen – but I need new allies. I need people who can get their own way with men – starting now.

Language 2

Paul

I like it. I like it a lot. And do I like *her* – girl like that could make a man of me! Could make a *fucken* man of me, you *cunt*, hah-hah-hah! Terrible. You've got to laugh at the end of the day. Unless you're Moby Brennan, that is – tee-hee!

But I need to think this one out. She hasn't said as much, like, but she don't need to. I don't fucking *need* people to tell me what to do. I *need* to think how's the best way to off the pair a them and make it look like something else. It'll come. I know it will. The shame of it, though man, what's really a terrible terrible shame about all of this is that people *won't* know it was me. Know what I mean? It's a pity that, at the end of the day – people *should* get to know what sort of a man I really am.

The Horrors

Moby

There's only one or two times I can really remember feeling last about things what I've done – things what I've *had* to do, in fairness. The one that obviously still makes me thingio today was the Aldi job. Lad half deserved what he got and that – end of the day, the money he's getting paid and that, there's no need for the soft cunt to be acting the hero. Cunt fucking half deserved it – but obviously he never. No cunt deserves to get killed for going to work. Still gives us the horrors, that one. Soft cunt comes running out after us, tries to fucking rugby-tackle myself. I only hit the cunt the once, but I knew from the sound his head made when he hit the deck he was in a bad way. Poor fella croaked in the hozzy the next day. I felt last. Still do, in fairness.

I feel last about what I done to Paul the Hom today and all, too. What I fucking said and that – that more than anything. Out of order, that was – no need for it, at the end of the day. Bang out of order. I'm not going to apologise to the cunt, but I do feel last on him.

I must be half thingio, must be getting soft in my auld age because I sees aul' fucking Mini Me sat on the wall outside with a couple of his little mates. I thinks to myself: 'Here y'are, Moby lad. You can do some fucking good in your life for once.'

So I goes to the door and I shouts out to him. At first, they're on their toes, half ready to do one. They're thinking I'm going to give them loads. But I just shouts: 'Here y'are, lad. Call round here on Saturday and I'll take you round town and that – introduce you to some of the lads on the doors.'

Fucking kip on him by the way – fucking made up, he is. And his little mates. Fucking all over him, they are – do you *know* him, and that. Do you know Moby Brennan? Telling you, man, I've made their fucking day for them. Fucking state of them! Don't feel so sly on Paul now, in fairness.

The Leveller

Paul

I don't have any second thoughts about what I'm going to do, by the way – I really don't. Ged maybe – it's always a shame to see a lion felled – but Moby Brennan, no. He's brought all this on himself. What he's done with me and little Gavin and the way he's spoken to me back there – no thank you. He's getting levelled. Big bad bald Moby Dick is getting rubbed out, man.

Just Another Saturday

Cormack

I'm not exactly surprised at the news – but I have to say I'm a little taken aback by the bearer. I open my front door at 10.40 a.m. not to the postman or to Ms Walker or to any one of a dozen welcome callers, but to the

Bishop. I should have known. As soon as I saw him there, this entire dream crumbled to dust. Ah, well – there may indeed be others who live to fight another day, but not this old warrior. And in that instant of realisation, I feel a strange and simultaneous surge of relief – of *release*. I feel as though my fight, my good fight for my dear desperate sister Annie, has come to a close. And I feel fine about that.

I ask the Bishop in. He, of course, accepts. He also accepts the Madeira cake even though it's a little bit early for him, along with the rare and ancient Bowmore I offer and the crumbly, almost mouldy Stilton and biscuits. He tells me it's over – *quel surprise*! He *knows* I'd rather hear this from himself than from some faceless (!) council lackey. He hopes dearly that I shall agree to attend the grand walkabout and the fireworks and the gay dinner dance for all the Brussels wallahs tomorrow. I nod and say little and wonder quietly about Kelman – the shit – and slowly it dawns on me. I'm being counselled. This particular Bishop is giving me grief counselling! That cheers me up no end.

Margueritte

Paul seems to have it sussed. His take on it is that it happens *now*, today, and it has to happen outside Moby's. It makes it more random, more like a gangland execution – which is exactly what this is, by the way. The bit I don't like is my own involvement. My own take on it has been that I'm keeping as far away from the business end as fucking possible – but I see his point. We need to make it so as Ged arrives at Moby's carrying. We want him packing heat, man! The only way that's happening is if *I* make it happen. Don't know. Might use Debs somehow – get her to do my bidding. Or I might just one last time make Ged fall in love with me. Can I do that? Course I fucking can.

Or maybe I do all three.

Moby

Weird call and that. Nice one, to be fair – but fucking weird and all, too. Got me fucking stoked now, she has. Phone goes. It's her. Margo. Sounds thingio, to be fair – half sounds like she's playing with herself, know where I'm going. To be fair on the girl, I don't know. Just whenever Judies in films is doing phone sex, they sound like that – half rasping, knowmean.

'You on your own there?'

'Just getting ready to go out and that.'

'Anywhere nice?'

'Town. Said I'd show one or two of the little rats from round here how it works on the doors and that.'

'You're all heart. Where's Marie?'

I half tries one of them funny telly presenter voices.

'If it's Saturday it must be . . . BINGO!'

It don't come off, to be fair.

'Kids?'

'Fuck knows. Round and about. Be in later. They know the score.'

I said that last bit like I believe it. Truth be known, I haven't got a clue when they'll be in. That's her job. State of me, by the way – there I go again, 'truth be known' and that. That's that fucking arse bandit, that is!

'Moby?'

'What?'

'I'm really wet, honey. I really, really need your cock inside me. Can that be taken care of?'

Kinell, la! Can that be arranged! I've got a hard-on already. I do a bit of a voice thing myself, to be fair. Bit gruff and what have you, let her know what she's got coming to her.

'Get round here. Now.'

'Moby?'

'What?'

Pause. Can hear the girl breathing and that. Pure doing my head in now, she is. That girl is getting it, no two ways about it.

'Don't answer the phone. Don't answer the door. I'll ring three times. I'm coming now.'

Telling you, la, it's as much as I can do to keep my hands from off've my cock.

Ged

Could not take it in proper when Margo first phoned us about it, but she wouldn't've brought her in on it if there weren't nothing in it. And in all fairness, there was that little half tremble in her voice, knowmean. She did half sound like she was shitting herself.

What she's saying is that Moby's going to do that Paul in. Our Anthony's going to kill a man. Don't know what to do, in fairness. Pure do not know what to do about this. Then the phone goes again and it's Margo wanting to talk to Debs. Can hear the girl screaming down the phone from here.

'Stop him! Please, stop him from doing this thing!'

She's in fucking bits now.

Moby

Wish to fuck she'd get down here. I'm going up the wall, here – badly need to get it on with the girl and do one. Saturday's a big night for YT. Fucking phone keeps going. Rings, like, half a dozen times then rings off. Ignore it, she's said. Is right. To be fair and that, I am that little bit thingio – little bit nervous. Likesay, she's a fucking Big Shag that Margi. If you're going to get nervous about anyone, you'd get nervous over her. I goes into the bathroom and gives my dome another once over with the Mach III, just for something to do with myself. Wish she'd fucking get down here!

I'm already half thinking about where to go once I've give her one and got rid. I usually save Cooper's and the First National and that for Sundays. Telling you, kidder, that is one depraved scene that fucking Cooper's on a Sunday! What? Every fucking lunatic that ever went the match comes down, every Judy in town that's over thirty or over thirty fucking stone – it's the end of the fucking world, I tell you! Sex in the bogs, big mad fights, lads getting bottled, girls throwing up all over their mams – and that's all before pork pie and roasties comes out! Fucking love it down there, man. Might just take Mini Me down there tonight to show the kid what a wild door's like. Is right.

Fucking phone *again*! Better pick up. Might be one of the binlids in lumber somewhere. They don't usually bring bollocks to the doorstep, but I better answer the fucking thing. Fucking Margo better get down pronto, mind you, or I'll be having to wank myself off before I goes out.

Ged

At fucking last! I've got through to the lad and he's laughing it off, saying she's off her head and that, but I know he's lying. He sounds thingio – lad don't sound himself, to be fair. He can't wait to get us off've the phone. She thought that and all, too – and Debs has known Moby as long as I have, in fairness. She knows he's a gabby bastard. I'm going round there.

Margueritte

I have to say, she was the last person I was expecting to see. I'm glad she came. I'd only just come off the phone with young Paul, tell him it's ASG. What I actually said to him – fuck knows why – is 'the butter is in the fridge'. I'm staring at the phone like some bint out of a B-movie when she walks in. Jade. Looking utterly divine. My fanny's only twitched for women on rare occasions. That time in the pan-American was one of them – and now she's done me again. Our eyes say it all. Sooner or later, they say – sooner or later.

'I need to speak with you,' she says.

I'm like any girl. I've often wondered what it'd be *like* to be pleasured by a woman. But this is different. This goes way, way beyond mere curiosity. This cuts straight through to my solar plexus and burns deep down below. I want her. I really fucking want to kiss this girl – powerfully. I want to devour her. My face tries a stab at stress, vulnerability, something that will make her see me as a woman, a sister, a fucking friend. It works.

'You look tense,' she says.

I yawn and stretch and try a smile.

'It's all this,' I say. I sweep an arm at my desk full of papers.

'Is it worth it?'

I pause for dramatic effect.

'No,' I tell her.

She smiles. She has a devastating smile that goes right through your groin. Nose is a little too broad and sluttish, but her eyes, those green, green eyes and her tiny waist and her long legs – I can't take my eyes off her. She's fucking gorgeous. She comes across.

'Never mind,' she says. 'We'll talk about it some other time. I had a proposition?'

I usually find that adolescent Aussie soap-style of talking does my head in – but not with her. Her voice is so cracked and smoky. I want to fuck her.

'Lean right back,' she says. I do just that and then her fingers are dry-shampooing my scalp, kneading and teasing and taking away all that pressure, all that shit. I let out a sigh. Her fingers stroke the back of my neck. She scratches the nape of my neck and runs her fingertips behind my ears and pinches my earlobes and I'm lost, slumped back in my ergonomic leather office chair, eyes closed, groaning. She comes around and faces me. I open my eyes. She looks deep inside me and reads my thoughts.

'Bring me off,' I'm saying. 'Finger me. Fuck me.'

Paul

I'm superstitious as it is, but that's just gone through me, that has – that was just like a ghost walking through me. I've left the house at 5.55 p.m. on the nose – no two ways about it. I checked every clock – it was 5.55. I walked around to the lock-up to get the shooters and that's when I seen him. Mickey Ryan. Jesus, I nearly fainted!

Mickey Ryan was the hardest lad round here by a long chalk. He was rock. He was three years older than me but for some reason he was always all right with me.

More than all right, he was *lovely* with me. There really, really was not anything I wouldn't have done for Mickey. This one summer, Bri'd come into a few bob and he was taking us to Talacre not just for a week, but for a fortnight. We'd never been away nowhere as a family before. I couldn't think about nothing but Talacre – my head was full of it. But as it got nearer, this weird nightmare kept coming to us. What if, while I was away, Mickey Ryan made friends with some of the other lads? By the time I come back, he might not want to knock around with us no more. In the end, it played on my mind so much, the idea that Mickey'd sack us while I was gone, that I begged Mam and Bri to let him come with us. They never, like. And they wouldn't let me stay behind, neither. Looking back, I ruined that holiday for everyone. All's I wanted to do was get back and carry on being Mickey Ryan's run-around. I was right, though. When I got back he'd teamed up with some lads from Balliol Road and they were like a proper little firm, up to no good. It broke my heart, that did. I thought the world of him.

I only seen him for a second as he was crossing over the road and I was just about to shout out: 'Mickey!'

Then I remembered what I was about to do. I would've loved to've told him about it, but obviously I couldn't, like.

Ged

Hitting the tunnel approach I am going that little bit faster than what I ought to be, in all fairness, and it's as much as I can do to slam the brakes on. Just stood there, he is. It's not even dark yet – it's that half green sort of twilight that you love when you're little, playing out late on the block and what have you. Just stood there he is, right in the middle of the motorway – like as though he knows something. What I know is I'm half fucking certain it's the same fox that cut in front of us in the winter. Grown a bit, in all fairness – grown a fuck of a lot, he has. He's fucking beautiful. Just stands there, looks us right in the eye, then trots off. That's exactly what he does, by the way – he trots like a horse, little paws almost tripping into each other and that. Fair enough, it isn't like there's loads of traffic at this time of the evening, but he wants to be a bit more careful, standing in the middle of a motorway like a knobhead.

Paul

Sorry it has to come to this, by the way, but needs must. Maybe one or two people might sit up and take notice now – and not before time, neither. Things I've done for this city, by the way. I've been one of the good ones, I have. Whoever I've worked for – worked *with*, Paulie, worked *with* – I've been a good soldier. I have. I've been a good fucking lad. Not just fucking loyal. No, not just fucking loyal, by the way – it goes *waaaay* beyond loyalty what I've done since I've been on the scene. Fucking – what about that lad of Fat Franner's? The big fat fucking yard dog that never says fuck all – fucking skip man. Who was it give him his name? *W9*. Maida Vale. *Made of Ale*. See? I'm not just one of the lads, me – I'm one of the fucking *top* lads. I can do a bit, me, but I can have a laugh and a joke and all, too. I know how it works. One of the fucking top lads, I am.

This thing that I've got to do now – there is not a fucking shred of doubt in my mind. I'm ice, la. I'm fucking steel. It's them Brennan shitehawks that's getting iced.

Ged

Little firm of rats scallying around on the corner of Mill Street. Only kids they are, but they're fucking lethal at that age. Where we park up for the match just off've Lambeth Road, the mind-your-car kiddies round there are fucking horrible. *Horrible*, they are. All in Lacoste trackies, skins the lot of them, and they look at your wheels, laugh in your face and go: 'Nice alloys them, lad, but they're doable. Little sports brace set I've got, they're fucking well doable, they are. Gone in sixty seconds, lad!'

Lad, by the way! The fucking age of them! What they're basically telling us is, here y'are, give us three pound and when you get back from the match your car'll still be here. And your fucking wheels and all, too.

I drives past them towards Moby's. One or two of them looks up, gives out the standard 'who the fuck are you' look and gets back to whatever it is they're plotting. There's two or three other lads up ahead, walking towards Moby's. The biggest one of them looks like a mini doorman. Makes myself smile, that does – half reminds us of that *Bugsy Malone*. Good film, that was. Fat Sam's Grand Slam and what have you. Very true to life, by the way.

Moby

Ah, fuck it! That's all we fucking need! Not only has she not shown – can't've been *that* fucking desperate by the way – fucking Mini Me's only turned up, hasn't he? Good fucking half-hour early and all, too. The lad is fucking obsessed, man. State of him, dressed up in his black bomber and his black jeans and fucking *gloves*! Leather gloves he's got, in this weather! Can not wait to be a fucking doorman, can he? His little life is dedicated to that one fucking thing – being a doorman. Being a hard cunt. Wish to fuck I hadn't got myself involved with the little dickhead. Half a hour fucking early, he is. Try and do somebody a favour, man, and look what happens – they take the fucking piss!

Goodfellas 2

Mini Me

Now's it's come down to it, I feel a bit of a cunt bringing these two down with us. They're all right and that – they won't shit out. But they're kids at the end of the day. Moby, man – he respects me. It's myself he's always letting to, myself he's offered to take around the gaffs and that. He can see it in me, man – he knows I'm on the up. Fair enough, he is a big name and that but the smart fellas are the ones that know who's up and coming. He can see it in me – he knows that in a couple of years' time I'm going to be a fucking Player. Is right. That's why he's making a bit of a fuss of myself now. These two, though – they're fuck all. I can see it now – they're going to make a cunt out of me, asking mad questions and getting dead excited 'cos they're knocking round down with fucking Moby Brennan. I've said they can come now, so there's fuck all I can do about it – but when I'm up there, these'll have to be binned. You wanna survive in this business, you needs quality around you. Fucking right you do.

Paul

Well, well, well – I take my hat off to you, Margueritte. As predicted, one highly aeriated Ged Brennan pulls up outside his cousin's gaff. Okey-dokey. Over to you, Paulie, lad. Over to you. Seven fifty-five. Not exactly perfect circumstances. By the time we're ready to roll it'll be, what – seven fifty-seven. That's better. That has symmetry. Not perfect either, but it'll do. Seven fifty-seven it is, then.

Out he gets. Oh, look at you, you big, daft cunt! It hasn't even entered your fucking empty head, has it, Gerrard? You're getting it, lad. You're fucking getting it.

Endgame

Ged

They've left us no with alternative. With all of what's went on back there, they really have not give myself a choice in the matter. It is what it is. I went down that road before with the other fella – forgive and forget. Not this time, by the way. Fuck that. Will not make the same mistake twice. They've give us no choice.

Don't know if the lad's dead. The kiddie is – the doorman kiddie is gone. Stepped right into it, he did. Can see the poor little lad now, stretched out on the pavement in all his black clobber. People starting to crowd around him. Ghouls, they are – fucking ghouls. Don't think that Paul's dead, mind you. He's lying there by his car where I got him, but I don't think I got him clean.

Can see our Moby wandering around in the road like a knobhead. You and all too, eh, Moby? Didn't quite work though, did it, lad? You've left us with no choice.

Mersey Paradise

Cormack

Somehow, I thought it'd hurt more. I'm here of course
– call me a ghoul but I really could not keep myself
away – taking the guided walk and listening to the
bright young thing who's telling us all how wonderful
and fresh and dynamic this part of the city is going to be.
I thought I'd feel anger or pain or something – but the
closest I come to all that is when the dishy Marc Kelman
takes me to one side and says: 'You didn't really ever
believe we could make that *happen*, did you?'

And that cuts. To be honest that cuts through me for
a split second, because I did. I did believe we were
going to do this marvellous and ground-breaking thing,
right here, on this land. But we're not.

We walk on towards the Stables.

The Art of War 4 – The Attack by Fire

*In order to carry out an attack with fire, we must have means
available; the material for raising fire should always be kept in
readiness.*

Ged

One of the better things about being in my profession is
that you can get your hands on any fucking gear you want
– anything at all, by the way – but especially gear like this.
I've planted it fucking everywhere. I feel last, if the truth
be known – I do, my kids'll be in bits when they see it on
the news. All that 'Stop the Rot' campaign in the *Echo* –
it's been all about preserving buildings like this. But fuck

it. What can you do? Twice in a fucking year your own family tries to rub you out, and for what? It's thingio, isn't it – it's one of them? It's not personal. Your own fucking flesh and blood and it's not personal.

So, knowmean, somebody somewhere has to stand up for the little man. That's what I felt that night when we was all out for Coley. We lost that one, but no way in the world am I myself losing out on this one. That Shelagh Cormack made a mistake the day she brought me in on all of this. You bring in the likes of myself, you've got to know what it is you're dealing with. You're dealing with a fella that's not going to get fucked around. That's all's it is – too many of the cunts tried to take the piss. Not any more, they won't. It's game over on this one.

I lays in the last fuse – there's probably well too much gear but it'll look fucking boss on the telly – and I gets the fuck out of there. I can hear that soft bint with the megaphone going on about this, that and the other. They're on their way. Fucking treat in store for that shower, by the way! Fucking Margo – you never expected none of this, did you?

From where I'm going to detonate it, I can be in the jam jar and out of there in half a minute. Fucking Chinatown's rammed of a Sunday by the way, plus there's all this delegation ballyhoo – I'll be home watching it on the news with the binlids before they can even get a squad car out there. I do feel sorry for our Stephen and our Cheyenne, but there you go. Some things you just have to do. They've give myself no choice in the matter. End of.